SNOW KILL

A Mystery

by

Tom Eslick

Withdrawn

A Write Way Publishing Book

Write Way Publishing
PO Box 441278
Aurora, CO 80044

First Edition; 2000

All Latin phrases used in this novel are attributed to Christopher Marlowe's *Doctor Faustus.*

ISBN 1-885173-18-0

1 2 3 4 5 6 7 8 9

For Lil and Tom,
my mom and dad

Author's Note:
Readers will be hard-pressed to find the town of Dunston on a map of New Hampshire but will easily recognize other place names. DHART is an actual organization as well, and I am indebted to them for their help. Although I have strived for authenticity at all times, any errors in protocol, including those involving the practices of working EMTs, are entirely the fault of the author.

CHAPTER ONE

Snow was predicted by early afternoon, and I spent all Sunday morning getting the wood in. The wind had died a bit since last night but was still gusty. The mid-November sky was gun-metal gray. I'd been stacking about an hour when the pager on my belt toned and dispatch requested FAST squad members to respond to a hunter wounded, shot in the leg.

I headed for Damon's house. I pulled into his driveway and gave a good honk on the horn. Damon Pill's my younger stepbrother, son of the woman my father married after my mother died. I was lucky to swim in a different gene pool.

I had to wait a bit for Damon to get himself together. I could see his head bouncing in the windows looking for whatever he couldn't find. When he finally came out of the house, he was dressed in a fireman's full turnout gear. He bumped his head on the side rail getting in the cab and knocked his helmet akilter.

I got on the radio. "Memorial dispatch. This is Eighty-nine R-thirty."

I fiddled with the volume and the radio squelched

I tried again. "Can you repeat location?"

"Back it off," Damon said. "We'll never be able to hear anything."

He reached for it, but I snatched it away. "I know how to work a damn radio."

I adjusted the knob. Then through the static: "... on the east end of the Turner property near the curve before the interstate."

"What is it?" Damon said. "What's happening?"

"You got the call, didn't you?"

"The message broke up. I'm in a dip and the waves don't get through too good."

"You're in a dip all right."

He ignored my comment and messed with his fire helmet.

Dunston, New Hampshire, has an all-volunteer fire department and FAST (rescue) squad—I'm FAST, Damon's fire—with the protocol that one covers the other. So if you didn't know what the call was for, it was hard to know how to dress. I was still in my work clothes—boots and wool pants.

"Is it a fire?"

"Hunting accident."

His eyes fixed on me. "Shit."

I knew what he was thinking and I didn't like it, either. I hate gunshot wounds. As a medic in Vietnam, I'd seen enough of them.

"Probably some Masshole," Damon said.

I nodded. People around here tend to blame everything on assholes from Massachusetts. Since they can't hunt on Sunday in their own state, they flock up here.

We bounced along the dirt road that led away from his property and onto Route 30. When we hit the highway, I pushed the accelerator to the floor and watched the speedometer wind towards sixty. The sky ahead was angry. Snow swirled in front of the truck.

"What held you up this time?" I asked. "What were you looking for?"

"Weren't looking for nothing."

"Christ, Damon. You've got two trucks sitting in your yard and neither work a hoot. If you'd just fix one of them you could drive yourself to these calls."

"Waiting for parts."

"You're always waiting for parts."

We turned off Route 30 onto 125A. It's about three miles to the Turner property from the intersection.

By the time we arrived at the scene, Lawrence "Bumps" Lebeau, Dunston's police chief, was already there. The blue lights on his cruiser washed over us as we got out of the truck. He was talking to a man on the side of the road dressed in a long wool coat, a green scarf around his neck and something that looked like a crushed stove-pipe hat stuck on his head.

Bumps turned his head at our approach. "Morning, Chad," he said to me.

"What've we got?"

"Well, I don't know yet. I just got here."

I looked at the man with the crazy hat. "Did you make the call?"

He drew himself up straight. His face was ruddy, and he looked like he'd had a snootful. "I did, sir. It's my friend. Shot himself in the leg." He patted his thigh. "Left leg." When he stood up, it looked like the blood had drained out of his face. "I think it's pretty bad."

"How long's he been out there?"

"About an hour I guess."

Already I knew we had trouble. My training preaches the

principle of the "golden hour," the time you reasonably have to save a trauma victim. We had already lost valuable minutes. I turned away from him and searched for others on the squad. It looked like Damon and I were first to respond—probably because it was Sunday and people checked their pagers at the church door—if they weren't home with a hangover. As first EMT on the scene, I was in charge of the medical stuff.

"When the pumper comes," I said to Damon, "you get the Stokes litter and put the long board in it. You and whoever else shows follow me and this man." I nodded to him. "What's your name?"

"Glenn Chambers."

"Me and Mr. Chambers."

I put my hand on Bumps' shoulder. He looked up at me, his cheeks littered with acne scars, like he'd been branded with a waffle iron. "You'd better call DHART and put them on standby," I told him. "We may need a chopper."

"You bet," he said.

Because local hospitals like our Memorial couldn't afford trauma units, The Dartmouth-Hitchcock Air Response Team, just a year old, had been created to get critical patients to medical care as fast as possible. Response time to our part of New Hampshire was less than ten minutes from Lebanon, while an ambulance would take a good forty-five minutes over the interstate.

As Bumps went to the cruiser, the pumper showed up. It lumbered to a halt, and I saw Neil Striker driving. Striker was a certified firefighter and also a First Responder. I liked working with him.

I went to the truck. "Get your bag, Neil," I said. "I need your help."

"How far in is this hunter?" he asked.

"About a half hour, I think."

Damon started yelling for the litter, and I got two blankets out of the back of the pumper. I returned to Chambers. He still looked a little pale. If I could get him doing something, it might take his mind off things. "I want you to carry these," I said, handing him the blankets.

He took them from me without saying anything.

"You feeling okay? You think you'll be able to lead us to him?"

He blew out some air and forced a weak smile. "I'm okay." He pointed to the northwest at a pasture perimetered by a stone wall. It ran up a hill to the tree line. "We have to go back up across that field."

Striker joined us. "Let's get going," he said.

I turned to Damon. "You ready?"

By this time, others had shown up and had gathered around the litter. I counted six not including Damon. If we had to carry the hunter out, we would need at least that number, espe-cially in this weather. The litter is as light as it can be, a basket-weave of metal alloy, but with a full grown man aboard it can be pretty unwieldy.

I asked Chambers, "How much does your friend weigh?"

"I don't know. He's pretty big."

"Over six feet?"

"Yeah. Used to play round ball in college. Now he's gone to pot."

We headed across the road and stepped over the stone wall that bordered the field, Striker leading the way. I carried my med kit and Striker lugged an oxygen tank in a pack over his shoulder.

Some people don't like Striker because he's so grumpy, and he scares them because he's big and strong. At just a shade over six feet, he has the girth of an overweight accountant, but the grip of a grizzly. There's a story about the first time he met his ex-wife's father. The father always liked to greet people with a firm handshake. Striker squeezed back. There was a standoff. Striker broke two bones in the man's hand and split the webbing of skin between thumb and forefinger before they called it a draw. The marriage lasted six months.

I checked my watch. Even though it was only a little after noon, it was dark enough to worry about light. The wind had picked up and the snow was getting heavier. It gusted across the field as we walked, a cold, dry snow.

Chambers held the blankets pressed against his chest and struggled up the hill. He puffed like a forge bellows, and we had to stop about fifty yards from the tree line.

"Why don't you give me one of those blankets, Mr. Chambers?" Striker asked.

"No. It's all right. I just need to catch my breath."

I took one from him anyway. "We have to keep going," I said. "Have to find your friend."

"Fucking bastard," Chambers muttered.

"What?"

"Not you. Rodriguez."

"That's his name? The guy who shot himself?"

"I'm going to kill him for putting me through this."

I grabbed the other blanket out of Chambers' hand. "You go ahead and set the pace, Mr. Chambers."

We reached the tree line and hunkered low. My face stung from the wind. I looked back down the hill and spotted Damon with the others coming up with the litter. The whirling snow made them look like walking ghosts.

Striker said, "How much farther?"

Chambers scouted the landscape. "We have to walk that way," he said pointing west. His head spun back. "I think."

"What do you mean, 'you *think*?" Striker said.

Before Striker could say more, Chambers said, "Yes, over here. I'm sure this is the way."

Striker and I caught up to him and we headed through a stand of birch. The terrain opened up into a selected cut area and we once again had to push against the wind and snow. Chambers reached the edge of the clearing and said, "Through here. Just a few more yards."

We were about to follow when something caught my eye. Farther north up the clear-cut, there was a body slumped on the ground, the lower half still in the woods. It had to be Rodriguez. He probably tried to crawl into the clearing so we could find him easier.

We reached him. He lay face down. He was close to six-six, and I wondered if he would fit in the litter. He was hatless, and the snow that covered his hair gave the odd impression he was wearing a veil.

In his outstretched hand was a pistol. It looked like a semi-automatic of some sort. What the hell was a hunter doing with a pistol?

I found a pair of Latex gloves in the pocket of my jacket and put them on. I uncurled his fingers from around the pistol. I took a pen from my pocket, stuck it through the trigger ring, lifted the pistol out of his hand, and put it in my med kit.

"What's his first name?" I asked Chambers.

Chambers didn't respond. He just stared at Rodriguez.

"I said, what's his first name?"

"Joseph."

I got on my knees and put my head close to Rodriguez's ear. "Joseph, can you hear me? My name's Chad. I'm an EMT and I'm here to help you."

Rodriguez let out a groan. His breath came in short gasps. From what I could tell, his airway wasn't pinched off. He was conscious, but his pale, cool, clammy skin told me he was "shocky." He was dressed like a hunter. His jacket was bright orange and it had a hood.

I opened his jacket and made sure there were no other bleeds. "We have to roll him," I said to Striker. "Spread one of those blankets on the ground by his side. I'll stabilize the head."

While Striker unfolded the blanket, I caught a glimpse of Chambers. He was looking pale again. I said to him, "We could use your help, too."

"Me?"

"You come up here by his shoulders and grab hold of his coat. Striker will get his legs."

"I don't know. I don't think ..."

"Do it!"

When they were in position, I held Rodriguez's head and checked his neck for deformities in his C-spine. It looked okay. "Ready to roll." I said. "On my count. One ... two ... three ..."

Rodriguez groaned again as we turned him. "Okay, now you two take hold of the blanket at the bottom and drag him into the clearing." We moved him about ten yards. We could work on him now without getting hung up in branches and deadfall.

I let Chambers take over my job at the head to keep him busy and told Striker to put the other blanket over Rodriguez and get his oxygen tank. I would also need scissors, gauze, and a trauma dressing from my kit.

I palpated Rodriguez's radial pulse: 86. On the high side—rapid and thready. Then I checked his respirations: 38. He was sucking wind too fast. We had to help him breathe.

"High Flow?" Striker asked.

"We need to bag him. Fifteen liters."

Striker searched his kit for a bag valve mask. This device has a triangular arrangement that fits over the mouth and nose attached to a hollow barrel-shaped piece of plastic. You attach the barrel end to oxygen, place your hand around the middle, and squeeze it every five seconds or so, literally breathing for the patient to get the respirations back to what they should be.

With Striker busy doing that, I finally had a chance to look at the leg wound.

Rodriguez's pant leg was drenched in blood above the knee. Striker handed me scissors and I began cutting from cuff to thigh. I didn't see his rifle nearby—which only made sense since I doubted he would have dragged it out with him. A deer rifle would be a high-velocity .30-06, maybe, or .30/30. You have to think about the weapon involved. In low-velocity firearms, like .22s, the slugs tend to penetrate and bounce off bones, raising all sorts of internal havoc, while the bigger stuff blows right through you, ripping organs and blood vessels.

I finished cutting off his pant leg. I took a look at his lower leg and found the entrance wound, but my biggest concern was where the bullet came out.

The exit wound was large and ugly—it had blown out the back of his thigh. Palpation revealed the bullet probably crashed through his femur, no doubt severing the femoral artery. This man was in deep shit. Bleeding inside and out. I used Striker's oxygen bag as a prop to elevate his leg. I applied direct pressure with a trauma dressing and wrapped gauze around it.

I took his blood pressure: 110 over 45.

Diastolic was in the toilet. The numbers confirmed Rodriguez's biggest problem. His heart was working like a water pump getting down to mud in a cellar hole, and his skin felt like he'd spent the night there. He was hypovolemic—no volume left to pump.

"His eyes are closed," Chambers said, suddenly. "I think he's dead."

"He's not dead," I said. "Keep holding his head straight!"

Chambers let go of Rodriguez's head. "I'm not touching any stiff!" He walked away and stood hugging himself against the cold.

I ignored Chambers and shifted my focus back to Rodriguez. The snow hadn't let up at all and my hands felt numb as I took another blood pressure: 95 over 42.

Chambers said, "I want to get out of here."

"Stay put!" I said.

"But I'm freezing."

"Tough!"

Chambers walked away from me. He was headed down the hill when I saw Damon and his crew coming up to meet us. "Chambers!" I yelled.

He turned to say something, but as he did a shot rang out from behind me. Chambers lurched, then fell hard, like one of those old wall-hung ironing boards that come crashing down if you look at them crooked.

I'd seen it before.

That son of a bitch was dead before he hit the ground.

CHAPTER TWO

The guys toting the litter dropped it like it was electrified and dove for cover, leaving it in the middle of the clearing. Striker started toward Chambers, but I grabbed his elbow. "Stay down. Leave him," I said. "Come on, help me pull Rodriguez behind that tree."

Striker nodded, but he didn't move at first. "Take hold of the edge of the blanket, there." I showed him by grabbing a fistful of cloth.

He gripped the blanket, then suddenly let it drop. "Fuck that!" he said, and took off down the clearing toward where Chambers had fallen.

For a minute, I was stunned. Why Striker would put himself in the line of fire to check on Chambers was beyond me. I tugged on the blanket, shimmied Rodriguez downhill, and sought cover behind a gnarled maple. I retrieved the bag valve mask that Striker had dropped and pumped oxygen into Rodriguez.

Striker bent over Chambers. I could see him testing for a pulse. I kept expecting any minute to hear another shot, but none came. Finally, Striker looked up. "He's dead," he yelled.

I could have told you that, you stupid bastard. "Striker!" I yelled. "Bring the litter back with you."

I grabbed Rodriguez's wrist and found a fluttery pulse. He was slipping away. We had to get him out of there.

Striker grabbed the rail of the litter and lifted it with one hand. He ran with it like he was carrying a Styrofoam surfboard.

I yelled to Bumps across the clearing, "Everybody okay over there?"

"Yeah."

"You got backup coming?"

"On their way."

Knowing Bumps he'd probably contacted the world as soon as he knew that Rodriguez was down—State Police, Fish and Game, even the damn FBI.

Striker threw the litter in the snow and took over bagging Rodriguez.

I watched Rodriguez for a sign he might come around, but his skin remained a pasty blue. All the while I was thinking we were being watched, that whoever had shot Chambers was circling around, ready to zero us in his sights.

I looked at my watch again. It had been about ten minutes since Chambers fell. My feet were numb, and I had to slap my hands against my thigh to keep the blood moving. If it was this cold for me, Rodgriguez had to be sliding into a freezer.

Across the clearing, Bumps rose to one knee and leveled his .45 up toward the north where the shot had come from. From the sound of the report, whoever fired had been just a few yards to our right, close to where we first found Rodriguez.

Bumps moved into the clearing, the crew rose slowly, then stumbled over each other to catch up to him. Soon everyone had made it up the hill and gathered around Rodriguez.

"He still alive?" Bumps asked Striker.

"Barely."

"DHART's on the way," Bumps said. "They want to know where to land."

"Tell them right in the field where we put in," I said. "You got someone you can talk to below?"

"Haskell just signed on."

Blaine Haskell was Bumps' assistant, a recent graduate from the technical college. He was good man to have on communications. "Tell him to gather as many vehicles as he can and drive them onto the field. Form a circle and turn on the headlights."

"How wide a circle?"

"About a hundred feet across should do it. And when the pilot's making his descent, turn the headlights off. We don't want to blind him."

"What about the other guy?"

I caught a glimpse of Chambers' body in the clearing collecting snow. "We'll come back for him."

Bumps got on the radio while we rolled Rodriquez onto the long board. I heard him groan a little and my heart jumped. *Hang on, man.*

We laid out some blankets on the bottom of the litter and lowered Rodriguez into it. His feet hung over the long board so we had to prop them up in order to fit him in the litter—then we wrapped him up good, strapping the oxygen bottle between his legs. Striker kept bagging him.

I tried not to think about Chambers and whoever it was who had gunned him down. I couldn't shake the feeling we were being watched.

Finally, we had Rodriguez trussed up like King Tut and were ready to move. I organized the men around the litter. "Three on each side," I said. "Damon. You're the lead man. You walk ahead and call out if you see a chuck hole or something. We'll take a break every fifty yards. Then you take over a litter position and the one you replace becomes the lead man. Okay?"

I wrapped the litter strap closest to me over my shoulder. The others got in position to lift. We raised him cleanly. Rodriquez was a load.

We headed out of the clear-cut and back through the stand of birch, Bumps sweeping in back with his pistol drawn. I was at the rear end of the litter and couldn't see much ahead. With the snow spitting around us and the clouds hanging like gray udders, I had to feel each roll of the earth with shuffle steps. Just before the edge of the field, we set Rodriguez down.

"Good job." I said. My arms felt stretched.

"Listen," Striker said. He held up his hand like a traffic cop. "I think I hear it."

Overhead, it sounded like faint thunder, and the grumbling was deep-throated and rhythmic and grew louder as the helicopter circled. I looked down in the field below and saw the lights from the trucks jockeying into position. Before we got going again, I checked Rodriguez's neck. The carotid pulse was weak but regular.

We started down the field. I was still in the rear and the strap cut into my shoulder as gravity dragged the litter away from me. We moved down the slope toward the ring of trucks. Their lights formed a halo that seemed to pull the helicopter softly down toward its center, like a large bird settling into its nest.

When we arrived at the landing site, the side gull-wing door to the chopper was already open. The rotors were still turning hard. The Dartmouth-Hitchcock Air Response Team likes to load hot.

I approached the door with my head down. It's a small, maneuverable rig—an Agusta 109 C MAX—which is why the response time is so fast. A paramedic was hooking up a tube to his oxygen supply. His name tag read Lefty Birch.

"You want us to keep him on the long board?" I asked.

"Right." He tested the oxygen to see if the line was secure. "What've you got for vitals?"

I recited the latest set.

Birch shook his head. "Let's load and go."

Birch's partner, a registered nurse named Henrique Alonzo, helped us transfer Rodriquez to the aircraft stretcher, a special litter on wheels.

As we rolled him toward the chopper door, Birch said, "Get another pulse."

I couldn't reach Rodriguez's neck because Birch was at the head of the litter. He had taken over bagging Rodriguez from Striker. I grabbed hold of Rodriguez's wrist.

The turning rotor roared as the blades whipped above my head. I couldn't find a radial pulse. "Hold it a minute," I yelled above the engine noise, "I'm not getting anything. Check his carotid."

Birch palpated his neck. "Nothing," he said. He put his hand on Rodriguez's chest, then looked at me. "He's in cardiac arrest. Start compressions."

I parted Rodriguez's coat and ripped his shirt open. The buttons flew. I found my landmark on his chest above the xiphoid process, placed the heel of my right hand on his sternum, left hand on top of the right, fingers interlaced, and pressed down on his chest with a five count: "One—and—two—and ..." When I got to five, Birch squeezed the bag valve, giving Rodriguez one breath. Then the process began again.

It was difficult doing the compressions on a moving litter, but we made it to the door of the rig on the second cycle of CPR. We had to interrupt the operation momentarily as we pushed him head first through the open door. The wheels traveled along a track and locked in place with a metallic click. Rodriguez barely fit, his body extending over the full width of the cabin.

There was a bench seat alongside the litter, so we could reach Rodriguez while sitting. Birch got in and motioned for me to get in beside him. "We need you for compressions," he yelled. "Alonzo has to run lines."

I hesitated. I hadn't bargained on a helicopter ride. I'd had enough of them in 'Nam. These days I like keeping both feet on the ground.

"Come on," Birch said.

Alonzo gave me a shove from behind, and I landed in the seat beside Birch, who was busy transferring the oxygen tube from the bottle to the cabin supply.

Alonzo got in quickly. He put on his helmet and handed one to me. The helmet served for communication as well as safety. I could hear them talking and the drone of the heavy 'copter blades became muffled.

In the light of the cabin, Rodriquez's face looked like a death mask. If he could just hold on for another ten minutes ... We recommenced CPR as the pilot shut the cabin door.

The rotors sang in a high-pitched wail, the prop wash beating the snow against the window in concussive waves. I felt a tug in my stomach as the helicopter rose above the ring of truck lights to a cruising altitude. Then the pilot kicked it into gear, this souped-up hot rod, over-torqued, built for speed, and the cabin shuddered as we flew through the darkness. Above the clouds, the stars were bright and winking at us.

Rodriguez was in such bad shape that it took all our hands to try to stabilize him. Doing compressions is tiring, especially if you can't lock your elbows, and, squeezed in between Birch and Alonzo, I couldn't get directly over Rodriguez without standing up, something I wasn't about to do in the small confines of the cabin. "One—and—two—and ..." I kept watching Rodriguez for signs of life, but I knew that the odds of his making it weren't good. He was slipping into the deep weeds.

"One—and—two—and ..." My arms were blowing out, but I was determined to keep going. Right now, Rodriguez was really a dead man. With any luck I was keeping the blood pumping through his body and Birch was sending oxygen to his brain. The brain dies without oxygen within six minutes and if our CPR wasn't working, Rodriguez was done for.

What his heart really needed was a good kick start, a run down the hill with a popping of his clutch. Alonzo was busy pasting on the electrodes of the portable de-fib unit, about the size of a small beer cooler, to do just that.

"Clear!" he said over the headset.

The machine gave Rodriguez a jolt, but the graph on the LCD screen was still a flatline.

"Again," Alonzo said.

The machine revved up.

"Clear!"

The screen suddenly came to life, and a dot of light began tracing a line with sharp peaks and valleys, followed by regular beeping. Rodriguez's heart was working again.

I sat back on the seat. I felt a bead of sweat roll down my face.

Alonzo began poking Rodriguez's arm to find a vein for an IV drip, and it didn't take him long. He got my respect at that moment. Sticking a line into anyone given these conditions is tough. I know. He hooked the IV bag on a rod above his head.

Then I heard the pilot's voice over the headset talking to headquarters. We were making our descent.

I felt a lump rise from my stomach to my throat, and in an instant we were on the ground, and the gull-wing door was open.

A gurney was at the ready and we downloaded him. I walked beside him as the gurney rolled through double doors into a trauma room where a team was waiting to pounce.

Birch talked vital signs and Alonzo reported on the treatment thus far.

The ID badge on the doctor in charge read Sabim Kummalo. He looked Pakastani or Indian.

"All right," Kummalo said. "Strip him down and let's see what we've got." Suddenly, he looked at me over his mask. "Who the hell are you?"

"An EMT," Birch jumped in. "He did compressions for us on the ride in."

"Great. Now get him the hell out of here."

"Yes, sir," Birch said. He grabbed my arm to lead me away.

"I was the one who found him," I said.

"That so? Talk to me. Make it fast."

"Gunshot wound, probably a fractured femur."

"Tell me something I don't know."

"Internal bleeding."

"I can see that. Any other trauma?"

"None that I could find."

The nurse had pretty much cut away all of Rodriguez's clothes. His skin looked like a freshly plucked chicken's.

Kummalo separated the gauze from Rodriguez's leg. "Cute tattoo," he said.

At first, I thought what Kummalo had pointed out was a bruise on Rodriguez's hip, but a closer glance did indeed reveal a small star-shaped tattoo.

Exposing the wound yielded few surprises—it was still ugly and mean-looking.

"Femoral artery is severed," Kummalo said, more as a note to himself than to anyone in the room. I could see him reaching in, trying to pinch the artery.

Kummalo's question began to eat at me. Was there any other trauma? Anything I missed? I was so focused on his leg that I hadn't bothered with a complete survey. With Rodriguez fully exposed on the table, it was an easy visual check. There was nothing obvious, no discoloration or limbs at odd angles, and his other leg disclosed only a few small scars on his knee where it might have been 'scoped. No. I hadn't missed any other obvious trauma.

CHAPTER THREE

With Rodriguez in surgery, my work was over. Birch and Alonzo went back on standby, and I left word at the nurse's station that if anyone came looking for me I would be up at the snack bar grabbing a cup of coffee. I figured it would gradually dawn on Damon that he needed to come pick me up.

The snack bar was quite a way from Emergency, and I played ring-around-the- corridor a few times before I stumbled into an area buzzing with people. Walking among them down the wide hallway lined with specialty shops and food concessions was strangely comforting, like I was suddenly allowed back into the world of the living where none of the events of the past few hours had any meaning at all.

I chose a table at the snack bar near the window so that I could see Damon when he showed.

The coffee was hot, gourmet, and cost a buck. All I wanted was Juan Valdez, but what I got was Heavenly Farms Hazelnut. It came in a paper cup with a fancy dome lid and raised spout that looked like a child's training mug. I ripped the lid off, placed both my hands around the cup, and watched the steam rise.

The warmth on my hands felt good. What had happened in those woods was still a blur, and the helicopter ride had spurred images of Da Nang and Tri Lai—of rice paddies, of hauling up a kid on a hoist and having him machine-gunned in mid-air, of leg wounds that multiplied and grew, tumbling over each other in memory—but I could handle all that. I had long since settled on that war.

I focused on the coffee. Took a sip.

Rodriguez. And what about Chambers, for crissake? Who the hell shot him?

I looked up and out the window and saw Damon talking to a nurse. He was still in full turnout gear, his damn fire helmet stuck on his head. I got up from the table and stood in the doorway, trying to catch his eye. He finally saw me.

"This is embarrassing," I said as he slid into the booth. "Couldn't you have changed into something else?"

"I can't help it if this is all I've got to wear. I didn't have time to put pants on underneath."

"You could have at least left the helmet in the truck."

"It would be too cold to stick on my head when we came back out."

"So now you look like some refugee from Halloween."

"It doesn't bother me. What do you care what I'm wearing?"

I stared at him where the hedgerow of his brows grew together. It made him look like he was perpetually scowling.

He looked down at my coffee. "I'm hungry," he said.

"So get something to eat."

He didn't move.

"What's the matter?" I said.

"Lend me some money?"

"What?"

"I told you I didn't have time to put my pants on. My wallet's in my pants."

"You already owe me. When are you going to pay that back?"

"Come on. Don't be a dickwad."

Hopeless. I didn't have the energy. I gave him a fiver.

"How 'bout the twenty?"

"What?"

"I saw it in your wallet," he said. "I'm going to pay you back, anyway. What difference does it make if it's a twenty or a five? I'm hungry. Besides, it's really expensive here and ..."

"All right. All right." I pulled out the twenty and shoved it into his hand. "Gorge yourself."

I watched him as he headed for the snack bar, DUNSTON FIRE written over the back of his coat. The turnout gear made him waddle like an arthritic penguin. It reminded me of an absurd play by Ionesco we put on back in high school. It had a fireman in it. Nobody understood it.

Damon returned with a large pepperoni, sausage, and onion pizza. He had a Coke the size of a trash can. The doughy smells hit me hard, and I felt it in my gut. I suddenly realized I was hungry. I reached for a slice.

"Hey, get your own!" Damon said.

"I paid for the damn thing."

"So what? I ordered it."

I pulled two napkins out of the holder, spread them, and took two pieces. "Deal with it," I said. "And don't think I don't remember the other five. You owe me twenty-five bucks."

We ate in silence for a few moments, except for Damon's gnashing and slurping.

When I finished I said, "So, what were you and that nurse talking about?"

Damon took a big bite and chewed for a moment. "Nothing," he mumbled.

"You trying to pick her up, or what?"

"Naw. Naw." Damon's face began to turn red. I knew damn well he wasn't trying to pick her up. He gets flustered talking about women.

I winked at him. "Nice ass, huh?"

"Come on, Chad. Cut it out."

"You think she might have a sister? Maybe you could fix me up."

"Fuck you!"

He said this a little too loudly. Two women at a nearby table snapped their heads up.

I smiled at them, then turned back to Damon. "Keep your voice down," I said.

"Well, stop teasing me."

"Come on, finish up. Let's get out of here before we get kicked out."

"She and I was just talking, that's all."

"Okay, forget it."

"I don't know if she has a sister."

"Damon. Forget it."

"She was concerned, that's all."

"Concerned? About what?"

He stopped chewing for a moment, then bit off a huge piece of crust. He muttered something.

"What?"

"She was concerned that there might be a fire in the building." He blinked at me, then continued chewing.

I tried to control my smile. "Oh," I said.

"You okay?"

"Yeah, sure."

"You look like you're sucking a lemon."

"A little indigestion, that's all."

Damon took a long pull on his straw. "Serves you right for taking my pizza."

I shook my head and watched him eat. Soon after Damon came to live with us, it was clear there was something wrong with him. He hadn't developed according to the charts. In his school years, Damon was labeled "slow" when they didn't have a better name for his "condition." A doctor once hung a "savant" sign on him, something I believe because he always could feel the heart and soul of anything mechanical or electrical. He used to win lunch money from kids who challenged his pinball prowess in the back of Finsby's General Store. He still claims he can feel the mercury swaying in the tilt trigger.

Problem is, he's so good mechanically, he tends to make do when there's nothing left, like two trucks he pirates parts for, but none that works. Drives me crazy.

"So what happened after I left?" I said.

"Nothing much. They were getting ready to go back and get that dead guy. They were waiting for Woo when I left."

Woo was the state medical examiner.

"Oh," he said, "and Bumps told me he wants you back as soon as you can make it."

"He did?"

"Yeah."

I leaned forward, elbows on the table. "Damon, for crissake. Why didn't you tell me that before?"

"I was going to."

"Then why are we sitting around eating pizza?"

"Because we're hungry?"

***

It was still snowing, and I had to brush the windshield of the truck with a gloved hand. We sat in the cab a few minutes while the defroster melted a swath big enough for me to see. The noise of the fan was like a long exhalation, while above us and to the left, the snow danced in front of a large halogen streetlight.

Damon groaned beside me.

"What's the matter?"

"Ate too much," he said.

"Serves you right."

I pulled out of the parking lot and headed toward Interstate 89. The plows had been out, but the secondary roads were covered with a skin of snow. The flakes were falling faster than local crews could scrape. I knew about this stuff. I make part of my living plowing driveways. It reminded me that this day, which had now turned into night, wasn't over. I would be pushing snow into the early hours.

Okay by me. I was tired, but I was too jacked to sleep. "Bumps say what he wanted?"

"Be there for questions."

"That's all he said?"

"That's all."

I pulled onto the ramp that led to the interstate. Here the highway was clear. "Staties there before you left?" I asked.

"What?"

"State Police. Were they on the scene?"

"I don't know. I guess so."

"Well, did you see them?"

Damon groaned. "Jesus-Christ-all-go-to-hell!"

"What's the matter?"

"Will you just shut up with the questions! I'm not feeling so hot."

"Sorry."

"I'm going to sleep now."

And he did. In a few minutes he was nodding, his arms crossed over his chest. It was always something I marveled at, a skill he had cultivated in school. His teachers got tired of trying to keep him awake. They'd let him doze in the back of the room, occasionally having one of the kids poke him because of his snoring.

So, I drove into the darkness listening to Damon play his nose trumpet.

I knew that Bumps wanted me there to fill in the gaps. He wasn't on the scene when we first found Rodriguez, and I realized I hadn't told him about the pistol in Rodriguez's hand. I wondered about my med kit. What had I done with it? It was probably still there where Striker and I first found Rodriguez. It bothered me, though, thinking about it.

I ticked off the events of the day. When I filled out my run sheet I would focus on the medical emergency itself, how we'd walked in with Chambers who had called rescue, how we'd found Rodriguez in the clearing—here a recitation of his early vitals, his skin temperature, moisture, BP—how I'd packed his leg wound, how Striker had bagged him—High Flow-15 liters.

Then it had become police business. Chambers felled. Striker checking on him. At least he did that. He made sure he was dead. I would continue the report with the evacuation of Rodriguez. Was that police business, too?

As I reviewed these events, I felt good about the way I'd

reacted to the emergency. Clarise Traynor would call it a success.

She's my shrink. She would be especially happy that I didn't freeze, that I'd been able to make decisions under pressure.

Not too long ago I wouldn't have been able to perform like today. Maybe there is something to this analysis crap after all. Traynor doesn't like it when I talk this way. Denial, she'd say. Calling it "crap" wraps language around a process that, if it fails, wouldn't be so discouraging to think about.

This is what we talk about, the event that I don't like to talk about, but that she makes me talk about anyhow.

After the war, I'd shifted around a bit. I landed in Boston working for an ambulance company. I met Meg. We fell in love. We were married two years later. She got pregnant. We were happy.

One night shift, we got a call. Two persons were down in a convenience store. We responded. It was the store manager and Meg. Her face had been blown away by a shotgun. She had just happened to be in the way. Our unborn child died, too. So did I.

They never found the guy who did it.

I came back to New Hampshire to live with my ailing grandfather. Caring for him didn't help me take my mind off what happened to Meg and our child because I had no recollection of what happened. It's hard to be distracted from something you can't remember. All I knew was there was something cold at the center, and it had physical dimensions, like I was carrying a rock or something. It was a rock of guilt. Traynor says I couldn't have saved her.

It was a girl, they told me. We hadn't settled on a name yet, but I always see her as Natalie, after Meg's mother.

Traynor thought it was the sum total of all my war experiences, capped by the trauma of losing a loved one, that caused the psychic paralysis. Through analysis, hypnosis, and whatever witchdoctor stuff she could come up with, the cold center began to melt.

Traynor still tries to get me going, "to confront it," she says, but I still hold back. I know I'm healing. I want to take my time.

Last year, Traynor said a true test of how far I had healed would be to become an EMT again. "You are a caregiver," she said. "You shouldn't stop giving care." She makes it sound good.

So, that's what I did. And today—well, I did okay, eh Doc?

When I got back to the scene, I could see the lights on the hill. I left Damon sleeping in the truck and walked over to the parked cruiser. Blaine Haskell was still manning the radio. He rolled down his window.

"Tell Bumps I'm here," I said.

"He'll be glad," Haskell said.

"How are things going up there?"

"Not so hot."

"What happened?"

"They can't find the body."

CHAPTER FOUR

Despite the accumulating snow, the walk up the hill took less effort than the first time because the trail had been packed by Fish and Game snowmobiles leading to where Chambers had fallen. Someone had dragged up a gasoline generator, and it growled at the edge of the clearing. The scene was lit like a movie set, with yellow police tape cordoning off the area.

Bumps saw me as I approached. I could tell by the urgency in his stride that he wanted to get to me before I answered any questions.

"How's that fellow?" he said.

"Still alive, I think. Left him that way, anyway."

"Real piss-ass situation here."

"So I understand."

"Tierney thinks we botched it," he said. "Says we ought to have left somebody with the body."

"Guard the body? You tell him we were busy doing other things?"

Bumps shrugged. "I don't know. Maybe I should have left somebody there." The harsh white light accented the lines of worry on his forehead.

"Come on. How were you to know?"

He grabbed the sleeve of my jacket. "He was dead, right?"

"Sure. Striker checked him."

"He couldn't have made a mistake?"

"Did you ask Striker?"

"Didn't get a chance. He drove the pumper back to the station before we came to pick up the body."

I lowered my voice. "Look. If Tierney's saying Chambers wasn't dead and just walked away, then he's full of shit. When they talk to Striker, he'll confirm. I'll guarantee it."

Bumps let go of my jacket. "Then what the hell happened to him?"

"No clue," I said.

We started walking toward the cordoned-off area.

Bumps seemed a little over-sensitive to Tierney's criticism, but I wasn't surprised. A few years back Bumps arrested Tierney's brother Roland for growing marijuana on his back forty. I was involved in the discovery. I had stumbled onto it one day out bird hunting and reported it to Bumps. We both had to testify against Roland, and he got five to ten in the state pen. Bumps thinks Tierney hates him because of it, but I haven't seen any signs. I always liked Tierney. A real professional.

We stepped underneath the yellow police tape, and I recognized Arronson from Fish and Game, and the state medical examiner Woo standing next to Trooper Manfred Tierney—tall, square-jawed, with Arm and Hammer biceps, so much the poster cop that he sometimes worked public relations, showing up at schools to talk about the evils of drugs. Kids listened to him as they would a comic book superhero who stepped off the page—he filled out his pressed and creased uniform like Spiderman his tights.

Tierney shook my hand. "Well, Chad Duquette. As I live and breathe."

I nodded. "How you doin' ?"

"Well, I'm just ducky." He put his hands on his hips. "When are we going to have that chess match?"

"Soon," I said. "I'm still practicing." Tierney was a hell of a chess player. He used to dominate my grandfather, who had been considered an expert. Since I had studied under my grandfather's tutelage, Tierney was always trying to get me into a game.

"If I didn't know better, I'd think you were avoiding me." He winked and turned to the assembled group. "You know Arronson," he said. "And Ms. Woo." We shook hands.

Amy Woo was dressed in a long purple coat with a stylish, patterned scarf slung loosely around her neck. She had soft, delicate features. I always found it hard to imagine such a fragile-looking woman being in charge of all the detritus of jealous rages, knife fights, and trailer fires from the Massachusetts line to the Canadian border, but she was all business when it came to bodies.

Tierney glared at me. "Maybe you can tell us what happened here, Chad."

"A man named Rodriguez was shot," I said. "So was a guy named Chambers. One's being operated on as we speak. The other's dead."

"Are you sure he's dead?" Tierney said.

"I saw him fall."

"And as I understand it," Woo broke in, "your partner checked on his status."

"That's right. Striker."

"So, how do you explain this dead man getting up and walking away?" Woo asked.

I thought a moment. "Somebody could have picked him up after we left."

"In this storm?" Arronson said.

"Whoever shot Chambers could've waited until we left, then dragged him off." I hadn't thought through this theory, but it made sense as I said it.

"Dragged him off where?" Tierney said. "You'd have to be pretty strong to carry him any distance."

"I don't know. Maybe he didn't have to. Maybe he used a snowmobile."

"We would have heard him," Bumps said.

"Think about it." I said. "You remember how loud that chopper was. Maybe he waited until it was thundering to the ground. We wouldn't have heard a thing."

"Interesting," Tierney said.

I hesitated. "Look," I said. "I'm just suggesting a possibility, that's all. I don't know what happened and don't pretend to."

Arronson studied me. His horn-rims gave him a bookish look. "So," he said, "if someone used a snowmobile, then we should be able to pick up the trail."

I shrugged. "There may not have been any snowmobile at all; I'm just guessing. I'm no detective." This was getting ridiculous. I ought to keep my mouth shut.

"Don't know if you could find anything under these conditions, anyway," Bumps said.

"Well, we do have something," Tierney said. He walked over to a snowmobile and came back with the squashed hat. "We found this."

"That belonged to Chambers," I said.

"Problem is, the snow's going to cover the scent."

"And tracks and snowmobile trail, if there was one," Bumps added.

Tierney looked up at the sky. "Weather's supposed to roll out of here in a few hours. We'll begin our search at first light."

I turned to Bumps. "Did you find my med kit?"

"I haven't looked."

"Where'd you leave it?" Tierney asked.

I pointed to where we had first found Rodriguez. There was clearly nothing there. I told them about the pistol.

"And you put it in that bag?" Tierney said.

"That's right."

"One thing for sure," Tierney said. "This guy Rodriguez wasn't out hunting deer."

When I got back to the truck, Damon was still asleep, curled in a ball like a giant possum. He didn't stir until I turned off 125A and got back onto Route 30, heading for home.

He sat up and rubbed his face. "Guess I must have dozed off," he said.

"Dozed off! You were unconscious."

"Did I miss anything?"

"Naw, not much. Chambers' body disappeared, that's all. Other than that, things are pretty quiet."

Damon was silent for a moment. "You're shitting me, right?"

"Wish I was."

"Come on, Chad. You're teasing me again. You know I hate that."

"Fine, don't believe me. You can read all about it in the papers tomorrow."

As soon as I got home, I hooked up the Fisher plow. I had to take time to grease the hydraulics, a chore I had usually completed long before the first snow.

My grandfather's house, where I now live by myself, was willed to me. It has no mortgage—hasn't for over fifty years—so that isn't one of my expenses. I make ends meet by doing what many in New Hampshire do: I plow snow, mend roofs, haul wood, sweep chimneys. I don't have a boss, that's the important thing. Hell, this is the land of "Live Free or Die"—no state income tax, no sales tax, just property taxes that go through the roof, and, on one occasion, made a wild-eyed citizen with a shotgun storm the town hall to blow away a few selectmen. Other than that, things usually work out fine. "Live Free or Die" or "Live Free or I'll Kill You." The bumper sticker says it best: "Live, Freeze, and Die."

The snow had let up quite a bit, and the northern sky showed a hint of stars through thinning clouds. I plowed my own driveway first. The snow felt light and feathery against the push of the plow, and the bumping and rumbling kept me focused. I didn't want to think about anything. I regretted opening my big mouth about what might have happened with Chambers. Who the hell cares what I think, anyway.

I just have six regular customers—all local—and it usually takes about an hour and a half to get them cleared out. Most of the houses I service are on the property that belonged to the first Duquette, a transplanted Quebecois, who left the homeland with Christ gnawing into his head like a worm to form a commune based on the principles of piety and polygamy. From what I've read in his journals, Great-Great-Grandfather Ezekial Duquette wanted to find a way to enter into a state of mystical fucking under the guise of the Biblical edict to be fruitful and multiply.

He was, in other words, a flim-flam fornicator. If my grandfather Willy Duquette heard me talking like this, he would curse me in French Canadian about insulting the family heritage, but the journals don't lie. Ezekial spent a great deal of time flagellating himself over the sins of the flesh.

As a result, there are many who carry the Duquette name who look nothing like each other, and our family tree resembles a briar patch with branches intersecting in odd and mysterious ways. So it's not unusual, given my family history, that I would have a stepbrother named Damon Pill.

All this sweating and fornicating couldn't last forever, and the commune eventually broke up, the lands below my grandfather's house near the village, along with the falling-down buildings, sold to an enterprising young educator who named the school he founded after the town—Dunston Academy—a generation after Ezekial was put into the ground. The school stands today, independent and thriving.

My mom died of scleroderma when I was two. I was four when Dad took up with Willa Pill—who did not take Dad's name—and Damon was two when they both arrived at the farmhouse. For as long as I can remember, Grandpa always lived there.

The last house on my route was an ancient Cape belonging to Miss Martha Pegram, a woman who had turned one hundred and three last spring. She's been a good customer. My grandfather used to see that she was plowed out before I took over his route after he became ill. Why she needed her driveway plowed is another question. She doesn't drive and hardly anyone comes to visit. She's outlived all her friends. Perhaps she just likes company, even if it's only the plow driver. I knew that she was awake, watching me work.

I didn't want to go back to my own empty house, so I drove into town. Nothing was open. Dunston has just one combination general store and gas station, and that closes at 8:00. But I wanted to see if Rachel had made it back from Boston.

I'd met Rachel Spires in my EMT class. We'd been seeing each other off and on for a few months. She was an English teacher at Dunston Academy who also coached girls' soccer and ice hockey. She had been divorced for two years and had come from Massachusetts to work at the school soon after the papers were signed. We didn't have a relationship so much as an agreement. It was a physical one of the Ezekial kind, but without the marriage or the guilt.

She supervised a girls' dorm, which was situated right on the main drag. The lights in the windows meant that she was there and probably hadn't turned in yet. I drove to the post office parking lot and used the public phone. She didn't like me coming to campus because it was ticklish, a dorm parent having a back-door man. I kind of liked it, though.

She picked up.

"You made it back," I said when she answered.

"Barely." She sounded tired.

"How's your mom?"

"She wants to move to Florida."

"Is that good?"

"I guess so. I'd like her closer, that's all." She paused. "Where are you?"

"Across the street." I heard static on the line. "I won't come over if you don't want me to," I said.

"It's not that. It's just that I still need to prepare my class for tomorrow."

"That's okay. It's late."

"Are you all right? Something's wrong. I can hear it in your voice."

"No. I just wanted to talk a little, that's all."

"I'll unlock the door," she said.

The back door opened into the kitchen. Rachel was at the table reading her literature text and writing notes on a yellow legal pad.

She stood and came to me. We embraced. I could feel through her bathrobe that she wasn't wearing anything underneath.

"Want something to drink?" she said. "I'm having tea."

"No. Nothing, thanks."

She led me by the hand to the kitchen table. "What's up?" she asked.

I told her. As much as I could piece together. I struggled with the detail. It sounded fantastical, like I was making it all up.

When I finished, she said. "So, what happens now?"

"They search for the body."

"And what if they don't find it?"

I shrugged.

"Jesus Christ," she said.

I looked down at my hands. "There's something screwy here."

"This Rodriguez guy. He's still alive?"

"He was when I left him. I hope he hangs on; I'd like to ask him a few questions."

She reached over and ran her hand lightly through my hair. "You've had a day, haven't you?"

I took her hand and kissed it. "Rachel. Can I ask you something?"

"Sure."

"What exactly did you hear in my voice? How did you know something was wrong?"

"I don't know. You don't usually call at this hour, for one thing. I guess I just knew."

I smiled at her. "I think we're starting to know each other too well."

She leaned over the table and kissed me lightly on the lips. "Does that scare you?"

"No."

"I'll tell you something else about yourself, too."

"What's that?"

"You've never called me up just to talk."

"That's not true."

"Liar."

"How do you know I'm a liar?"

"I can hear it in your voice."

I laughed. "You're hearing things. I just wanted to talk, that's all. I can do that. Now I'll leave. See? I'm leaving. Now go prepare class."

She looked up at me. "You're really going to walk out that door?"

"Sure. You have work to do."

She stood up and kissed me again. This time she flicked her tongue in my mouth. "It's just John Donne," she said. "And he's dead."

Upstairs, she drew the shades in her bedroom but kept a table lamp on in the corner by the closet. Unlike Meg, Rachel likes to make love with a light on—she wants to watch my face, she says, and as many times as we have done this, I am always moved by her openness.

I undressed in the half-light. I felt the unevenness of the wide floorboards under my bare feet, the coolness on my skin as Rachel came to me. I parted her bathrobe, dropped to my knees, ran my mouth across her belly.

She slipped off her robe, took my hand, and led me to the bed by hand, guiding without speaking. She leaned against the edge of the bed and opened her legs. She held the back of my head, guiding the rhythms of my tongue. She tasted sweet, like she had just bathed, and I was a different man from the one who had died with his wife. I imagined Meg smiling, happy that I was reconnecting.

Then Rachel pulled me on the bed with her—urgent tonight, no lingering. I entered her, her legs thrust wide, her hips pushing against me. It didn't take long. We remained locked after our motions ceased. Neither of us wanted to be the first to relinquish the other. Finally, I fell away from her.

We lay with the quilt pushed aside without talking, still touching each other.

"You know something funny?" she asked.

"No. Tell me something funny."

"In the seventeenth century, 'to die' meant to have sexual intercourse."

"What?"

She raised herself up on one elbow. "It's true. Donne played with that image all through his work."

"Great," I said. "A literature lecture." I closed my eyes.

Donne.

Done.

I slept.

CHAPTER FIVE

I dreamed I was aboard a Huey near Da Nang running lines on a legless kid in a blissful morphine sleep. The scene shifted, and I was in the back of an ambulance, careening down Canal Street in Roxbury trying to get a pulse on a gangbanger who'd overdosed on Angel Dust. There was a floating, seamless quality to the whole thing, like morphing, but through it all I felt grounded by the warmth of the body sleeping next to me.

Then I felt the hot tongue on my face—it wasn't Rachel's, but Cob the dog's.

Cob is a yellow Lab, a chunky male connoisseur of garbage cans who doesn't like it when I stay over and assume his place on Rachel's bed.

There was no clock in the bedroom—Rachel woke up by internal rhythms—but the November light slanting through the window told me it was late. Rachel had long since gone to class.

I went downstairs. The clock on the stove in the kitchen read 9:00. This started the old Yankee in me shaking a finger, but I took my sleep as a good sign. Yesterday's events had not controlled me. I had, despite the dreams, got my snoring in. I would remember to tell Traynor this.

Rachel had left the coffee on, and I poured a cup. I heard

Cob's nails on the wooden stairs. Anything going on in the kitchen gets his attention. He came to me and I patted his broad skull. "Thanks for waking me up, buddy."

Cob wagged his tail and sniffed my crotch. I pushed his nose away. "I know what you want," I said, "and it's not that." I found the box of dog biscuits in the cupboard. I shook the box and Cob's ears stood at attention. Drool hung from his dewlaps. I gave him two, which he devoured standing. He cocked his ears for more. "That's it, Cobbie."

I sank in a chair at the kitchen table and sipped my coffee. Cob watched for a minute to see if more food would appear, then decided it was time to make the garbage-can loop. There's a leash law in town—not strictly enforced, especially if Cob sticks to the campus. He has his own doggie door, a big heavy oak thing he pushes with his thick skull, and he roams, the free spirit of the campus, Cob the King, the color of corn.

The coffee was strong and black. The sun was bright and pleasant streaming through the window. My thoughts soon drifted to what had happened in the woods. I thought about the run sheet I had to write. The sooner I got to it the better; I needed to put this baby to rest. I dumped the dregs of the coffee in the sink and phoned Striker.

Striker makes custom furniture, and as I suspected, he was at his shop.

"Can't you just fill the thing out yourself?" he said.

"This isn't your ordinary run-of-the mill. I'd appreciate your input." I could hear the whine of a table saw in the background. His assistant Jimmy was having at it with something tough— maybe cherry.

"You know as well as I do what happened. I'd just be nodding my head."

"Humor me, will you?"

We agreed to meet at the fire station in an hour.

I left the dorm. The air was crisp, the sky a bright blue, scrubbed clean by the storm that seemed to have happened not yesterday but at least a week ago.

There wasn't much movement on campus because it was school assembly time, and I made it to my truck at the post office parking lot without running into anyone except Cob, who was strutting around near the admissions building with what looked like half a loaf of bread in his mouth. I checked my mail—flyers, and blissfully no bills—and headed for the fire station.

I punched in the code for the combination lock and let myself in. The empty fire station had a musty smell of damp fire hoses, and with the high ceilings, my steps echoed like in the halls of a mausoleum. I glanced at the wall clock. Striker wouldn't arrive for another half hour.

I found an empty run sheet in a steel cabinet and sat down at a long folding table in the back room. This was where I usually went to write these things. Something about the starkness of the place helped get me thinking clearly.

A run sheet is a simple document, official-looking and state required. It has spaces for vitals—blood pressure, pulse, respirations—as well as a large empty box where you're supposed to compose a narrative of events.

Since I had already thought about what I would say on the truck ride back from Lebanon last night, I was eager to get started, and my pen moved freely as I reviewed how Chambers had led us to Rodriguez, how he was shot, and where and when we evacuated him.

I stopped writing where we loaded Rodriguez onto the chopper. My focus drifted to Chambers, and in my mind's eye I could see him lying in the cold. I imagined someone coming out of the dense growth, lifting the body on his shoulders, then toting it off. He had to have been watching us all along.

I heard Striker's footfalls in the station and walked out of the back room to greet him. "I was about to make a pot of coffee," I said. "Want some?"

"Thanks, but I don't have time."

"I appreciate your help." In the back room I showed him what I had written so far.

"Perfect," he said. "I told you I didn't need to come over."

"I'm not finished yet. I still have to talk about the chopper ride."

"So talk about it." Striker blew on his hands. "Why is this room always freezing?"

It was clear that Striker thought this a waste of his time.

"You in the middle of a project or something?"

"Yes."

I returned to my chair, sat down, and picked up the pen. "What happened after I took off on the chopper?"

"Nothing happened."

"Did you go right back to check on Chambers?"

"Not right away. Bumps called in the medical examiner. We just kind of hung around a little."

"Five? Ten minutes?"

"Fifteen, at least."

"Christ. It took that long?"

"We were all kind of dazed, I guess. Tired from carrying that damn litter. Nobody was in a hurry to drag a stiff out of the woods."

"What did you find when you got there?"

"What do you mean what did we find? We didn't find anything."

"I know Chambers' body was gone. I'm just wondering if you saw anything else unusual, you know, out of the ordinary."

"It was dark as hell. We almost got lost finding our way back."

I watched Striker fidget with a button on his coat. It was obvious he wasn't going to add much to the report.

"Look, Chad," he said. "I really do have to get back. Don't want to leave Jimmy by himself for too long."

"What do you think happened, Striker?"

"I don't know."

"You think the same guy who killed Chambers shot Rodriguez?"

Striker hesitated, then shrugged. "Could be."

"You're not saying what you think."

Striker smiled. "Why speculate?" He paused in the doorway. "We'll probably never know one way or another."

"You really think we won't ever find out what happened?"

Striker pulled his coat closer. "I try not to think, Chad. I make furniture. That's what I do."

"Aren't you the least bit curious?"

"Sure. But making wild guesses about what happened has nothing to do with any run sheet."

"I just wondered if you had anything to add, that's all."

He glanced at the paper in my hand. "It looks pretty good, Chad. I wouldn't say anything else. Just hand it in and forget about it."

Striker left. From what I knew about him—a loner—he didn't

like to get involved with much of anything. I usually had trouble carrying on a conversation with him because he was so damn tight-lipped. Having been holed up alone for the past few years with my own demons, I could relate. Thank God for Rachel.

I read through the run sheet again and was satisfied with the straightforward chronicle of events. It was accurate, and nothing stood out as being obvious trouble if I had to take the witness stand.

But as I drove back up to Lebanon to deliver the thing, the discipline of writing it all down only opened up more questions for me. I knew my description didn't come close to explaining why Rodriguez and Chambers had been shot, and especially why Chambers' body had disappeared.

I suddenly felt tired. I mentally checked the date of my next appointment with Traynor. Two weeks away. Shit. I could always call her, but it would be like admitting failure, a sign that I had suffered a relapse. I didn't need that on top of everything else.

By the time I reached the parking lot of the hospital, I was determined to just drop off the run sheet and be done with it. My responsibilities ended, I could get back to plowing and gathering wood, what I do best.

I didn't ask anything about Rodriguez when I handed the nurse the run sheet, but she said that he was in a coma.

"So, he never came to at all?" I asked.

"Not that I'm aware of." The nurse was pixie cute, with pageboy dark hair and a round face. Her build was short, athletic, and her skin had the taut tone of an aerobics instructor.

"But he's still alive?" Amazing. Rodriguez had looked like he had been dipped in chalk last night. I didn't think he had a chance when they rolled him into the operating room.

"Thanks to you."

"Me?"

"I guess you're quite the hero," she said.

"Who told you that?"

"Lefty and I are good friends."

"And he called me a hero?"

"He was impressed with the way you handled your end of it."

I could feel my face coloring. That Lefty thought I was a hero meant something, and despite my modest tendencies, I had to admit I liked what she said. "I did what I could."

She smiled at me. Her eyes were smiling, too.

"The femur's fixed, I guess."

She nodded. "He's stabilized."

"Any idea when he might come out of it?"

"Doctor's optimistic. That's all I heard him say."

Her eyes were earnest now, as if waiting for the next question. I checked myself. Why was I asking her all this? The hero crap threw me off. She had the run sheet; it was over. "If he comes to, tell him I send my best."

"I'm sure he'll want to thank you."

"No need to. Like I said, I just did what I could."

I had to pass through the Emergency waiting room to get to the parking lot, and I was surprised to spot Tierney sitting next to a dark-haired woman with a balled-up handkerchief in her hands. He motioned for me to come over.

"Didn't expect to see you here," he said.

I mumbled something about the run sheet.

He turned toward the woman. "This is Manuella Silva. Mr. Rodriguez's sister."

I took her hand. It was damp from her handkerchief. She

had long fingernails, polished a glossy purple. "Pleasure meeting you," I said.

"Chad is the one I was telling you about," Tierney said to Manuella. "The one who did so much for your brother."

Manuella's face brightened. "Then it is indeed a pleasure." She squeezed my hand tighter, and one of her nails dug in.

I wanted to pull it away, but her look was so intent, I thought I might offend her. "I wasn't the only one," I said.

"God bless you," she said. "He's alive thanks to you." She held on to my hand for awhile, and I started to feel really stupid standing there.

Manuella Silva, by her mannerisms and speech—her broad A's—placed her around Boston. She looked to be in her early thirties, stocky, olive-skinned, with dark sloe eyes that looked half closed. She wore a long overcoat with a fake fur collar that she pulled about her as she shifted in her chair. Finally, she let go of my hand.

There was a moment when neither of us said anything, and I wasn't about to open my mouth because I didn't know how much the doctor had told her.

Tierney clued me in. "As I was saying, Ms. Silva. The doctor really can't tell how long it will take your brother to come out of it, if he does at all."

"I know that. He told me that."

"So anything you can tell me about your brother might help us get to the bottom of this."

"I know. I know. I just can't believe he got shot."

"And you're sure he's no hunter?" Tierney asked.

She batted the air to dismiss the idea. "Joseph couldn't hunt a rat in a toilet."

"You have no idea why he was in the woods?"

"No."

"You knew the other man, this Mr. Chambers?"

"Never met him. Joseph talked about him, though."

"Did Mr. Chambers like to hunt?"

"I don't know."

I felt the odd man out in Tierney's interrogation, and I was sure he'd forgotten I was even there. "Excuse me," I said. "I have to be leaving."

Manuella Silva smiled up at me. "Of course. We must be keeping you."

She looked like she was going to get up and take my hand again, so I stepped toward her and patted her on the shoulder and said as sincerely as I could manage: "I hope your brother recovers."

I couldn't get out of the hospital fast enough. Having been considered a hero twice in the span of a half hour left me sullen and more than a little angry. I didn't like the role. I'd seen too many heroes with their guts spilling over their belts.

The sun was bright on my face. Gradually my mood began to change.

My job was done.

CHAPTER SIX

On the ride home, my thoughts shifted to Damon. With all the run sheet business, I had forgotten all about him. I was concerned with how this murder was settling with him the day after. He thinks I worry too much about him. Maybe I do.

When I came back to live with my grandfather after Meg died, I found Damon living in the same place I'd left him before I joined up—one of the original buildings in Dunston, a caretaker's cottage that had been part of the infamous commune. There was one big difference, though: He was living alone.

My father died while we were both in high school, and soon after my graduation, Willa Pill moved out of the old farmhouse into that smaller cottage, leaving Grandpa by himself. She said the old place was too much to care for, and besides, she had Damon to look after.

Willa died during my second tour in 'Nam. Damon didn't take it well, I guess. The story goes that Damon started giving away all his stored-up deer meat. Bumps, a bit curious, paid him a visit. He found Willa in the freezer. She was a little bit of a thing, so, with the shelves out, she fit without being folded. Damon had wrapped a blanket around her so she wouldn't get cold. They figured Damon had kept her that way for about a month.

There was then some talk of institutionalizing Damon, but Grandpa fought for his custody and freedom. He got him psychiatric help, and Damon soon settled into a routine of hunting, fishing, and fixing things. Some people are born caregivers, and my grandfather was one. When he died, I figured I owed it to him to watch out for Damon.

Damon worked out of his house, and every time I drove up, the sight gave me pause. On the lawn were the two '75 Ford F-150s I had yelled at him to get fixed just the day before. They were up on blocks. One was yellow and rusted out with its hood open, engine-less. The red one with the good body had just received the transplant. But that one didn't run, either.

Damon was too busy to finish the truck job, fixing the TVs, ham radios, cell phones, microwaves, computers, washing machines, vacuum cleaners, Dustbusters—anything, in short, that had a current running through it or a part that had to flip, spin, or reboot. People just stacked things up on either of the attached closed-in porches, and Damon whittled away at the pile when he got around to it. If you showed up and bugged him, he'd paw through the junk and fix it on the spot and charge you a quarter. I joked with him once about hanging out a sign: *Savant Fix It.* He didn't understand, but he got mad because he could tell I was kidding him.

As if the fix-it business didn't bring in enough junk, Damon was best friends with Harold Barrow, the town dump-meister. There was an ordinance against picking, but Harold would tip off Damon if some precious treasure came in. Damon would drag the loot home and play with it, creating backyard Henry

Moores out of storm windows, satellite dishes, oil drums, re-frigerators—even a cast-off tractor, rusted a mottled red with two TV antennas sprouting like angels' wings from the engine well, a department store mannequin sitting demurely in the scooped seat, one hand extended with a cigarette holder, the other firmly gripped on the wheel. Damon called it "The Angel in Space." I preferred "Winged Pegasus."

He had something he called a "Tower of Tools," just a bunch of hand tools he' welded together, starting from the ground up that reached to a height of over eight feet before the ladder he had stacked against it slipped off, and he almost impaled himself on an old cross-cut saw blade that stuck out about halfway down the tower.

Lining the road in front of the house at Christmas was a series of old galvanized pipes driven into the ground, and into the top of each he stuck a branch from a silver, plastic Christmas tree. He illuminated his sculptures with tree lights, and last year he beamed with pride over his neon-lighted contraption that fizzled and popped and read "Bah Humbug."

But what he loved the most, and spent endless hours grooming, was the path that wound down by the stream near his house, punctuated with Chinese pagodas that had small wire baskets hanging from them, crammed with teddy bears and other stuffed animals—a purple zebra, two yellow giraffes, a black, hairy-chested ape—some even hanging from nooses, swaying in the wind in a surreal *danse macabre.* Damon liked to think of this as his children's park, which is sad because children were told to stay away from Damon.

I found Damon inside having lunch. He was frying up some hash from a can, and was about to mix in the *pièce de résistance*—miniature cocktail hotdogs—when I walked in the door.

He look up above the sizzling hash and waved his wooden spoon at me. "There you are. Where the hell have you been?"

"Why? What's the matter?" He usually wasn't this animated about seeing me. I figured something was up.

"I tried you at home," he said. "I even called down at the school."

"I was in Lebanon."

"Jeesum Crow! You're never home when I need you."

"Will you tell me what's going on?"

"I must have left three calls on your machine." He shook his spoon at me. "I can't believe I forgot to tell you last night."

"Tell me what?"

"It was because I fell asleep in the truck. That was it. I got all messed up. I was going to tell you at the hospital, too—but that was before I saw the pizza. And that messed me up, too." He slammed the spoon down in the hash. "Shit!" He beat a tattoo with his spoon on the edge of the pan.

I had to step around a pile of *Life* magazines to get to him. You could barely move around the place without confronting a monument to the publishing industry, all neatly stacked according to date. He had copies of *The National Geographic* that went back to the early 'forties when Willa had started collecting them.

I put my hand on his arm to calm the spooning staccato. "It's okay, Damon. I'm here now."

"But, you weren't there then," he said.

"I know, and I'm sorry."

"You mean it?"

"I'm sorry, and I mean it." I could feel his hand relax. I took over the wooden spoon. "Now, why don't you sit at the table and let me serve you."

He looked up at me with the doleful eyes of a kindly dancing bear. "You going to eat, too?"

"Sure. I'm kinda hungry." I spooned the hash, pushing hard against the burned part that smoked hot in the middle like a signal fire. I worried about his diet—there was nothing green in it; his plate was usually full of browns, pale yellows, and whites.

I waited until he settled in his chair. "Now, why don't you just say your say."

"It happened when we went back for that guy."

"Chambers?"

"Yeah. The dead guy. Jeez! You should have seen it."

"You saw somebody out there?"

"Not somebody."

I stirred the hash and kept calm. Damon got this way when he had a secret. It was almost too much for him to keep it inside, but he hated to let it out because then the fun would be gone.

"You going to make me guess?" I said.

"It was a buck!" he blurted, the strain obviously too much to bear.

"A buck? You saw a buck?"

He made like his fingers were antlers and stuck them on his head. "Yeah."

"I know what a buck is, Damon." I stirred the hash.

"No you don't. Not until you've seen this one."

"What's so special?"

"It's huge."

"How big?"

"Size of my truck."

"The yellow or the red one?"

His eyes narrowed. "Come on, Chad. They're the same size. You're kidding me."

"Maybe a little."

"Well, don't kid me. I don't like it." He rose from his chair. "You always do that. Why do you always do that?"

"Don't get started again."

"But you always do that."

I got two plates out of the draining rack near the sink, utensils from the attached plastic well, and placed them on the table. I spooned the hash onto the plates and sat down in the chair next to him. "So, tell me about this buck," I said.

Damon's eyes lit up when he spoke, and I knew I was going to hear about this beast until we either found it or they lowered me in the ground.

"So, that's why you called. You want to go hunting."

"You should see his rack." Damon spread his arms.

"Let's wait for the weekend. We planned to go on Saturday, remember?"

"No. Somebody else will get him."

"The property might be posted."

"We didn't see no signs."

"I know. But we'd better check it out, anyway."

"Come on, Chad." He stabbed the hash with his fork. It stood upright in the middle of the dish. "If you won't go with me, I'll go by myself."

"Let me look into it. We don't want to get arrested, right?"

Damon didn't say anything. He stuck out his lower lip.

"Okay. I'll take you after you get that truck fixed."

He grinned at me. "She turned over today. Should be running by tomorrow."

Shit.

***

Grandpa's farmhouse had green shutters and white clapboards, typical of New Englanders, with the requisite built-ons that led out the rear to the barn so you could do winter-time milking without stepping outside. The cows had since gone the way of Grandpa, though, and the buildings no longer served their function, except perhaps as a backdrop for Kodak-wielding flatlanders on a quest for the "quaint."

It felt as if I had been away for a few weeks when I walked through the back kitchen door. Familiar objects had taken on a patina of change, but I knew time was playing tricks. So many things had happened in a short span that it felt like I had been on a long trip.

I made coffee. The clock on the fireplace mantle in the living room chimed once, and I checked my watch to confirm it. Rachel wouldn't be out of class for another two hours, and thinking about her made me remember our dinner date tonight. We had planned to go out to a new restaurant in Concord, reputed to have a live blues band. Tonight was an open mike. Just what the doctor ordered.

I grabbed the paper from the front stoop, curious over what it had to say about Chambers and Rodriguez, and sat down on the sofa in the living room. The headline read: Two Hunters Shot. The coverage was thin, though, and the article didn't mention names because the next of kin hadn't been notified. I remembered Manuella Silva. Those long fingernails. I put the paper down. The next edition no doubt would have more info. I took one sip from my cup, lay my head back on the couch, and fell asleep.

I awoke to the phone ringing. It was Rachel. "I'm sorry. I don't think I'll be able to make it tonight."

"You won't? Why not?" I glanced at the mantle clock. Almost four. I had slept three full hours.

"I'm sorry, something came up," she said. "You okay?"

"Yeah. Sure. Just a little tired, that's all. And disappointed."

"I thought about you a lot today," she said softly.

"You mean you worried about me."

"Not really."

"Darn."

"Okay. I worried about you."

I told her about turning in the run sheet in Lebanon, about Rodriguez in a coma, about Damon and his buck, about not needing to worry because I was fine. "So, how come we can't go out?" I said.

Rachel sighed. "I really love my job, but sometimes it's a pain."

"All your students flunking?"

"I wish the problem were that easy. Remember I told you about Angela?"

"Yeah, your advisee. The one into leather and body piercing."

"I found a bag of marijuana in the washer when I went to shift her clothes into the dryer."

"You were doing her laundry?"

"No, stupid. I needed to use the machine."

"So now you have to narc on her?"

"There's a court session tonight. I hate this job."

"No you don't."

"It would be so easy to look the other way."

"You'd be dead meat in the dorm. No credibility."

"I know. I know."

"Want to come over here?" I asked. "I can whip up some

eggs or something. Might do you good to have a break from the place."

"Thanks, but I have to stay."

After she hung up, I walked around the house, growing increasingly aware of my disappointment. I needed to be with her tonight. The aloneness of the place was beginning to take on a shape of its own. I turned on the TV for company. Montel Williams had a Jack Spratt show—fat women and skinny men. One woman was six-six, three-fifty, and her mate looked like Barney Fife without the badge. Before I met Rachel, I had read ads in the Personals and even began to understand what they meant. Never answered any, though. *Height/Weight Proportional* always got me. I suppose you could argue six-six, three-fifty was just that.

I snapped off the TV and switched on the scanner in the kitchen.

After a supper of scrambled eggs, I decided to clean my firearms. With Damon chomping at the bit about his buck, I knew it was only a matter of time before we were in the field.

It's not like I had an arsenal—it's mostly stuff I inherited from Grandpa. The stock of his Marlin .30/30 lever action was worn smooth with use, but the rifling was still accurate. He'd bought a Redfield 5-Star 4x scope for it when his eyes started to go, but for most of his life he hunted without it, reminding me constantly as a young boy growing up that there's "a fine line that separates the true hunter from the mere killer of animals." You're a hunter if you track well and get one good shot. I suppose that's the reason I became a medic and didn't pick up a rifle in the war. There's no sport in carnage.

I get my deer every year, now, but I hunt with a bow—and

I'm pretty much a hunting snob about that, too. No fiberglass compounds. I'm a dedicated longbow and recurve hunter, a hopeless romantic.

The State of New Hampshire allows bow hunting from September 15th through December 15th, quite a stretch compared with the Muzzleloader (November 2- November 12) and Regular Firearms (November 13-December 8). Why so long for bow hunters? Because it's damned hard to shoot a deer with a bow. You have to know how to track, you have to have patience, you have to think like a deer. The gutted six-point buck I shot the previous week hangs from the swivel ring of my hayloft door. One shot, right behind the left shoulder.

Damon hated it when I got my deer first, and I knew why he was so excited about this big buck. He wanted to show me up. I taught him how to shoot a bow. He had a tree stand in one of his favorite spots, something I refused to use, but he was still a lousy shot with a bow.

All through the evening, I worked at the cleaning, including the Colt M1911 pistol Grandpa carried during the war. There was not much going on with the scanner except for a chimney fire the next town over, and I settled into the routine, thinking about my grandfather and his gifts to me.

He'd left behind more than his imprint on the firearms. This house and the objects I inherited paled against the gift he gave of himself. He took me in and asked no questions. He read to me in those first days after my return to this place when I was too paralyzed with ennui and a deep sickness in the heart to do much of anything except lie in bed. When his glaucoma got so bad that his eyes bulged like billiard balls, I read to him.

I had never been much for books, but Grandpa changed all

that. He read everything he could get his hands on, and the weight of his library literally caused the floor in the living room to sag. From him I learned about Odysseus, Virgil, and the Hegelian Dialectic. He died in bed, hearing the words of Keats and his Nightingale's sweeter unheard melodies as I read him into the beyond.

My reverie was broken by Bumps' familiar voice on the scanner. Through the crackle and the back-and-forth chatter, it didn't take long to figure out they had found another body on the Turner property.

CHAPTER SEVEN

I hopped into my truck and headed out. I switched on the radio—the one I carry for EMT calls—to channel three, the municipal channel, and listened to the back and forth of Bumps and the state police. Tierney was on his way.

The stars looked like ice crystals, sharply defined in the cold, dark sky, and there was no wind anywhere, just a stillness where the only thing moving seemed to be me and my truck.

Bumps and Tierney grew pretty tight-lipped over the air waves, as I suspected they would. You don't say much about such things over the radio, not in this age of manic jurisprudence and nosey people like me listening to scanners. My mind was racing, though, and the conversation in my head filled the void. What was going on here? Who the hell was this guy they found? What, if anything, did he have to do with Chambers and Rodriguez?

I was vaguely aware of the tires humming on the highway, but I was so much inside my head I didn't realize that I was drifting toward the shoulder. I caught the right rear tire on the lip of the highway. I jerked the wheel back to the left and the truck lurched and bucked. I braked and slowed. The damn plow. I still had the plow attached. I pulled off the side of the road and lay my head back against the rear window.

This was not good. What was happening out there was none of my business. A car sped by and honked its horn. I made a U-turn and headed slowly back toward Dunston. It bothered me that I could be so easily lured toward trouble.

I used the phone in the post office parking lot and was relieved when Rachel picked up right away. "How did it go?"

"Not over yet," she said.

"I see. Bad time to call?"

"You could say that."

"Sorry. I'll hang up." But I stayed on the line. "I just wanted to talk. Did they kick her out?"

"Headmaster's mulling." Rachel lowered her voice. "She needs help. Parents are in denial."

"She's sitting right there, isn't she?"

"Yes."

"Maybe later we can get together and talk."

"I'd like that."

"Good."

"But I can't. I just can't. There's too much going on."

"Look. I'll let you go."

"I'm sorry."

"Watch the news tonight."

"Why?"

"They found another body on the Turner property."

"Jesus Christ."

"Amen."

When I got home, I switched on the 11:00 news. A late-breaking story but few details. A news chopper was on the way. I didn't watch any more of it.

***

There is a silence that settles on the house at night after I burrow beneath the quilt that kept my grandfather warm for nearly a century, and it bores into the spaces of my consciousness where secrets are harbored; they whisper in a sibilance, their rhythms like an erratic heartbeat that says all is not yet well.

My wife sometimes comes to visit in this troubled silence, and I see her clearly, at times feeling I am holding her, her belly pushed against me, hearing the small thump of the child, mittening to get out—and I sometimes wonder what it would have been like if she and the child had lived.

This was not good. Not good. Traynor says it is fruitless to think of what might have been. But was it really that bad?

Sometimes I am blessed in this silence seeing my child, dancing. She is in a studio of mirrors, multiplied, her moves graceful, her legs muscular and supple as a thoroughbred. She spins toward me, her smile growing. She stops, places a hand on my shoulder, kisses my cheek.

In the morning, I was just finishing up the dishes when I heard a knock at the door.

"Are you Chad Duquette?"

A woman smiled at me from the stoop. She looked to be just out of college, dressed in a classy camel-hair coat, her face rouged and eager.

"That's right."

"My name's Natasha Wright. I'm with *The Concord Patriot.* I wonder if I could ask you a few questions."

"About what?"

"I understand you were the EMT in charge when those men were shot."

I stood in the doorway and studied her. I wiped my hands

slowly on a dish towel. The morning sun behind her fell warm on the doorstep, and wispy puffs of condensation rose from the brick walkway.

"I suppose you could say I was in charge."

She hugged herself against the cold. "Could I talk with you?"

It wasn't very neighborly of me to keep her standing there, but I didn't like the idea of her showing up uninvited, either.

I was about to tell her I was too busy, but she piqued my curiosity. "Do you think the body they found last night is connected in any way to those shootings?" she asked. Her eyes met mine directly.

Inside the house, I caught a whiff of her perfume as I helped her off with her coat, and I felt a bit self-conscious over the maleness of the place—my Early Brewery decor—empty beer bottles, peanut shells, hunting magazines and such.

I made another pot of coffee. We exchanged inanities in the kitchen, then adjourned to the living room where she sat in the overstuffed chair and arranged her scarf, sipped her coffee, and made a *hmm* sound.

I pulled up the desk chair and faced her. She crossed her legs and tugged the edge of her skirt toward her knees. She had nice legs.

"Can you tell me your version of what happened?" she began.

"My version? There's more than one?"

She put her cup down and removed a steno notebook from her purse. "From the beginning, please."

I sipped coffee and thought a minute, then began my story. She wrote in long, loopy scrawls, flipping pages while I talked.

"And as far as you know Mr. Rodriguez is still in a coma?"

"That's right."

She waggled her pencil. "He's key here, isn't he?"

"I don't know what you mean."

"He's the only one who can tell us what really happened."

I drained my coffee cup and held it in both hands on my lap. "That's supposing he knows."

Her face broke into a smile. "Come on, Mr. Duquette. You must think he knows."

I shrugged. "You're probably right."

She sat back and uncrossed her legs. She bit the tip of her eraser. "Let me get this straight. You don't think Rodriguez knows the person who shot him? What about Chambers?"

"Wait a minute. I never said he didn't know who shot him. It was just an offhand comment." I cleared my throat. "The point is, none of us knows what really happened out there."

She thought about that. "But in cases like this, most likely those involved know each other."

"You're the expert."

"I know that there's killing and carnage because of jealousy, anger, that sort of thing." She waved her hand like she was churning something up.

"Rodriguez probably does know. It makes sense."

She recrossed her legs. "But let's just suppose you're right, that neither Chambers nor Rodriguez knew who shot them."

"Yeah?"

"Then there's only one other answer ... that someone randomly picked them out and tracked them down."

I stared at her but didn't say anything. I felt like I was being led someplace I didn't want to go.

"You have to admit it's a logical conclusion to make." She seemed pleased with herself. The clock on the mantle chimed ten times. "Don't you think?"

"You're not going to write that, are you?"

"I don't know."

"I wouldn't."

"Why?"

"For one thing it would stir up trouble. Get people scared around here."

She smiled at me again. "I know I must look pretty young to you, Mr. Duquette, but I've been in the newspaper business for over ten years. I'm just trying to understand what happened out there."

"Even if you have to make it up?" I looked closely at her face. There was a hint of crow's feet near her eyes, but other than that she probably got carded every time she ordered a drink. She had to be over thirty. For some reason, that changed my opinion of her—like she was some vamp who had lured me into something—and I wanted this conversation to end.

"I write what's in front of my face, Mr. Duquette. If you don't think they knew each other, that might be important."

"But you're twisting what I said." I felt myself getting hot.

She smiled at me. "You can calm down, Mr. Duquette. I'm not going to twist anything."

"Look, Ms. Wright, I would like you to tell me exactly what you are going to write in your article."

"I can't tell you that."

"Why not?"

"Because I haven't written it yet."

"I'd better not be misquoted."

She closed her notebook. "Is that some sort of threat?"

I ignored her comment. "If you write that I believe Rodriguez didn't know who shot him, you'd be telling a lie."

She stared at me hard. "Well. What *do* you think, then?"

It wasn't a question. It was a demand. "I don't know what I think," I said. "And you can write that."

She stood up and brushed at her skirt. "Thank you for your time, Mr. Duquette. You've given me an interesting slant. And the more I think about it, it ties in well with what I found out yesterday."

I got her coat from the closet and helped her on with it. "What did you find out yesterday?"

She thought a moment. "Okay. Let me run this by you: When I arrived on the scene last night, I got to talk to the man who reported the other hunter killed." She adjusted her coat. Her perfume hit me again, something sweet, like cinnamon apples.

"And?"

"I asked him if he found the body accidently—you know, just came across him while he was hunting. He told me he stumbled onto it when he was trying to run away from somebody taking pot shots at him."

"What?"

"Now, don't you think that's a little significant?"

Bumps visits a diner about a mile outside of Dunston for lunch most every day, and I puttered around after Natasha Wright left, killing time until 11:30 before driving down to meet him by looking through some old newspapers in the barn and rereading her stuff. She had an "in your face" style that was immediately engaging. And she was tough. She once took on a strip mall developer and stirred up enough support to save wetlands just outside Concord. I feared what she would write.

The temperature had risen steadily since early morning, and the snow was melting rapidly. This warmth, though, was a momentary respite, for another front was predicted to move through later on with more light snow expected tonight, roller-coaster weather, typical for this early winter time of year.

Across the street from Holten's Diner was the Dunston mini-mart. The building was divided in two. A combination gas station, small engine repair shop, and deer- weighing station occupied the other end. As I pulled into the parking lot of Holten's, I could see an old Chevy Caprice with a buck strapped over the hood, just making a turn into the station.

I chose a booth with a window view and watched the ritual of weighing-in going on across the street as I drank coffee waiting for Bumps. Driving around with the trophy on the car, showing the kill off at the weigh-in, telling the heroic tales of the hunt—this had been the stuff of New Hampshire men for eons. And what if there was someone out there hunting the hunters?

Bumps walked in right on schedule. He was by himself. I waved him over. "So, you've been busy," I said.

He slid into the booth and plopped his hat on the table. "I guess to Christ."

"I heard it on the scanner."

"You and everybody else. It's a real pisser, I'll tell you that."

"Who's the guy who was killed?"

"Name's Perino."

"Local?"

"From Massachusetts. Another one."

The waitress came and took our order—a bacon double-cheese for Bumps, and a tuna grinder for me. I'd hate to see Bumps' cholesterol level, and he'll never have it tested. He's almost sixty and hasn't been to a doctor since he had to have a three- penny nail removed from his foot when he was a kid. Doesn't believe in them.

"What's up?" he said. "You come down to pump me for information, or you got something on your mind?"

I told him about Natasha Wright. "I thought I'd warn you," I said.

"Jesus. That's all we need."

"I wanted you to know it wasn't my idea."

"You think she's right?"

"Do you?"

Bumps let out a sigh. "Here we've got two men killed, one in a coma, and another guy says he was shot at. It may be not be too farfetched to think someone's out there hunting them down."

The waitress came with the food. Cheryl Holten, the owner's daughter, was a petite thing with a bow in her hair, a recent high school graduate sometimes pulling double shifts to save enough money to go to Plymouth State in the fall. In addition to the burger, she plunked down a double-chocolate malt for Bumps. I had more coffee.

"Thank you, Cheryl." Bumps winked at her.

"I don't know," I said. "It seems to me that Chambers and Rodriguez and this guy Perino have got to be connected."

Bumps took large bites and still tried to talk. "Let me tell you something else. Perino was wearing a shoulder holster."

"A sidearm?"

Bumps shook his head. "Holster was empty."

I stopped mid-bite and put my sandwich on the plate. "Wait a minute."

Bumps aimed his burger at me. "You're thinking that the pistol you found on Rodriguez fits in that holster."

"You bet."

"The answer is, it could. But it could also just be coincidence—that both had been carrying handguns."

"What's the likelihood of that?"

Bumps shrugged and took a big bite of his burger. He pulled out a large piece of bacon with his teeth, and part of it lay over his chin. He worked it into his mouth with chipmunk-size bites, never letting go of his burger.

As I watched him eat I imagined a struggle between Rodriguez and Perino with the former wresting Perino's sidearm and shooting him.

"Do you know what killed Perino?"

"Gunshot."

"I know that. What kind of gun?"

"Have to wait for ballistics." He wiped his mouth with a napkin. "You know that."

"So, if the bullet that killed Perino matches the pistol I found on Rodriguez, it stands to reason that Rodriquez shot him."

"Stands to reason." Bumps' cheeks imploded as he sucked heavily on his straw. "If we could ever find that pistol."

"Then that means these killings aren't random."

"Maybe so. But we still don't know who shot at the guy who found Perino."

I took a bite of my sandwich. "Oh, yeah."

Bumps drained his malt with a slurpy rattle. "Like I said. It's a real pisser."

When I got home there was a message on my machine from Damon. The light snow tonight would make tomorrow morning a perfect time to go after that big buck. He was hoping I would join him.

I decided a phone call wouldn't do it. Damon would need some face-to-face convincing to postpone the trip until more about what was really happening on the Turner property came to light.

As I drove to Damon's house I thought about the Turner property. Before I left the diner, I'd asked Bumps if he knew if the land was posted, and he said he thought it was in "current use," a trade-off the state makes with landowners which basically says you can have a tax break if you allow others to traipse across your property. The kicker is that the Turners didn't own it anymore, and Bumps thought the new owners were from out of state.

I was also curious about another discovery Bumps had let slip: cocaine was found in both Chamber's and Rodriguez's blood. I wondered how many more coke snortin' hunters were out there banging away at anything orange.

I found Damon laying out his gear. He was meticulous about everything he carried, and his eyes glimmered with expectation as he arranged his boots near his bed.

"I can see you're ready to go," I said.

"We've got to get a real early start. I'm setting my alarm for three-thirty."

"I don't know if tomorrow's such a good time."

He sat on the edge of his bed and looked up at me. "Why not?"

I told him about the hunter who got shot at, the one who stumbled over Perino's body.

"So?"

"So, I don't think it's safe out there right now."

He grinned at me. "Come on, Chad. You're kidding me again."

"Nope. This time I'm serious."

His eyebrows furrowed. "We've got to go after that buck."

"And we will. Like I said before, this weekend. We planned to go anyway."

He got up from the bed and stared at me. "You aren't kidding," he said. He turned on his heels and stormed into the kitchen.

"Hey, it's not my fault," I called after him.

I could hear him rummaging around in the cabinets. When he got upset, he usually went after something to eat. I found him with his hand in a Cheerios box. "Just calm down," I said.

"I'm going anyway," he said.

"No, you're not."

"Am too."

I put my hand on his shoulder. "Look, Damon. Somebody might be out there shooting at hunters."

"So what?"

"So what? Doesn't that bother you?"

He crammed another fistful of Cheerios into his mouth. "You can track him. You can see him before he gets us."

"I don't want to."

"I'm going. I'll shoot him before he can see me."

I watched him eat. It was hopeless; there was no stopping him, and there was no way I was letting him go out there alone. I had to admit, though, I was a little more than curious about what we would find out there.

CHAPTER EIGHT

I picked up Damon right at 4:00 AM, and we headed out to the old Turner property. It's legal to start hunting a half hour before sunup, and we wanted to be in the woods by first light—about 6:20. We doused ourselves with deer scent before we left the house. It was still dark by the time we reached the spot where he'd seen the buck. The moon was full and we had light enough to see.

Our breaths condensed in plumes as we crunched across a frosty popcorn snow, about three inches of night powder on top of a frozen crust. I cradled the Marlin under one arm as we walked.

Grandpa taught me long ago there are two types of hunters: stump sitters, who sit and wait for whitetail, and still-hunters, who go out looking for them. Still-hunting is harder, for you must get inside the deer's head, get to know his habits, where he feeds, where he beds down for the night. And you've got to outsmart him if you're going to see him at all. When I was ten I got my first buck, still-hunting with my grandfather. Everything I know about tracking I learned from him.

We had worked our way up from the highway across the field—spaced out about fifteen yards from each other—and were at the edge of a copse of thick fir at the top of the hill when Damon sneezed. He gave a good honk into his handkerchief.

"For crissake, Damon," I whispered. "Can't you make any more noise?"

"Sorry. I couldn't help it."

"You sure this is the spot?"

"This is it."

Damon's nose was red from the cold, and it looked like it might be enough to designate him as a hunter without his neon orange knit cap. He had his rifle, a bolt-action Remington, another one that had belonged to my grandfather, slung over his shoulder.

I bent down to examine the area more closely with my flashlight and brushed away some of the snow. The new snow pretty much negated picking up any sign that may have been left behind when Damon first spotted the buck, but knowing that it had been here was a valuable piece of information.

Whitetails tend to follow a set routine, and if you could somehow hover above them and study their habits, you'd be able to draw their peripatetic route on a topo map, and the shape might look something like an amoeba. Inside the lines, you'd find all the deer needed to survive—water, food, and places to hide. The idea was to find his tracks, follow him, see him before he saw you.

"Why don't you go over to the east," I said. "See what you can find. I'll take this line." I motioned dead ahead.

Damon nodded without saying anything. He was in his hunting mode now, and when he set his mind to it, he could move with finesse in the woods. I knew the two of us working together had a good chance of catching sight of the beast. In the back of my mind, I wondered what else we might run across.

It's impossible to move in the woods without making any noise, and it was especially difficult under these crusty conditions. The trick is to move like a deer and you'll sound like one, one or two steps, then hold your position, look around.

We worked our way up over a ridge in this deliberate manner, and it was down in a small saddle, after a half hour's work, that Damon found fresh tracks. He was pretty excited.

"I told you. I told you."

I knelt down and followed with my eye where the tracks led uphill across another ridge. This was a big buck all right. Maybe not Damon's, but a big one. In light snow, a buck drags his toes so the path is pretty easy to follow—like this one—while a doe has a tendency to pick them up and set them down clean.

"Look at the size of that thing," Damon said.

I examined one nicely formed track, a deep impression in a boggy area where dark mud showed in sharp relief against the snow. At its heel, the footprint was as broad as my fist, and the dewclaws speared the ground a good three inches behind the heel. I broke off a piece of twig that measured the distance precisely and stuck it in my pocket for future reference.

"Look how deep that heel goes in," Damon said.

"That's where he carries all his weight."

"I know that."

"He's been rutting."

"No shit."

I followed the tracks a little farther up out of the saddle to where I could assess the wind direction. We were in luck. The wind was still in our faces. Deer tend to move to higher ground in the early morning when the thermals are still flowing downhill. When the sun heats the earth, the thermals shift, and if you're caught in the middle of it, the deer can pick up your scent and bolt before you know it.

Damon assumed his position on the flank, and we hunted in our usual take-a-few-steps-and-freeze style, using the cover of trees and bushes as much as possible. About halfway up the rise, I ran across some dribbled scat, still moist, another sign that this was a buck we were following. A doe tends to take her time and drop her stuff in a clump.

Athletes talk about a zone they get in when things are clicking on all cylinders, and that's what it was like for me when I got hot on the trail. We must have hunted a good hour before it crept into my mind again that we were on the land where the shootings had occurred, where, at least according to Natasha Wright's theory, we were in danger of being shot at. I didn't buy it, though. We had seen no signs of any other hunters, and I felt confident that my senses could pick up anything peculiar. It would be nice, though, to have a deer's nose at times like these.

We reached the top of the ridge and the tracks skirted to the left, traversed the ridge and led through a recent clear-cut. The wind at this point dropped.

The sun was up now and glared off the snow. We reached the edge of the clearing and were back in the woods when I spotted a ground scrape, a place the buck probably visited at night when he was out on patrol. Overhead there was a branch that showed signs of wear. Most likely he nuzzled, licked, and marked it with his scent.

"What are we stopping for?" Damon asked.

"Just checking this out."

"Come on. We're going to lose him."

"This isn't a race. You hydrating?"

"What?"

"Take some water."

After more coaxing, Damon finally took a swig of his water bottle. He put it away and flapped his arms against his coat.

"You okay?" I asked again.

"I'm okay."

"You look pretty cold."

"I'm cold because we stopped, stupid."

"You're cold because you haven't been drinking. When it's cold, you can get more dehydrated than when it's really hot."

"Oh, shut up, will you? You have to be such a damned expert about everything."

"All right. Forget it."

"Always yappin' about something."

I walked away from him, back out into the clearing again.

He followed close behind. "Where are you going? You're mad at me, aren't you?"

"About what?"

"About what I said. You know, yappin' all the time."

"I probably deserved it."

"You did?"

I didn't answer him but looked out across the valley to the northeast.

"Does that mean we can go now?"

"I'm not mad at you, Damon. I'm waiting for the wind to shift."

"Oh."

I pointed across the valley. "Look. You can see the back part of that old mine."

Tinderhook Mine on Tingly Mountain was mostly an open pit, but there were also giant rooms with arched ceilings dug out by Amos Tinderhook and family back in the early 1800s when he discovered mica on his land. From our angle and height on top of this ridge, two open tunnels appeared as sunken eyeholes of a skull, an open expanse of granite above serving as the forehead.

"That's Tinderhook?" Damon said. "Jeez. We've walked pretty far."

"It's deceiving. We've taken a slight curve to the southwest since this morning. It's not the same distance as it would be walking the highway."

"How do you know?"

"Because on the highway you have to go around Tingly Mountain first." I felt a chill standing there. We had lost the sun temporarily behind a fair-weather cloud. The wind had definitely shifted and was running pretty strong uphill. "I guess we can get back to business," I said.

We followed the track as it led us directly downhill for a few hundred yards, then turned westerly. The prints still looked fresh. I motioned for Damon to reconnoiter again, for I wanted to slow our pace down even more.

"Did you find something?" he asked.

"I think we're close to him. I'm going to take a line off the track, too, and scallop back every now and again so I don't run into him."

Damon's face was flushed from the cold. "Chad, you've got to promise."

"What's that?"

"If you see him first, don't shoot."

"I promise."

We followed a line that led us southwesterly again through old pasture land, now overgrown with hardwoods—oak, maple, and hophornbeam. Parts of old stone walls sprang up like the remains of Druid altars, and I imagined what it might have been like a hundred years ago in these hills, when cows were marched to upper pastures, wide open and cleared for miles around.

That one cloud hiding the sun at the top of the ridge had been a harbinger. It was just after one-thirty in the afternoon, and a stillness had settled on the land. The sky had turned musket gray, and the wind had picked up. My pace had settled to a crawl, and I could see Damon off to my left matching my steps.

I loved this. I could almost feel this buck. From this point on, I knew we could lose him easily. Just one mistake and he would bolt. That's the trick. Shoot a standing buck. If he's running, it means you didn't do your job. He saw you before you saw him.

We continued working carefully downhill and picked up a stream to our right, water rushing over ice-capped rocks. An ideal place for the buck to stop. I waved for Damon to hold it while I watched and listened.

A smart buck often walks straight downwind for a few hundred yards, then travels back parallel to his tracks before bedding down—a good way to see, hear, and smell if anyone else is in the area. The stream bed leveled off with the land just a football-field length away, and I felt that if we were going to run into this buck it would be here.

I waved to Damon and pointed to the stream bed. With other hand signals I finally got him to understand that I wanted him to take a wider swath and cross the water above the leveled area. I'd follow a more direct line.

I watched him move before I took another step, thinking it best to stand my ground until he made up the distance. We could both stalk in tandem once we were closer together.

He was tracking quietly and slowly, something I gave him credit for because I know he was churning to get this buck. I could just make him out as he moved from tree to tree. The sound of the rolling water was more than enough to hide his footfalls. The wind was still pushing uphill, and I shifted my glance ahead on the flattened area for evidence that the buck might be around. I spotted what looked like another ground scrape, but I was too far away to be sure.

I checked back to see if Damon had curled down toward the stream, but I couldn't find him. I waited. A red squirrel chattered above my head. Still no Damon. I hadn't thought about our being in danger hunting on this land since earlier in the morning, but now it settled like a chill in the bones. Someone might be out there watching us.

I fought the urge to call out Damon's name. Then I saw a flash of orange. He must have made a pretty wide turn. Relief rushed through me, and I chastised myself for being stupid enough to believe another hunter was out there except Damon. We had been hunting all day without a sign of anyone else in the woods.

Then a shot.

I waited and listened. "Did you get him?" I yelled.

There was another report. Damon screamed. "Chad! Oh, shit! Help!"

I froze. The sound of the rifle forced an image of Chambers falling to the ground like a cut log, and I couldn't shake it free.

"Damn it! Help me!"

I crashed toward Damon's position. I kept thinking as I lurched through pockets of deadfall that someone might be drawing a bead on me right now, and I half expected to be dropped in my tracks. But I pushed away that thought and stumbled forward toward his screams. It didn't take long to make up the distance, and as I came up over a small rise, I immediately saw the problem.

Damon had fallen off the rise into what looked like an abandoned cistern—water storage for livestock that no longer browsed these hills. There was probably an old channel from the stream somewhere that led to it.

A rotten tree limb sticking out from the side of the cistern had broken Damon's fall, and he stared up at me now.

"You okay?"

"Get me out of here."

"Can you move?"

"I think so."

"Wiggle your fingers and toes."

"What?"

"Just do it!"

Damon moved his fingers. When he tried his legs, the tree limb shifted slightly, and he almost lost his balance.

"Damn it! You trying to kill me?"

He was down about six feet, beyond my reach. The cistern itself looked to be a good fifteen feet deep. I took off my jacket. "You've got to get off that thing before it breaks. Can you sit up?"

"I don't want to move."

"Does it hurt anywhere?"

"No."

I dangled my jacket so the sleeve hung down close to him. "Grab hold of that."

"I can't."

"Grab hold of it!"

Just then, the branch cracked again and jolted him downward. It scared him enough so that he sat up and scrambled toward the sleeve of my jacket. He reached for it and held on with both hands.

I dug my feet in, using the concrete lip of the cistern as leverage. I leaned forward. "See if you can find a better foothold and get off that limb."

He was breathing hard. "I can't see anything."

"Are you sure? There's more deadfall off to your right. Can you get over there?"

"I can't open my eyes."

"All right. Just hang on." I scootched closer to the edge again and felt a strain on my back. "If you can just extend your right foot over to that other dead tree, it looks a lot safer. You'll be able to climb up and out from there."

"I will?"

"Just step across. I've got hold of you. You won't fall."

"I can't move my leg."

"There's nothing wrong with you, Damon. Piece of cake. Come on. On my count. One ... two ..." But I didn't get to three. The rotten tree let loose with a loud crack. I pulled Damon off to his right, hoping with the urging of the motion his foot would follow. I could feel him straining below toward the other piece of deadfall, and then I was thrown backward as I yanked nothing but jacket into the air.

The sound of the rotten tree crashing shook the cistern, and in the moment of stillness that followed I imagined Damon crushed at the bottom of it—but then I heard him.

"Holy shit."

I rushed to the side of the cistern and saw him clinging to the limb I had tried to guide him toward. "You're there, Damon. Just shinny up. You've done that before."

"I'm tired."

"You've got to do it."

It took him just a few minutes. When he was toward the top, I grabbed him by his belt and hauled him over the side. We both lay there for several minutes, catching our breath.

Then I put my jacket on and went looking for his rifle. I found it a few yards away from where he had fallen. It had been discharged.

"So, it went off when you tripped backward."

"I threw it away like I was supposed to."

"What about the first shot?"

"It was the buck. I saw him."

"You hit him?"

"No. I lost my damn footing." He slapped the ground, then gestured toward the cistern. "What the hell is that thing doing in the middle of the woods?"

"We'll see him another day," I said.

I flicked the safety back on, relieved that both shots had come from the same firearm.

I could tell Damon was still shaken by his fall as we walked out. He lagged behind and kept muttering to himself about the cistern. We followed a line out of the woods that took us close to the area where we had found Rodriguez.

Darkness was falling fast and I had to prod Damon to keep moving. When we finally reached the road, I told him to stay put. I would walk down the highway to where we had parked, get the truck, and return for him.

When I came back and swerved the truck across the road to back around in the opposite direction, something glinted in my lights. I stopped, told Damon to watch for cars coming, and got out of the truck to investigate.

Just over the edge of the road, a rifle barrel stuck out of the snow.

CHAPTER NINE

After lovemaking, I usually fall asleep quickly, but tonight my eyes were wide open, a deer caught in the headlights. I swung my legs over and sat on the edge of the bed. The old floorboards in Rachel's bedroom were cold under my feet.

Rachel stirred. Cob raised his head, then let it fall loudly on the wood floor, as if to say my insomnia was of no consequence.

I felt Rachel's hand on my back. "You okay?"

"Can't sleep."

She yawned. "Too much to think about?"

"I'm not really thinking. I'm just awake."

"Come here," she said. "You can think about me."

I lay back.

"Let's pretend," she said. "We're at the Cayman Islands, lying on the sand. The wind brushes over us ever so slightly ... back and forth ..." She moved her fingers over my chest in rhythm with her words.

"Why don't we just go there?" I said.

"Quiet. I'm imaging for you."

I closed my eyes and tried to let her voice take me away, but it wouldn't happen. "Sorry. All I'm getting is white noise."

"Not even a test pattern?"

I kissed her. "Spring break. Let's go there. Dunston's closing in on me."

"Great. What'll we use for money?"

"Plastic."

She rolled toward me. "Sorry. Visa's maxed." She kissed me.

"My treat?"

"Really?"

"Sure. Just call me Mr. Big Bucks."

"But we don't need the real thing. We can pretend."

Maybe it was lack of sleep, but for some reason, her words bothered me. "Is that what we're doing?"

"What?"

I sat up. "Nothing. Forget what I said."

"Is there something you want to tell me?"

"No."

"You're bothered by this hunter thing, aren't you."

"I'm sure that's it."

She paused. "Why do I think that's not it."

I lay back again. "Look. I'm tired. I honestly don't know what I'm talking about."

A silence settled in the room. I reached for her but she stayed my hand, brought it to her lips and kissed it. "You think we're pretending?" she said.

"No. I love us. I think we're great."

She let go of my hand. "Maybe we are pretending."

"What difference does it make? I like it."

"So do I." She touched my cheek. "You're sweet," she said. "And cute."

"Cute? I hate that."

"It's what you are."

"It's such a girl thing. You never hear a guy use that word."

"So, I'll never use it again."

"Did I say that?"

She straddled me and ran her hands up and down my chest. "You're cute 'cause you're hairy."

I laughed. "It's nice to know there's a reason."

"Cliff was bald."

"Who's Cliff?"

She stopped moving her hands. "You don't know Cliff?"

"I don't know Cliff."

She continued her massage. "Cliff was my husband. I thought I told you."

"Knew you had a husband. Never knew his name."

"I swear I told you."

"Was Cliff really bald, or just his chest?"

"His chest. I guess I need to talk to you about him."

"Some other time."

"You don't want me to talk about him?" she said.

"Right now I'm ready to do some more pretending."

The next morning about six, before Rachel got up, I headed down to Holten's Diner because I knew Bumps would be there. His daily routine began with a short stack and a side of bacon. I was curious about this other guy who'd been shot at. I also wondered if there had been a ballistics report on the rifle I had found. It was probably too early, but I was dying to see if the bullet they pulled out of Rodriguez's leg matched it.

My prediction about Natasha Wright's article stirring up trouble had been on target, but even I hadn't expected the extent of the hoopla. AP had picked up the story, and before you could say "Bang, you're dead" the networks were running features about some crazed hunter out for blood roaming the woods of New Hampshire.

Holten's was crowded and buzzing. Bumps was in his customary corner booth. Usually he ate by himself, but this morning there were three others—Wilfred Baines, town selectman; his brother, the very deaf Bill; and Josh Morgenstern, road agent—shoved into the opposite seat. Both Baines and Morgenstern were FAST squad members. They leaned forward intently, hands wrapped around coffee mugs.

I pulled up a chair at the end of the table.

"Well, speak of the devil."

"Talking about me again, Wilfred?" I said.

"It's not often I meet a celebrity."

I frowned at him.

Bumps said, "Natasha Wright. You read the article?"

"No. I've been avoiding it."

"Your name's all over it," Wilfred said.

"I'm sure. Probably all lies."

"What?" Bill Baines said, his hand cupped over his ear.

"All lies," I repeated.

"So, I take it you don't think these are random shootings," Josh said.

"I'll just tell you what I told Natasha Wright: I have no idea."

"She seems to think otherwise," Bumps said.

It didn't surprise me. All I had to do was look at the headline to realize the slant she was taking. It simply read STALKER. I knew if I read the article, I'd probably get my rifle and stalk *her.* Given who was at the table, I thought it best not to bring up the rifle.

"Getting back to what we were talking about, Bumps." Wilfred Baines wiped his mouth with a napkin. "I think we should call a special town meeting about this."

Bumps stuck a wad of pancake in his mouth. "Why stir things up, Wilfred?"

"Stir things up? They're already stirred up."

"A lot of folks are angry, I know that," Josh added.

"About what?" Bumps asked.

Josh sat back. "They're scared shitless. They're afraid to step out in their own backyards. And they're pissed off about it."

"Can you get Tierney to come?" Wilfred asked.

"Look, fellas," Bumps held his knife mid-air, "let's just wait a few days. See what happens."

"That might be too late," Wilfred said.

Bumps slammed his knife down on the table. "What the hell do you think is going to happen, Wilfred?"

"What's going to happen? People are going to get killed."

"Okay, let me ask you this." Bumps was clearly irritated over having his breakfast interrupted. "How many people have been killed since Chambers and that fellow Perino?"

Wilfred didn't answer. Nobody had been killed since those two. Rodriguez was still in a coma.

"What's your point?" I said.

"My point is that whoever's doing the shooting now is a lousy shot."

I thought about that a moment. "So someone's shooting and missing on purpose?"

"Could be."

"But, why?" Wilfred asked.

"To scare us."

"Why does someone want to scare us?" Josh said.

Bumps smiled. "Answer that one and you've solved the case."

While Bumps asked for his check, I pondered the implications of what he had said. It made sense. Whoever had been shooting at hunters wasn't shooting to kill. Which left only one explanation. Someone was setting a false track, trying to scare everybody into thinking one thing. Fear is a set of blinders.

I asked Bumps, "You think the same guy's taking pot shots?"

"That's my hunch. But the longer this goes on, the more likely we'll get some copycatting."

"So I take it you don't think we need a town meeting," Wilfred said.

Before Bumps could answer, John Riesling, the owner of the mini-mart across the street, came rushing in. "I think you'd better come over."

"What's the matter, John?"

"We've got a set-to in the making."

"Tell me about it."

"Well, you know that George Telleman who works in the pharmacy? He's squared off against Tub Marx."

"Tub's up to his old tricks, I guess," Bumps said.

"He claims he knows who's doing the shooting."

"He does, does he?"

"Says it's that animal rights nut. You know. The one—"

"The one who just moved in."

"Yeah. He says—"

"Okay, John. I'll take it from here." Bumps put on his gloves, adjusted his hat, and shot a glance at Wilfred. "How does Sunday evening for a town meeting sound?"

We three sat—Damon, Rachel and I—in the back row of the Grange Hall built by my great-grandfather. The Dunston population is a mix of natives whose ancestry goes back, like mine, to the early founders of the village, and newcomers, mostly artists—potters, weavers, painters—and, of course, Wallace Pegner, our local animal rights activist. You could pretty much divide the room between overalls and feed caps, and turtle necks and corduroys. It looked like the entire village had shown up for this one.

The TV crews covering the event made this meeting a little different. The place was lit up like a crime scene.

Bumps sat next to Tierney on the podium, looking scared to death. He'd rather pull double shifts than speak fifteen minutes in front of a crowd, and, under the glare of the lights, sweat was already breaking on his forehead.

In direct contrast, Manfred Tierney sat with his legs comfortably crossed, cool and crisp in his uniform. It reminded me of how he had sat in the courtroom at his brother's trial. I couldn't help notice his stony gaze as I gave my testimony of how I had stumbled onto Roland's cash-crop of marijuana. At first, as I told my story, I misread Tierney's demeanor as anger—I was sending his brother up the river, after all—and his eyes felt like they were boring into me. After his brother was convicted, though, he surprised me on the courthouse steps by clapping me on the shoulder, offering that it must have been hard for me to testify, and that he harbored no ill will. That

impressed the hell out of me. It takes a big man to do that sort
of thing, and I chalked up his hard glance to intense concentra-
tion over the details of my story.

Wilfred Baines gaveled the meeting to order. "Now, we're
here tonight to get some facts about what's going on. Bumps
and Trooper Tierney have kindly offered to give us what information they can." He paused and leaned over the lectern. "Now,
I'd like this to be an orderly discussion. Bumps will say a few
words. Then you can ask questions if you want. Bumps?"

Bumps approached the lectern and began: "About a week
ago two fellows from Massachusetts got themselves killed up
there on the old Turner property. Since then, there've been all
sorts of rumors flying because someone's been shooting at
hunters." Bumps emphasized that there had been no further
killings since the Turner incident, and he urged people to use
their heads when they were out hunting. He mopped his forehead with his handkerchief and sat down.

George Gosh stood up first, as he always did in town meet-
ings. He had a florid face, his chin thrust upward. He was
considered the oldest man in the village, but nobody knew
exactly how old he was. "That's it?"

"What else do you want me to say, George?" Bumps said.

"All these people come here," George said, his arm scribing
an arc, "and all you can tell them is to use their heads?"

"What else do you want me to say?"

"Well, is it safe to go hunting, or not?"

"Of course."

The crowd stirred, and Wilfred rapped his gavel. George's
eyes narrowed. "Then I must've missed something. Seems to
me, people are here because they're scared to death of gettin'
shot."

Tierney got up out of his chair. "You have to believe we're doing all we can here. The Major Crime Unit has been working 'round the clock on this thing. What Bumps is saying is that we shouldn't panic. We should keep on with what we're doing and not fly off the handle."

"What you're saying is you haven't a clue who's shooting at us," George said.

"We have some leads," Tierney said. He paced in front of the lectern, then turned dramatically. "You got your deer yet, George?"

"No. And it don't look like I'm going to."

"I was out hunting this morning. If you'd like to come with me next weekend, I'd be glad to have you along."

"Not me."

"You a chickenshit, George?" This from the back of the room.

George wheeled around. "Who said that?"

Jimmy Plowright, owner of the local sandpit, stood up. "It's just me, George."

"Well, I ain't no chickenshit." He pointed to his head. "I'm just using my bean."

"Yeah, well, I think it's gone to seed."

The place erupted in laughter. Wilfred pounded his gavel. "All right. That's enough."

Jimmy raised his hand. "Can I say one more thing?"

"As long as you don't insult George again," Wilfred said.

Jimmy pulled himself up straight. He crumbled his ball cap in his hands. "I don't know about the rest of you people, but I don't like the idea that some jerk thinks he can control our lives by shooting at us."

A few voices murmured their agreement.

"And I don't think we should stop hunting, neither. We should make sure we don't go alone, but we shouldn't let no one keep us from getting our deer. I say, let's take our woods back."

An outburst of applause followed and people started stamping their feet.

Tierney raised his hands for silence. "Thank you, Jimmy, for those comments." He stepped forward toward the crowd, maneuvering himself into a better camera angle. "What Jimmy has just said is the approach I would recommend." He paused and pointed his finger at the crowd. "We need all of you to help us," he said. "This is not the time to hide away, to cower in fear. The more we have out there hunting, the more likely we can catch this guy."

"You mean you want to use us for bait?" George said.

"If I felt like bait, I wouldn't go out there myself." Tierney smiled. "So, next Sunday, George. What time should I pick you up?"

CHAPTER TEN

Later that evening, I was dreaming about Meg when my pager went off: "This is Memorial dispatch requesting all Dunston Fire, FAST, and Police please respond to the Hanneford residence at the corner of Route 105 and Turnabout Lane for a seventeen-year-old female who is bleeding from self-inflicted wounds. Patient is conscious and alert and should be approached with caution. Time of the tone: 02:03."

My response time was usually pretty good, even in the middle of the night. We were issued jumpsuits, so getting dressed was a matter of stepping into a fancy coverall and throwing on a pair of shoes. By the time I started the truck, turned on the red flashing rack lights, and pulled out of the driveway, the clock on the dashboard read 2:06. I signed on: "Memorial dispatch, this is Eighty-nine R-thirty. I'm ten-one." Dispatch copied me.

Given the location of the Hanneford residence, a couple of miles to the east, I would probably be first on the scene, especially since Damon spent all yesterday getting his truck running, and I wouldn't have to stop for him.

I knew the Hannefords. Harry "Hap" Hanneford is an ophthalmologist, his wife Ellie, an Episcopal minister. Upstanding family. Their only daughter is another story—"troubled" would be an understatement.

When I arrived at the scene, the Hannefords were waiting for me outside, huddled against the cold. I radioed in: "Memorial dispatch, this is Eighty-nine R-thirty. I'm off at that scene."

I retrieved my new med kit from the tool cabinet in back and approached them. "Hap. What's up?" The red strobe lights from my truck punctuated Hap's face, but I could still read fear there.

"It's Julie," Hap said. "She was in her room all night. Then we heard her screaming."

"What did you find?"

"She was ..." Hap rubbed his forehead, then let his head rest on his hand.

"It's okay, Hap. It's going to be all right. Just tell me what happened."

"There was blood all over the place," he said.

"She still in her room?"

"Yes."

"And she cut herself?"

Ellie broke down. "It's awful. " Hap hugged her.

"Does she still have a knife?" I asked.

Hap looked up at me. "Yes."

"You two stay right here. You warm enough?"

"Fine. We're fine," Hap said.

I walked up the front stoop and opened the door.

"Upstairs," Ellie called to me. "In her room."

"Wait a minute, Chad." Hap approached, holding onto Ellie's arm. "You need to know something else: I think she took something."

"Like what?"

"Maybe acid. She's not herself."

"Thanks, Hap."

I gloved up and entered the house. Hap had done a nice job restoring the place. The hardwood floors gleamed with new urethane. I walked up the stairs that led to the second floor. I could hear some raucous "grunge" music coming from the corner room. I knew backup was on the way, but if she still had the knife ... My worst fear was that I was too late.

The door was partway open. Inside, the room was bathed in blue light. Slowly, I pushed the door. "Julie," I said.

There was no response.

I walked into the room. What caught my eye first was light flickering in the far corner. There were several candles burning on what looked like a makeshift altar. And then I saw her. She was sitting cross-legged on the bed, her head shaking violently to the pounding of the music. She had a knife in one hand. It looked like an ordinary kitchen knife with a serrated edge. She didn't have a stitch on.

I called out her name. She didn't respond. I walked closer to the bed. "Julie," I said again.

She suddenly jumped to her feet. Her eyes were ringed in black and there were cuts all up and down her arms. Smeared blood was on her stomach. "Who are you?"

"I'm Chad. You know me."

"Are you the man?"

"What man, Julie?"

"The dark man."

"There is no dark man, Julie." I took a step toward her. "Only me."

She jabbed the knife in my direction. "Stay there."

"Give me the knife, Julie. This is Chad. You know me."

She measured me, the knife shaking in her hand. She had also sliced her thighs. The wounds appeared superficial, but there was so much blood it was hard to tell.

"I have to wait for the dark man. He'll take me."

I took another step forward. "I'm here to help."

"No!" she screamed. She jumped off the bed and stood holding the knife, using the bed as a barrier between us.

I could hear others coming up the stairs. So could Julie.

"Stay away. Stay away," she said.

"Chad. You in there?" It was Bumps' voice from the hallway.

"Don't come in!" I said.

"Who's that!" Julie screamed.

"A friend." I lowered my voice. Slowly, I said, "Give me the knife, Julie."

"No."

It was clear she didn't trust me. I tried a new tack. "Julie. I am the dark man."

She stood still for a moment, but her hand holding the knife was still shaking. "No."

"Yes."

Then she dropped to her knees, her arms out straight in front of her, but she didn't let go of the knife.

I walked slowly to her side of the bed. She was sobbing. "I thought you wouldn't come. I summoned you with my blood."

"I am here."

"Then I am ready."

She sat back on her haunches and placed the knife at her own throat. "I yield to your powers."

"No. Don't." The pressure of the knife against her throat drew blood. My mind raced. The whole idea of identifying myself as "the dark man" had come in a rush. Now, it might be the thing that killed her. "I've changed my mind," I said.

She blinked at me, the dark circles around her eyes making the sockets look sunken, cadaverous.

I searched for more words to say. "I have other plans for you. Give me your knife."

She stared at me long and hard, then shuddered. "You're not the dark man," she said. Tears welled in her eyes. She let the knife drop and collapsed to the floor.

I grabbed the knife and put it on the bed. Julie sobbed, and I held her in my arms. "It's okay. It's over now," I said. "You're safe." I hugged her, trying to calm her down.

Bumps call out to me again. "Chad?"

"We'll need that slat stretcher," I said. Because of the twists and turns in the hallway, a soft canvas stretcher works better to manipulate a patient around doorways.

Julie moaned and I stroked her hair. I knew I was covered with her blood, but my jumpsuit provided a barrier. I had gloves on, but no protection for my eyes. I would have to be careful to keep my hands away from my face—things you have to think about in this age of blood-borne pathogens.

When help came I told them to leave the overhead lights off because I wanted to make the transition to the ambulance as smooth as possible. I removed a blanket from the bed and wrapped it around Julie. I talked softly to her as I maneuvered her to the stretcher. She lay back without protest, and we strapped her in. I stayed at her head as we jostled into the hallway and made our way down the stairs. She remained quiet for the ride except for the sobbing.

The ambulance stretcher was waiting for us outside. We

buckled her in, and as we lifted her into the ambulance, Julie suddenly raised her head and pointed to a group of Fire and FAST gathered around the scene.

"You!" she screamed. "You!"

I rode with her in the ambulance to Memorial and administered oxygen, twelve liters with a non-rebreather mask, while Lorraine Michaels, a registered nurse, began monitoring her vitals. Julie didn't fight the mask. I brushed hair away from her forehead. She was coming down from the bad trip. I left her to the care of the emergency room staff. Her wounds were superficial and non life-threatening.

I disposed of my jumpsuit in a red Hazmat (Hazardous Materials) bag, showered, and put on some borrowed scrubs. I chose to wait outside in the cold air. I knew someone would come to pick me up.

The night was a storybook of stars, and I took my mind off Julie Hanneford by reading the sky. I was in the middle of trying to locate Cassiopeia when I heard a vehicle pull into the parking lot. Of all the people I expected to see behind the wheel of my truck, Rachel wasn't on the list.

I opened the door of the driver's side, and she slid over.

"Ellie called me," she said. "I just missed the ambulance."

"You know Ellie Hanneford?"

"Yes. How's Julie doing?"

"She's okay. Going to be sore as hell from all those cuts." I pulled out of the parking lot. "How do you know Ellie?"

"She's my minister. Or was."

"You go to church?"

"Not anymore. She married Cliff and me."

"What? In New Hampshire?"

"No."

"I guess I'm confused," I said.

"Sorry. I'll back up a little. Ellie and Hap moved up to New Hampshire shortly after I married Cliff. She was a minister in Massachusetts before Hap found work up here. She really helped me sort out my feelings about Cliff."

"I see."

"And Ellie's the one who told me about the job opening at Dunston," she said. "She's the one responsible for my being here."

It was something to hear all of this coming at me at once. In a few short minutes I found out more about Rachel than I had in the past two months. She went to church. Ellie married her. But what feelings about Cliff needed sorting out? "Perhaps we should go thank her," I said.

Rachel touched the sleeve of my jacket. "I left my car at their house. Can you take me back? I told them I'd meet them at the hospital."

"Sure." A shortcut to Turnabout Lane was coming up, and I slowed down to make the left. There was hardly any traffic on the road. "It was nice of you to pick me up. You could have had Damon do it."

"I know. I wanted to see you."

"You did?"

"I feel awful about this. So responsible."

"Why should you feel responsible?"

"I was the one who suggested Julie become a day student at Dunston."

"You can't blame yourself for what happened."

"I know. I just have to convince myself."

"I thought Julie went to the regional."

"She did. Up until this fall."

I thought about Rachel's recent troubles with that girl in the dorm. "What's going on at that school, anyway?"

"I wish I knew. These drugs are coming from somewhere."

When I was five, the house was full of pumpkin smells on Thanksgiving, and to this day, a pie baking can trigger that memory. It had been a happier time, and even though I was getting used to a new mother and younger stepbrother, there was a renewed sense of family in the old farmhouse. At that time, my grandfather gave his upstairs room to Damon and moved into the parlor. He was glad to do it, pleased that my father had decided to remarry and make the house full again.

Perhaps this longing for family is why I baked pumpkin pies in the early morning before it was time to pick up Rachel. Her car was getting serviced.

The rich, fruity smells filled the house and made me temporarily forget the recent Hanneford call. I didn't get to sleep after returning to the house the night of the call, and last night I lay awake most of the night. I got up before dawn and started baking.

I put in the turkey, a twenty-pounder, about ten o'clock.

Damon walked up to the farmhouse at noon, and we all sat around the kitchen table drinking beer and wine until the bird was done. Rachel raved all through dinner about my cooking. After dinner, Damon retired to the living room and fell asleep watching the Cowboys-Lions game.

Rachel and I did the dishes.

"Why do you tease him all the time?" she asked.

"Damon?"

"Yes."

"I don't know. Something I've always done, I guess."

"You didn't have to tell that story about when he was in school."

"Oh, he doesn't mind."

"I think he does."

I ran water in the sink, took out the screen, and tapped it against the side of the trash can. "I guess you just have to understand what we were like growing up."

"Tell me about it."

"We were brothers. We were always fighting."

She wiped the plate slowly with the towel. "It just makes me sad sometimes. The way you treat him."

I turned and looked in her eyes. She was serious. "Okay. I'll try not to do it anymore."

"I'm only telling you what I feel. You don't have to listen to me."

I smiled at her. "Maybe I shouldn't tease him as much."

"I'm not asking you to change how you act with your brother."

"Yes, you are." Gently, I took hold of her arms and kissed her. "I want you to say things like that. I need you to say things like that."

She pulled away and gave me a playful snap with her towel. "Stop being so drippy."

"I'm not. I want your perspective. You soften my edges."

"Oh, shut up."

***

Damon left after the game, and I was about to pour some Remy Martin when the scanner picked up Bumps' voice. What drew my attention first was the urgent tone, something uncharacteristic given his usual flat, unaffected speech. He was trying to be coy, using ten-codes. Apparently, something was happening down at the minimart.

"What is it?" Rachel said.

"A ten-fifty."

"What's that?"

"I'm not sure."

I found the phone book in the cupboard and pulled out a ten-code sheet I had stashed. I scanned with my finger. "A homicide," I said.

Rachel didn't say anything. I stood closer to the scanner. "He's called in the state police," I said. I could feel her eyes watching me.

"You want to go down there, don't you?"

"Bumps might need some help. Come along with me?"

"Thanks. I'll stay here with my friend, Remy."

"I won't be long," I said.

I pulled into the parking lot of the mini-mart, and a cruiser skidded in right behind me. Bumps was waiting over by the deer-weighing station, waving a flashlight to show his location. Tierney got out of the cruiser and adjusted his hat. I let him pass before I opened the truck door.

As I approached, I could see what looked like the shadow of a deer dangling from the weighing hook. Both men aimed their flashlights, and I knew immediately this was no deer.

Glenn Chambers' nude body hung upside down, his hair

frozen in spikes, his face blue and bloated. He was gutted like a deer.

I felt my stomach lurch, but I couldn't take my eyes off him. I wanted to turn away, but I felt drawn closer until I stood next to both Tierney and Bumps. They didn't seem to notice me.

We left him hanging like that until Amy Woo showed up. We had just taken him down and were placing him into the body bag when my eye caught something on his hip.

A tattoo of a five-pointed star.

CHAPTER ELEVEN

By the time I got back to the farmhouse, Rachel was gone. There was a note: "Something came up. I'm with Ellie. I'll explain later."

I didn't sleep much that night. Glenn Chambers' body swung on a hook in the back of my mind, and I was trying to remember if the tattoo I saw on Rodriguez matched the one on Chambers' hip. Both were star-shaped, and it seemed too connected to be coincidental, like both men were literally joined at the hip. I had to tell Bumps about this. I finally fell asleep at five. I woke two hours later to temperatures in the thirties, snow predicted by early afternoon.

I knew it was too late to catch Bumps at Holten's Diner, but he might be at the station. The Dunston Police Station is a misnomer, but I guess it wouldn't sound as official calling it the "Dunston Police Room Inside the Firehouse." One tiny room doesn't impress with the full force of the law, but it's an improvement over the way it used to be when Bumps had to run the department out of his home.

Bumps wasn't there.

"You just missed him," Blaine Haskell said.

"Where did he go?"

Blaine was sitting at the desk, crisp and official in his blues. "Concord," he said without looking up.

"What's he doing there?"

Haskell wrote something on an official-looking form, then his head snapped up, and he finally made eye contact. "Police business."

I liked Blaine, but he sometimes took himself too seriously. In a youthful attempt to be professional, he tended to go overboard with protocol. "I don't suppose you can tell me what that business is."

"Why do you want to know?"

"Because I need to talk to him."

"About what?"

"Police business."

Haskell blinked at me. "I don't know when he'll be back."

"My hunch, he's with Woo."

"How do you know that?"

I wagged a finger. "You shouldn't tell me police business."

Haskell colored. "I didn't say anything."

I clapped him on the shoulder. "You tell Bumps I need to see him. Just tell him that, okay?"

I left the station and drove to Rachel's apartment. She wasn't at the apartment. I puzzled over her cryptic note and decided to give the Hanneford house a call. There was no answer.

During vacation periods, Dunston Academy had the feel of eerie emptiness, like a neutron bomb had hit and left the buildings standing, the people vaporized. But this morning, the feeling was worse—the whole town looked deserted. And I wasn't surprised. By now the news about Chambers must be out. I thought about the recent town meeting. I doubted whether Tierney would find anyone to go hunting with him.

On the way back home, I stopped at the minimart and filled up my truck with gas. The latest forecast called for a foot of wet snow by morning, and I knew I'd be up most of the night pushing the stuff around. I charged the gas and chatted with Tessa Mills while she rang me up.

"If it isn't one thing it's another," she said. Tessa was a squat woman in her seventies, with thinning gray hair. She wore an apron tied tightly around her midriff, an Exxon label emblazoned on the pocket.

"You talking about the weather, Tessa?"

"No. I'm talking about the new kind of deer meat we got hanging around." She placed her hands on her hips, as if Chambers' body was a personal insult. "Christ, that's all we need around here."

I didn't know how to respond, so I just said, "You bet."

"You were there, I hear."

"That's right," I said.

"So?"

"So what?"

"So what did you see?"

"What do you want to know, Tessa?"

She leaned forward, placed her hands on the counter, and screwed up her face like she was sucking a sourball. "What did the fella look like?"

I signed the charge slip and pushed it her way. "He looked dead."

I turned on my heels, shoved the door open, and left the building as fast as I could. Usually, I could tolerate small talk with Tessa Mills, but I never did much care for the woman. She and her husband Darl were ambulance chasers. They owned a scanner and often showed up on emergency calls, lurking in the background.

Back home, I picked up the morning paper on my stoop and put on some coffee. Chambers had made the front page of the *Patriot*—no pictures. Tessa Mills would be disappointed. As

I suspected, the article just reported the discovery of the body. Too early for anything more.

In a way, I was glad Chambers had finally reappeared, even though he was in bad shape. There would be no more speculation that the man got up and walked away the day he was gunned down on the Turner property. I can still hear Tierney challenging my version of the story. Finding Chambers also meant that Natasha Wright would probably go digging into his background. She might find something that would reveal what was behind the shootings.

I read the sports section and my eyelids began to get heavy. Even though I had stayed awake most of last night, I hated the idea of sleeping during the day. I'd done it too much after Meg died. But I knew I would have to plow into the night, and it might be good to rest up.

I opted for the sofa and quickly dozed off. My sleep was fitful. Instead of star tattoos, I dreamed of Julie Hanneford. She was coming at me with a knife, slashing away in violent downward thrusts. She forced me out the door and down the stairs of the Hanneford house. I ran to the porch and the ambulance was there, surrounded by a faceless crowd of people. Suddenly, hands grabbed me. I struggled to free myself. Julie came through the doorway. "Hold him!" she screamed. Then she pointed her knife at me: "You! You!"

I woke with a start. I was sweating. I stumbled into the kitchen, flopped down in a chair, and held my head in my hands. The dream seemed too real. Her words kept coming at me: "You. You." Then I knew why. In a sense, the dream *was* real. Julie had said those words while being carted into the ambulance. She had been pointing to someone in the crowd. Who?

***

I worked all night.

There's something therapeutic about plowing snow—the whine of the blade as it rises, the tug of the wheels as I back up, the thud of the plow as I drop it again, the vibrating rumble as I push, push.

I finished about 4:00 AM and had two hours to kill before Bumps would most likely show up at the diner. I didn't want to go home. Bumps never did call me yesterday, and I wondered if Blaine Haskell had remembered to deliver the message. I made my rounds of plow customers again, dinking around in their driveways. It turned out that I had some more work to do because the town plows had made another unexpected pass on North Eastman road, blocking a few entrances.

Bumps is a man of dependable habits, and I found him in his favorite booth at Holten's, a short stack in front of him. For a Saturday morning, the crowd of locals was thin.

"Ah, Chad," Bumps said. "I thought you'd be here."

"Haskell tell you I wanted to talk?"

"Blaine? No."

"Well, that little bastard."

"I didn't get back 'til late yesterday. He was gone by the time I got in."

"He could have left a note."

"Well, anyway, I'm glad you're here. I have a few questions myself."

I watched him stick a wad of pancake in his mouth. "Go ahead. Ask away."

"No. No. You go first," he said, chewing noisily. "I want to eat my breakfast."

"Wait a minute. If Haskell didn't tell you I wanted to talk, why were you so sure I'd show up here?"

Bumps waved his fork. "Plowing. You always come here after you get done."

"Oh."

He stopped chewing. "What's with you, anyway? What are you so nervous about?"

"What?"

"Your leg is jumping," he said.

"I just got something on my mind, that's all."

He gave another wave of his fork. "So, let's hear it."

I ordered a cup of coffee first. I told him about the tattoos.

He listened with interest. "And you think they're a match? The same star shape?"

"There's an easy way to find out."

"I'll call Woo and have her sketch it and fax it. Then I'll pay a visit to Mr. Rodriguez." He shoved a napkin and pen my way. "In the meantime, see if you can draw me what you saw."

It took a few tries, but then I realized what I was attempting was something familiar, what a child learns to sketch in grade school—a five-pointed star drawn with a continuous line. The act of reproducing it from memory on the napkin made me visualize more clearly what I had seen on Chambers' hip. My recall of Rodriguez's tattoo was still fuzzy, but my gut told me it had to be a match. I showed Bumps the napkin. "That's what I saw."

Bumps scratched his chin. "You sure about that?"

I looked at the napkin again. Something wasn't quite right, but it was close enough. "I'm pretty sure that's it."

"What does it mean?"

"Maybe they belonged to some club?"

"I'll look into it," Bumps said and pocketed the napkin.

I ordered breakfast, two poached eggs, toast, and homefries. "Your turn," I said.

"What?"

"You said you had some questions for me."

Bumps lowered his coffee cup. "Oh, yeah. Jeez, I got so caught up in the tattoo story, I forgot all about it."

"Woo found something, didn't she?"

"Well, I don't know. It could be something."

"What?"

"First, I want you to tell me again what happened the day Chambers was killed."

"You were there."

"Not really. I was with the litter crew, bringing up the rear." He leaned back in the booth. "Now, as I understand it, when you found Rodriguez, he had a pistol in his hand. That right?"

"That's right."

"And you took that pistol out of his hand and placed it in your med kit."

"Yes."

"Then you and Striker dragged Rodriguez out of the woods, leaving your med kit behind."

I stared at Bumps. What was this? "We've been through all of this before," I said.

"Just bear with me. Now, where was Chambers when you were working on Rodriguez?"

"Right with us. In the way, mostly."

"And you say he suddenly got nervous, said something like 'I ain't touching no stiff,' then started walking away from you downhill."

"That's the way it happened."

Bumps looked out the window to his left, then back to me. "What do you suppose he was suddenly nervous about?"

"Maybe he saw something."

"Or someone."

"Could be."

Bumps tapped the table with his pen. "Now, from that point on you were concentrating on Rodriguez so much you forgot all about your med kit with the pistol in it."

"That's right."

"And when you went back to find the med kit, it was gone."

I shook my head. "I didn't go back for it. I was so busy with Rodriguez I forgot about it."

"You didn't need the stuff that was in it?"

"No. We had the oxygen. The med kit wasn't that far away from me, anyway."

"'Bout how far would you say?"

"I don't know. A few yards, maybe."

"Two, three?"

I shook my head again.

"What's the matter?"

"You sound like a cheap imitation of Sherlock Holmes."

"I'm just trying to ..."

"Cut the crap; tell me what Woo found."

"Christ! Let me be the cop, will you?"

"I don't have that much time."

"All right. All right."

I leaned forward.

Bumps spoke slowly. "The bullet they took out of Rodriguez's leg matched the rifle you found."

I slapped the table. "I knew it."

"Chambers' prints're all over it."

"So Chambers shot Rodriguez?"

"Can't tell for sure."

"Why not?"

"Because he could have picked up the rifle after Rodriguez was shot."

"Come on. How likely is that?"

"Don't know yet."

"What about Chambers? What was he shot with?"

Bumps worked a toothpick in his mouth. "Now, that's the real interesting part," he said. "The slug Woo dug out of Chambers' forehead might have belonged to an automatic handgun."

I let the news sink in. "He was killed with a pistol?"

"Nine millimeter." Bumps sucked at a piece of food stuck in his tooth. "She has to run more tests, but that's her take on it now."

"What sort of tests?"

"Who knows? She yammered something about velocity and skull impact."

I sat back. "And you think the firearm was the one I found in Rodriguez's hand."

"What do *you* think, Watson?"

As I drove back home, I didn't know what to think. What I couldn't figure out especially was why Bumps just didn't come out and tell me the ballistic information. Why the questions?

That Rodriguez had been shot with a rifle with Chambers' prints on it made it seem likely that Chambers had done the deed. But if that were true, why would he go for help?

And the pistol? If it was a 9MM handgun that did Chambers in, it wouldn't necessarily bring anybody closer to discovering who pulled the trigger, but it was significant. I had always felt Chambers had been floored by a high powered rifle—from a distance—and I'm sure Bumps had always thought that, too, even though we never talked about it. In my mind's eye, I tried to replay the scene.

The shot had come from uphill to my right, near the same location where I had left the med kit. It meant two things: the guy was really close to us when he fired and he was a hell of a shot. I remembered flinching at the sound of the report, then watching in horror as Chambers fell. It must have been a few seconds before I looked back up the hill, time enough for the guy to skirt undercover.

When I got home there was a message on my machine: "Hi. It's me. I'm home now. Thought I'd let you know." I didn't even bother showering or changing but drove directly to Rachel's.

When I walked through her back door, Cob was there to greet me. He jumped up, and I grabbed his paws. I let him lick my face. Rachel was sitting in her bathrobe at the kitchen table, a newspaper spread out in front of her. She didn't get up.

"I was worried about you," I said.

"I'm sorry. An emergency."

"What happened?"

"Georgette Salmon. She had a stroke."

I walked to the kitchen table, pulled out a chair, and sat down. "How's she doing?"

"I don't know. It doesn't look good."

Georgette Salmon was the wife of the former headmaster. She lived in a house on the edge of campus that the trustees bought for her and her husband after he retired. For a minute I wondered why the FAST squad hadn't been called out, but then I remembered that Georgette's house was just over the line, in another town's jurisdiction.

"You knew her well, didn't you?"

"She was a friend of my mother's. Old friend."

"I'm sorry."

"Thanks. I went over there first thing yesterday to see what I could do. I spent the day fielding phone calls."

"How's your mom taking the news?"

"I haven't told her yet."

I was about to suggest she should make the difficult call, but I was still measuring her mood. I didn't want to upset her. I changed the subject. "I thought you'd run out on me."

"Why?"

Cob came over and nuzzled his head in my lap. I gave him a pat. "Because I left you alone."

"I'm a big girl."

"I'm falling in love with you. You know that?" I didn't know where that came from. Maybe it was the way the light from the window played on her face.

She smiled. "No, you're not."

"You're blushing."

She turned away and stared down at her empty coffee cup. "I don't understand why you get so involved. You're a volunteer. You don't have to go chasing after murder and mayhem."

"So, you *were* angry I left you."

"No. I'm just trying to figure you out, that's all."

I felt my face color. "I don't usually get this involved."

"Then what is it?"

I thought a moment. "It's personal, I guess."

"Personal?" She gestured at the newspaper on the table. "What does Glenn Chambers have to do with you?"

"It's just that I feel something's going on here that I don't know about."

"Like what?"

Cob flopped down on the floor. He lay his head on my shoe. "Can I see that pen?"

Rachel slid the ballpoint across the table.

I leaned over and drew her the star shape on the newspaper. "Ever see this before?"

"A pentagram?" she said.

"A what?"

"That's what you drew."

"I thought it was a star."

She counted the points. "It's a pentagram."

"What does it mean?"

"It's a religious symbol. Why?"

"Both Rodriguez and Chambers have this tattoo on their hips."

She studied the symbol. "So what does this have to do with you?"

"Aren't you the least bit curious about why the tattoos are there?"

"Of course. But why is this personal?"

I didn't have an answer for her, at least one that made sense. "I just have a feeling that I'm being sucked into things, that's all. I try to tell myself to forget about Chambers and Rodriguez, but every morning I wake up something else happens that draws me back into it."

"Okay."

"Okay what?"

She took my hand. "Now I know better what you're thinking."

CHAPTER TWELVE

Sunday morning marked two weeks since we'd answered the call of a hunter shot on the Turner property, and I woke thinking of Damon. I expected he would have called yesterday to ask if we could go hunting for his buck. It gave me hope that Chambers' body hanging at the mini-mart had quelled his hunting lust, at least temporarily. I drove out to his place and found him at his workbench, fiddling with an old black-and-white portable TV.

"That thing worth fixing?"

"Mabel Campbell thinks so," he said.

"I'm guessing you heard about Chambers."

"Yup."

I waited for more, but he was so focused on tracing two wires, I didn't know how much he had heard. "That all you've got to say?"

"Aha," he said, pointing with needlenose pliers. "These suckers were shorting out."

"If you're not going to talk to me, I'll just leave."

"Okay."

"Come on, Damon. Talk to me."

"Sorry. I'm trying to catch up on this stuff." He waved in

the general direction of his workroom. The place was piled with old mahogany consoles, stand-alone radios with large dials, tubes, coils of wire, toasters, vacuum cleaners (mostly parts), and a special area for electronics—VCRs, cell phones, fax machines. In contrast to the maelstrom of parts, Damon's workbench was immaculate. His tools were neatly placed on a pegboard behind the bench.

He wiped his hands on his shirt. "What do you want?" he said.

"To make sure you don't go into the woods."

He placed the needlenose pliers back in a wire holder on the pegboard. "I ain't going nowhere."

I studied him. "I'm glad to hear that."

He looked directly at me. His eyes were red-rimmed. "They gutted Chambers, didn't they?"

"Yes."

"Ain't nobody going to gut me."

Then I understood. Chambers' body had scared the willies out of him. "How long you been sitting here, Damon?"

"I don't know. Couple days, maybe."

I didn't think he was lying. Damon either eats when he gets upset or gets busy doing something—or both. I took a step closer and noticed the empty cereal boxes underneath his workbench. He had been living on dry Cap'n Crunch and Cocoa Puffs.

"You must be tired," I said.

"A mite, I guess."

"Come on. Why don't you get some sleep?"

"I'm okay."

I put my hand on his shoulder. "It's going to be all right, Damon."

He looked up at me. "Why is somebody shooting at us?"

"I don't know."

"It's not fair."

"He'll get caught. Don't you worry."

He leaned his head against my hip. "I'm tired, I guess."

"Come on. You should go to bed."

"I don't want to close my eyes."

I let my hand rest on his shoulder. "Come back to the farmhouse with me. You can sleep on the couch."

"That's okay."

"Come on. I'll be there all afternoon. I'll cook us up a good supper."

As I drove him to the farmhouse, I kicked myself for not getting in touch sooner. He had been so spooked by the whole incident, he was afraid to go to sleep for fear somebody would break in and gut him. I should have known. All I would have needed to do was remember Willa in the freezer. Damon didn't take kindly to deaths, and a graphic, grisly end of someone he had known, even briefly, would set his mind off in a chamber of horrors. It might have been better for him to have actually seen Chambers' body than to endure what his imagination had concocted for him.

In the farmhouse, he lay on the living room couch, his jacket draped over his torso. I drew the shades and went into the kitchen.

"Hey, Chad," he called, a few moments later.

When I returned to the living room, he was sitting up. "What are you doing out there?" he said.

"Seeing what I have for supper."

"Can you stay in here for awhile?"

"Sure." I walked back to the living room and sat down in the rocker. "I'll be right here."

"I want to go hunting, you know that," he said. "That buck's mine."

"I know. And we'll get him."

"As soon as they catch that bastard, I'm going."

"Just try to sleep." God, he was wound tight.

Damon lay back. "I want to tell you something else."

"Try to relax."

"I almost forgot. I was working on a cell phone last night. I overheard somebody talking about Rodriguez and Chambers."

I leaned forward in my rocker. "What? What did they say?"

"They were talking about the kids."

"What kids?"

"I don't know. Something about keeping them quiet."

"They say anything else?"

"No. They hung up real quick." Damon rolled over on his side and looked at me. "It's the voice that's driving me crazy. I think I know one of them."

"You do?"

"I can't remember. I'm sleepy now."

Damon drifted off. I set the rocker into motion. A cell phone conversation. Two innocent people talking about the news? Or two people who knew the truth?

Damon slept through the afternoon and all night long. He was better in the morning, but he still couldn't place the voice he'd heard on the cell phone. I had to keep my appointment in Lebanon with Dr. Traynor and gave Damon the choice of riding with me or going back to his house. He opted for the latter.

"You sure you're okay?" I asked, dropping him off.

"Sleep helps."

"It usually does."

He got out of the truck and slammed the door. As I drove away, I watched him in my rearview going back into his house. He did look better, but I was badgered by misgivings over leaving him by himself. I wondered if he would ever remember the cell phone voice. Just realizing it was familiar, though, was enough to preoccupy my thinking on the trip to Lebanon.

Damon didn't know many people who weren't local, and if these cell phone talkers were discussing Chambers and Rodriguez then at least one of them—somebody we would both recognize on the street—might have been involved. Involved in what, though? And what did "the kids" have to do with it?

Dr. Clarise Traynor worked out of the psychiatric wing at Dartmouth-Hitchcock. The wing was tastefully decorated with potted greenery, antiseptic-white walls, and contrasting oak panelling. Seeing Traynor wasn't like going to a dentist—more like an orthodontist for straightening and adjusting.

Traynor was on schedule and she saw me right away. She greeted me with, "I've been reading all about you."

She shook my hand lightly. Her hands seemed always cold, the thin bones of her fingers, fragile. She was slim, thirty-something, always impeccably dressed in a shade-of-gray business suit, the dullness offset with a flourish of colorful, patterned scarves—this time it was yellows and pinks.

I must have sent her a puzzled look, for she said, "I'm talking about Natasha Wright's article."

"I haven't read it," I said.

"Really?" She walked back to her desk, and I watched her. "Sleek" came to mind. A tiger's saunter. "That's interesting," she said.

"Everything's interesting in this office, Dr. Traynor. Everything is significant."

She smiled and gathered her note pad from the desk. "Well, maybe not everything." She found her half-glasses that had a beaded chain attached to the stems. It was the one detail I didn't like about her. It was bad enough she chose to wear half-glasses, but with the beads, she looked—well, dowdy, like somebody's mother who played Bingo Tuesday nights at the firehouse. She was nobody's mother. "Shall we begin?" she said.

I took my customary place on the couch. Yes, she had a couch. I didn't lie down, though—just sort of lounged as she talked to me.

She drew up her chair. She had the newspaper with Natasha Wright's article with her. "So, what would you like to talk about, today?"

"I just have a few things."

"I imagine you do. If the article's any indication, a lot has happened since our last meeting." She glanced at the newspaper. "Why don't you start by telling me why you haven't read this."

"I can pretty much guess what it says."

"You don't want to read about yourself?"

"I don't want to read fabrications."

"Oh. So, she doesn't tell the truth?"

I placed my hands behind my head. "It probably says that I think Rodriguez didn't know who shot him. That's not the truth. The truth is I don't know what happened."

She looked at the paper, then over her half-glasses at me. "Interesting."

"I was right, you mean." I put my hands down and cradled my fingers in my lap. "I bet you thought I was afraid to read it," I said.

"I thought it odd that you hadn't read it."

"It's a matter of principle. I don't particularly care for Natasha Wright and her tactics. You should be proud of me for taking a stand."

She watched me for a moment, then wrote something on her pad.

"What'd you just write?"

She pointed her pen at me. "You know the rules. You can't ask me that."

"Come on, Dr. Traynor."

"Tell me more about this shooting you were called out on."

"I will if you tell me what you wrote."

"I wrote down that you appeared defensive."

Her stating this directly caught me off guard. Usually, I don't get squat out of her about what she writes on her pad. "You think I'm defensive?" I said.

"Well, you sure walked in here with an attitude. You want to start again?"

I let out some air. "Sure."

"Tell me what happened in the woods."

I related the whole story of Rodriguez and Chambers. I watched her as she took notes and thought about how relaxed I felt the more I opened up. I marveled at how she could turn me around.

She wasn't my first shrink. I'd started off with Dr. Weiler, a porky, bearded fellow with a permanent scowl. Talking to him had been like trying to unload a truck full of manure with the tailgate stuck. When I switched to Clarise Traynor, the stuff just poured out, much like what was happening now. Clarise, the natural cathartic. It took a woman like her to get me to remember Meg at all.

When I finished my story, Dr. Traynor said, "And you're angry about all of this."

"I'm angry?"

"Yes. It's in the stiffness of your gait, the way you hold your shoulders. You're angry."

"Sure. Okay."

"Tell me about it."

"I'm angry that ..." I looked up at the ceiling at a black light fixture in the shape of a rhombus. I tend to focus on it when the words won't come. "I'm angry because I don't feel like I'm in control."

"And that's a familiar feeling, isn't it?"

"Yes."

"Like you're a victim."

"Yes."

She waggled her pen. "You think someone's out to get you?"

I took a minute to think about that. "Oh, I get it," I said. "You think I feel paranoid?"

"That's not what I asked."

"Well, if I'm not really a victim, then I must be paranoid."

"Let me do the analysis," she said. She shifted in her seat, crossed her legs, exposing a white kneecap. "Tell me more about feeling like a victim."

I looked up at the black rhombus again. If I stared long

enough at it, maybe I might get some answers. It would have
been refreshing if just once she would tell me why she thought
I felt like a victim. Just tell me! "It's like something's out of
balance. I have this urge to find out what's going on, yet I
know I shouldn't stick my nose in."

I told her about hearing the news of Perino's body being
discovered, driving halfway to the scene and turning the truck
around, and about going down to the mini-mart when I suspected Bumps had trouble, only to find Chambers hanging on
a deer hook.

"Do you feel danger?"

"Danger? You mean, to me, personally?"

"Yes."

"Why should I feel that?"

"I'm reading a strong sense of urgency here, like if you
don't find out what's going on, you could be in trouble."

I pondered that. "I suppose it's dangerous going into the
woods with a lunatic loose, but personal danger? No. I don't
feel someone's out to get me. It's more like I'm part of a game
where I don't know the rules."

"So. Simple curiosity drives you to find out what they are."
It was a statement, not a question.

"If that were true, I wouldn't have turned around when I
heard about Perino's body being found. No, it's more than
that. I would like to forget this happened, but I can't. Things
keep nagging at me."

She wrote again. "Talk some more about those things."

"I have trouble believing there's a phantom killer out there
shooting hunters down, for one."

"What do you think happened?"

"I think Rodriguez knows who shot him."

"And Chambers?"

"Him, too." I told her about the tattoos, how that seemed to affirm some sort of connection.

"And you feel responsible for finding out the truth?"

I ran my hand through my hair. "I feel responsible for Rodriguez."

"Why?"

"Come on. You're a doctor. You know what it's like. If it weren't for me, Rodriguez would be dead. It's the old medical worker problem of becoming attached to the people you help."

"So, you owe it to him. You're still helping him."

"Yeah. That's not too weird, is it?"

She didn't answer me but wrote again on her pad. "Do you dream about him?"

"No. I dream about other things." I told her about Julie Hanneford coming after me with a knife and her seeing someone in the crowd who spooked her.

"You think that has anything to do with Chambers and Rodriguez?" she said.

"No. It's just something else I don't understand. I don't go looking for any of this. It just shows up on my doorstep."

"What have your other dreams been like?"

"Well, I've had a lot of them."

"More so than usual?"

"They do seem to be coming with more frequency, yes." I could feel her eyes on me, watching. She didn't write anything. "Is that important?"

"Not necessarily."

"But it could be?"

"It means your mind is active. You're feeding your subconscious."

"Munch, munch."

She put her pad down, a sign that this session was almost over. I hated this part. It was always tough to leave. "So do you have a plan?"

"Stay out of trouble." I smiled at her.

She looked up from her pad. "So, tell me about Rachel."

The shift in conversation was so abrupt, it took a few moments for me to respond. We had talked quite a bit about Rachel in our last session. "What do you want to know?" I asked.

"Anything you want to tell me."

"I have nothing to complain about."

"Then what's the problem?"

"There's a problem?"

Traynor waved her hand. "Come on, Chad. I can tell when you're not being forthcoming."

I stared at my hands. The "being forthcoming" sounded a starchy way to refer to what I felt. "I don't know. I think I'm getting serious about her."

"And?"

"I don't know how to take it to the next level."

"You're considering marriage?"

"No. Not now, anyway. It's just that, well, like the other day, for example. I found myself telling her I was falling in love."

"What did she say?"

"She changed the subject."

Traynor took off her glasses. "I can understand that."

"It didn't make me feel good."

"We already talked about this. She has something she's dealing with, too. The divorce wasn't so long ago."

"Yeah. I even found out her husband's name. Apparently, she's still dealing with Cliff."

"You mean, directly? They still see each other?"

"No." I tapped my skull. "In here."

She wrote Cliff's name down on her pad. "Give her time, Chad. She'll come around."

I smiled at her. "You don't think she's just using me, then?"

"You mean, she just wants you for your body?"

"Hard to believe, isn't it?"

"Maybe not."

This wasn't the answer I expected. I sat forward. "You don't really think that."

"No, I don't. But Rachel's obviously sending you signals that she doesn't want the relationship to go beyond what it is. Not right now, anyway."

CHAPTER THIRTEEN

After a session with Dr. Traynor, it usually took some time to sift through what we had talked about, and I decided to unwind a little in the hospital coffee shop before heading home. I nursed a cup of Heavenly Hazelnut. I hadn't been there long when I heard a voice from behind me.

"Mr. Duquette?"

I turned in my seat and looked up into the heavily made-up eyes of Manuella Silva.

"I thought it was you." She reached for my hand.

I got up from my chair and felt her sharp nails once again in my palm. Instead of purple nail polish, she was wearing peach to match the pastel print of her blouse.

"I was just eating some lunch and spotted you across the room," she said.

"Would you like to sit down?"

"Why don't you join me instead?" She motioned to a corner table. "I'm afraid I'm so spread out over there, it would take an hour to move everything."

She wasn't kidding about being spread out. She had ordered enough for a family of four chicken fingers, two burgers, large fries, and a chocolate chip cookie the size of a Frisbee. It looked as if she had started on the cookie first.

"Can I offer you something to eat?" she said.

I took my seat. "Not hungry, thanks."

She smiled. "I didn't have breakfast."

"Good to have a healthy appetite."

"It's not healthy." She dipped a chicken finger into a plastic container of sweet and sour sauce. "But it sure tastes good."

"I imagine you're here to visit your brother."

"Yes. One of his doctors wanted to talk to me."

"How's he doing?"

"Much the same. His color is pretty good, I guess."

"Still hasn't come out of it, though?"

Her shoulders sagged. "It's so sad. I wish I could do something to help him." She took a huge bite of her hamburger.

It was irksome watching her eat. How she could follow chicken fingers with a bit of cookie, then chomp on a burger was beyond me.

"The doctor's optimistic that Joseph will recover," she said. "The CAT scan shows no brain damage." She suddenly reached across the table and took my hand again. "We owe it all to you; you kept him alive." She squeezed my hand, then pulled hers away. I could feel a residue of grease on my fingers.

"Well, that's good news," I said.

She smiled and ate some more.

I cleared my throat. "Better news than what happened to Glenn Chambers, that's for sure."

She put her hamburger down. "That was awful," she said. She wiped her mouth with a napkin. "That's the one thing I fear. Joseph coming to, how hard he's going to take the news."

"They were that close?"

She smiled at me, coyly. "You could say that."

My face must have registered a blank. "Oh. Didn't I tell you?" she said, and slapped the table. "Of course not. It was that cop I told. I just thought it was you." She shook her head. "Sometimes I think the screws are coming out of my brain."

"What exactly did you think you told me?"

She chewed, absently. "That Joseph and Glenn were lovers."

I don't know how long I sat there, stunned.

She pushed some fries my way. "Are you sure you can't help me out here? I'm getting full."

"No, thanks."

She shrugged. "Suit yourself." She didn't look full the way she got back to her eating.

"How long did they know each other?" I said.

"About five years."

"And they were lovers all that time?"

"I think so. Of course, I didn't see my brother much after high school, so I only knew about Glenn from what he had told me."

"You never met the man?"

"No."

"You have any idea what they were doing in the woods?"

She sat back and rested her hands over her middle. "Like I told the trooper, I think Glenn knew of a place, some sort of cabin or something."

"On the Turner property?"

"Turner property. Where's that?"

"That's where your brother was shot."

"Oh."

I couldn't recall ever hearing of any cabin even remotely near the Turner property. "Don't you find it odd that they were in the woods?"

"Not really. Joseph likes to go for walks."

"Even during hunting season?"

"I don't think they even thought about that. They're from the city." She licked her fingers, then wiped them on her napkin. I looked at the table. She had finished everything.

"Do you know if they belonged to any organizations?"

She frowned at me. "You mean like Triple-A?"

"No. Fraternal. You know, the Elks or the Moose?"

"I don't think so." She smiled. "You're full of questions today, Mr. Duquette."

"Just curious, that's all."

"Now, why would you want to know if they belonged to the Moose?" She laughed, and brought her peach fingernails to her mouth. "It sounds silly when you say it like that."

"I wondered because they both have the same tattoo. I thought it might signify some club or something."

Her laughter faded. "They have the same tattoo?"

"Yes. Do you know anything about that?"

"I knew Joseph had a tattoo, but I have no idea about Glenn." She thought a minute. "And he was pretty sensitive about it, too."

"What do you mean?"

"I saw it on the beach one day. Joseph liked to wear these skimpy tank suits, you know what I mean? It was on his upper thigh, just the edge of it, you know? So I asked him about it and he told me it was none of my business."

"You never found out what it was?"

"No. He grabbed a towel and wrapped it around himself. He never took it off the rest of the day." She worked her tongue on a back molar, trying to dislodge some remnant of her meal. "Come to think of it, he was *real* touchy about that tattoo."

***

Rachel finally got some time off from the dorm, but as it turned out Monday was also the night off for the blues band at Westy's Roadhouse. Her mood had been spirited on the drive into town. She chatted mostly about Julie Hanneford, and the conversation continued as we took our seats in a corner table far away from the jukebox.

"Julie's not coming back at all this year?" I said.

"Ellie thinks it's best."

I placed a napkin on my lap. "It was acid she dropped, right?"

"Yes."

"She say where she got it?"

Rachel smirked. "Yeah, right."

"Sorry. I wasn't thinking."

Rachel looked at her menu. "I think Ellie and Hap have tough times ahead."

"But Julie's okay?"

"She's home, recovering."

"And not saying anything about it."

"She called her parents a bunch of narcs."

A waitress came to take our order. Westy's was a steak and chop place, the laminated menus sporting dramatic color photos of sirloins, larger-than-life burgers, and mixed drinks with pastel umbrellas. I ordered the rib special, Rachel the surf and turf.

"So, tell me about your session," Rachel said.

"It was fine."

"That's it?"

"No. Dr. Traynor thinks I'm coming along." I laughed. "Then she said, 'that'll be a hundred dollars, please.' "

"Come on. What did she really say?"

I shifted in my seat. Westy's had cheap furniture. The back of the wooden chair was too low and pressed against my spine. "We talked mostly about the murders."

"And ..."

"And she thinks I'm handling it well. That's about it."

Rachel reached across the table and took my hand. "I'm glad."

Feeling her hand in mine almost made me want to press the issue about our relationship. I wrestled with whether I should bring up what I had told Traynor about taking it to the next level.

She gave me a playful kick under the table. "Hello?"

"Huh?"

"You checking out on me?"

"Sorry. Just thinking."

"About what?"

I deflected. "I ran into Manuella Silva in the hospital coffee shop."

Rachel looked puzzled. She pulled her hand away.

"Rodriguez's sister." I paused. "I told you about her, remember?" I leaned forward. "And she said that Rodriguez was real embarrassed by that tattoo. Didn't like anyone seeing it."

"Really."

"Yeah. What do you think about that?"

"Nothing."

"Nothing?"

"Why is it so unusual? Some people get tattoos when they're young and regret it."

"True. But I think this is different."

She toyed with her fork. "Who is this Manuella Silva, anyway?"

"I told you."

"No, I mean what does she do? Does she work or just hang around the hospital waiting for her brother to come out of it?"

"Wait a minute. I can tell you exactly." I fumbled through my jacket pocket and pulled out the business card Manuella had given me before I left the coffee shop. "She's a C.P.A. Financial advisor."

"Why the hell did she give you her card?"

"She offered free financial advice, you know, as a way of thanking me for what I did for her brother." I studied Rachel. "Why did you ask about the card?"

She dismissed the question with a wave of her hand.

"You think what she does has any bearing on this tattoo business?"

"What? No. Of course not."

"Then why did you ..."

"Some woman talks to you in a restaurant," she said. "She gives you her card. I like to know these things."

Rachel jealous? I felt like clicking my heels. I thought about telling her that I didn't give Manuella my address but checked myself. Let her wonder.

The waitress brought a draft for me and the house red for Rachel. I took a sip of beer—a bitter pale ale.

"Speaking of those tattoos," she said, "I looked into that pentagram thing."

"You did?"

"Yeah. I knew I had read about it, but I couldn't remember where. It was driving me crazy until I thumbed through a copy of *Sir Gawain and the Green Knight.*"

"Sir Gawain? Ah, yes."

"You've read it?"

"One of Grandpa's books."

"The pentagram is also on Tarot cards."

"So it has to do with telling fortunes."

"Yes. Have you ever had yours read?"

"No. Have you?"

"In college. I'm supposed to have a long life."

I sipped my coffee. "What else did you find out?"

She sat back and looked to be gathering her thoughts. I prepared myself for a lecture. "It has various meanings. It was long associated with Christianity, with the five wounds of Christ, a protective glyph." She went on about how the Gnostics called it the Blazing Star, and then she branched into Pythagoras, Plato, and assorted Stoics until my head was spinning.

I put my hand up for her to stop. "Enough. Are your classes like this?"

"I'm not finished."

"I don't think I can take anymore."

"We really haven't got to the interesting part."

"But why do you suppose Chambers and Rodriguez had a religious symbol tattooed on their thighs? Neither one struck me as ascetics."

"Depends on the arrangement of the star." She took a pen from her purse and drew out a pentagram on the back of her placemat. "If the point of the star is on the top," she said, indicating with her pen, "then it has religious and mystical connotations." She spun the placemat around. "But if the point is on the bottom, it means evil."

"The same symbol means spiritual and evil?"

"Look," she said. "If the point of the star is up, then the direction is toward the heavens, or the mystical. If it is down, it's toward ..."

"Hell?"

"Or the physical and elemental." She pointed to the pentagram, that from where I was sitting was still pointing down. "With the two points at the top, the symbol is also emblematic of the Horned God. See its ears, it looks like a goat's head, a sign of Wicca."

"Wicca. Devil worship."

"Yes."

As I stared at the symbol it hit me what was wrong the day I drew the star for Bumps. Of course it didn't look right: I'd drawn the star with the point up. I closed my eyes and pictured the tattoo on Chambers' hip. The point had been definitely up. Something seemed out of whack, and it bothered me until I remembered I had been looking at the remains of a man hanging upside down.

CHAPTER FOURTEEN

I drove Rachel home. We were both tired and decided to sleep in our own beds. When I turned off 125A on my way to the farmhouse I saw the fire trucks. Damn! While I'd been in Concord, I had missed a call. I knew the house; it belonged to the animal rights activist. It looked as if the fire department had arrived in time to save the structure. When I got out of the truck and looked closer, the damage seemed to be limited to the side porch. The vinyl siding was curled and scorched like ribbon candy.

I found Striker coiling a hose. "Looks like we got some trouble, eh Neil?"

"You could say that."

"How'd it start?"

"Tub Marx." Striker picked up the hose and brought it to the pumper.

I followed close behind. "You mean he torched the place?"

"Tried to. Didn't get far, though. I guess he thought no one was home. He lit the porch and this animal rights guy inside— eh, what's his name?"

"Zander Cleese."

"Yeah, well anyway, it seems he didn't consider humans

animals 'cause he set off a blast and filled Tub's pants with
birdshot."

"Tub okay?"

"He's not sitting down too good. Bumps booked him."

"Bumps around?"

"Somewheres. Last time I saw him he was taking Polaroids."

I found Bumps around the side of the house. He was by the
garage, underneath a spotlight, staring at his camera like it was
the Rosetta Stone.

"Problems?" I asked.

He turned the camera flip-side. It was pink and looked like
it might have once belonged to his daughter. "Piece of shit," he
said. He tugged at a print that was stuck in the slot.

"Want me to look at it?"

"No! I can handle it."

I stepped back. "Okay, fine."

"Where you been, anyway?" He pulled on the stuck print
and part of it ripped. "Damn."

"Out to dinner."

He held the camera loosely in both hands and glanced up
at the sky.

The sky was pretty hazy. "What are you looking at?" I asked.

Bumps lowered his head and glowered at me. He face was
red from his efforts with the camera, and the acne scars looked
like white moon craters. "I'm not looking at anything," he said,
measuring his words. "I'm counting to fucking ten."

"Oh."

"I guess this isn't a good time to talk about tattoos," I said.

"Tattoos?" He scowled. "No. I haven't found out anything
more about them."

"You mean you didn't call Woo?"

"No, I didn't." He went back to tugging at the stuck print.

I told him about what Rachel had discovered about point-down pentagrams. "So, you think it means anything?" I asked.

"Rachel? What does she have to do with this?"

"I told her about the tattoos."

He grunted. "Who else did you tell?"

"Nobody."

"You didn't talk to that reporter again, did you?"

"No."

He gave a mighty wrench on the stuck print. A bracket popped off and plastic pieces flew in the air. "Shit!" he yelled. He raised the camera above his head and threw it to the ground. The camera shattered on impact. We both stared at it, neither of us saying anything.

Bumps finally broke the silence. "I had to put it out of its misery," he said, and ran a hand across his mouth.

I turned to leave. "I'll call you tomorrow about the tattoos."

"Don't bother."

"Why?"

He stepped closer to me. "I don't care if the point was up, down, or sticking in somebody's poop chute." He wiped his mouth again and spat. Chewing tobacco. Bumps hadn't chewed in years.

"I'll wait for a better time." I smiled. "You know, when you're not so busy."

"Look, Chad." He turned his head and spat again. "I've got a redneck setting fires to houses. I've got a Bambi-lover shooting birdshot into his ass. I got a body hanging in the center of town. You think I've got time for friggin' tattoos?"

"Right. Like I said. Bad timing."

"I'll tell you one thing," he said. "We don't find Chambers' killer soon, this town's going to explode."

I don't know if Bumps' tantrum shook the heavens and caused the universe to shift, but I woke to news that a man named Roger Pierce had confessed to killing Glenn Chambers and wounding Joseph Rodriguez. A televised press conference was scheduled for later that morning.

Who the hell was Roger Pierce?

I got on the phone to Bumps, but he wasn't in. No doubt he had his role to play and was caught up in the investigation. As soon as I hung up the phone, Rachel called. We made a date to watch the news conference at my place. I put on another pot of coffee. I was at the sink when, through the window, I saw Damon pull into the driveway. He waved, all smiles. He did a little jig, then came to the door.

"Did you hear?"

"Yeah."

He grabbed my arms. "It's over," he said. "It's over."

I hadn't seen him this happy since he potted a raccoon that had been vandalizing his garbage. I grinned at him, pleased with the change in his mood from the last time I had seen him.

"That buck is mine!"

"Let's get the details first."

He pulled back. "What are you talking about? They got the guy! They got him!"

At 11:30 AM, regular programming was interrupted at the ABC affiliate in Concord.

The cameras zeroed in on the podium as Trooper Manfred Tierney stepped forward. He placed some papers on a lectern and looked directly into the cameras. "This morning Roger

Allen Pierce confessed to the murder of Glenn Chambers and is being held on one count of first degree murder. He has also been charged with assault with a deadly weapon against Joseph Rodriguez—intent to kill."

Tierney was in his element. The cameras loved him. "We are still interviewing Mr. Pierce, and more details will be forthcoming." He grasped the podium with both hands. "I'm afraid that's all I have for a statement. Now, I'll take your questions."

A man in square, black-rimmed glasses stood up. "Joe Castle—AP. Has Roger Pierce been under surveillance?"

"He's been a suspect, yes."

"Can you tell us why?"

"Mr. Pierce knew Mr. Chambers well. He had once been his lover." Murmurs ran through the crowd. I sat forward in my seat. Did I hear right? Tierney continued: "And he didn't take kindly to Mr. Chambers and Mr. Rodriguez spending a weekend together."

Natasha Wright spoke up. "Then you're saying the motive was jealousy?"

"It appears that way, yes."

From the back of the room a woman representing the *Union Leader* asked, "You say jealousy *appears* to be the motive. Does that mean you're not sure?"

"It means that from what we know so far, Roger Pierce was distraught over losing his lover, that he followed both men that weekend with an intent to do bodily harm." Tierney picked up his papers from the lectern and smiled at the crowd of reporters. "You can be sure, if I find out anything more, you'll be the first to know."

Tierney left the podium, reporters firing questions at his retreating figure.

I snapped off the TV.

Damon got to this feet. "Let's go hunting." he said.

"Maybe this weekend."

"Come on, Chad. Let's go today."

"No can do."

I turned to Rachel, who was still staring at the blank screen. "Rachel and I want to be together this afternoon. Students come back tonight."

"Oh, you want to be lovey-dovey."

I met Rachel's glance. "That's right," I said. "Why don't you go clean your rifle. We'll get your buck Saturday."

After Damon left, Rachel and I sat at the kitchen table. She made Darjeeling tea, which I hardly ever drank. But it tasted good.

"You're awfully quiet," she said.

"Just thinking."

"You aren't convinced, are you?"

I ran my finger over the handle of the mug. "I guess it's possible."

"At least now there's a motive."

"And all that stuff about a hunter stalking hunters is bogus?" I said.

"It could have been Pierce trying to throw the law off the scent."

I sat back in the chair. "Damned clever."

"Too clever, you mean?"

"Just tell me this," I said. "How does Perino fit into this lover theory? Is this some sort of quadrangle?"

"Quadrangle?"

"Do we have four lovers all pissed off at each other? Christ, this is like *General Hospital Ate Chicago*."

Rachel looked up from her mug. "Maybe Perino was hired by Pierce to help him kill Chambers and Rodriguez."

"And why would he want to do that?"

"Money, sex, power?"

"Greed, anger, lust? No. I'm sorry." I took a sip of tea. "Unless ..."

"Unless what?"

"Unless Roger Pierce has a star-shaped tattoo on his thigh."

"And what would that prove?"

"They all got drunk one night and got the same tattoo." What was the connection? It was getting so that I saw pentagrams in my sleep. "And why all of a sudden did Roger Pierce step forward and confess?"

She sighed. "Why don't you just accept it?"

I caught her drift to drop the subject and reached across the table and took her hand. "I have this fantasy about you," I said.

"Oh, really?"

"Yeah. Want to hear it?" I brought her fingers to my lips and kissed them. "I come in the house and you're waiting for me on the couch. It's in the afternoon, and the late November sun is pouring through the window. You slowly undress for me. Then we make love right beneath the portrait of Ezekial Duquette, who, by the time we are finished, has spun himself upside down." I leaned over the table and kissed her on the lips.

"That's it?" she said.

"What do you mean?"

"You couldn't come up with a fantasy better than that?"

I smiled at her. "You don't want to hear the others."

"Oooh. I'm embarrassed thinking about them." She kissed me. "You know what I think?"

"Haven't a clue, most of the time."

"I think you didn't have that fantasy at all."

"No?"

"No. I think you made that up because you want to get in my pants."

I expressed mock surprise. "I can't believe you would suspect me of anything so foul."

"Let's go see what old Ezekial has to say about this."

That night, alone in my bed, I dreamed I was in 'Nam after a firefight, picking up the pieces. I found a soldier with his chest blown open. I reached in and massaged his heart. An artery starting spurting. I let go of the heart and tried to close the artery off. It grew another, only it was gushing harder. The heart lay flaccid, but my hands were full with another artery that had let loose. I was swamped in blood. Then the soldier came to and started screaming at me.

I woke and threw off the covers. The sweat on my chest began to cool, sending a chill deep in my spine. I started shivering, but I lay there another minute or so before pulling the covers back over me. I glanced at the clock: 4:00 AM.

In a few hours I was supposed to help my neighbor Joe Rand frame a basement playroom. I called him at 7:00 and said I was under the weather. I got back in bed and slept until 10:00. When I got up for the second time that day, I felt punch drunk. Strong coffee didn't help.

I went to see Damon, but his truck was gone. I stepped into his kitchen and hollered for him. I checked the gun rack by the kitchen door. His rifle wasn't there. Shit. He'd gone hunting by himself. Probably early this morning.

I dragged myself through the rest of the day, but I did

manage to get the remainder of the wood in. When I went back to Damon's house around supper time, he still hadn't returned. I ate meatloaf and gravy at the diner, then returned to see if he was home, but no lights were on.

I called Bumps. "I'm a little worried," I said. "Damon hasn't come back."

"When's the last time you saw him?"

"Yesterday, before noon."

"He say where he was going?"

"I think he went hunting on the Turner property."

"It's too early to be worrying," Bumps said. "Give it 'til morning."

"It's not too early. It isn't like him."

There was a pause on the line before Bumps spoke again. "I'll call the state police. See if anything's been reported."

"Okay, thanks."

That evening, it snowed hard, and I drove out to the Turner property to see if I could spot Damon's truck. I skirted the whole perimeter, but there was nothing. When I got back, Bumps had left a message on my machine that no accidents had been reported involving a pickup.

I made my plow rounds, returned to the Turner property and was tracking by first light. I retraced our whole route the day we went looking for the buck, but my search was futile. The heavy snow had covered any sign of his being there.

I sped back to his house, hoping to see lights, but there were none.

CHAPTER FIFTEEN

The next day there was still no sign of Damon, and he was officially declared missing.

State Trooper Manfred Tierney drove up to the farmhouse that morning and informed me that he would be in charge of the investigation.

He sat down at the kitchen table and began taking notes. "When did you first notice that Damon was gone?"

"Wednesday morning," I said. "I drove over to his house."

"Wednesday," he said and checked his watch. "That was November thirtieth?"

"That's right."

"God. Where's the month gone?"

I watched him as he wrote, his handwriting meticulous, i's dotted and t's crossed. Just knowing Tierney was in charge made me feel confident that Damon would be found. He was all business.

"And you say you think he went hunting?"

"He took his rifle." I went into detail about Damon's obsession with getting the buck.

"On the Turner property?"

"It's the only thing that makes sense."

Tierney clicked his ballpoint a few times. "He couldn't have just gone to visit relatives?"

"We don't have any, not around here, anyway."

"Where, then?"

"An uncle in California. But you know Damon. He wouldn't drive there. He hates traveling."

"No girlfriend?"

"Like I said. You know Damon."

Tierney put his pen down. He sat back in his chair and folded his arms. His biceps bulged beneath his shirt. "You mentioned you already went looking for him."

"Yes. On Thursday."

"Didn't you think it was a little early to be worried? I mean, so the man went hunting."

"He would never stay out overnight. No, what I think happened was, after Roger Pierce's confession, Damon felt safe to go into the woods again. There was no longer anything holding him back."

Tierney pondered the idea.

Mentioning Pierce's name had dredged up the misgivings I felt about why Pierce had suddenly spilled his guts. "Can I ask you something?"

"Go ahead."

"What do you think of Pierce's confession?"

"You mean do I believe it?"

"Yes."

Tierney hesitated. "I'm afraid I can't comment on that. It's still under investigation."

"Come on. I'm not the press."

He smiled at me. A consummate professional smile. "I'm sure you can understand."

"But it might have some relevance here."

He looked puzzled. "You mean with regards to your brother?"

"Think about it," I said. "No sooner does Pierce confess than Damon goes hunting and disappears."

Tierney sat forward in his chair. "And you think that Pierce didn't kill Chambers? That the real perp is still out there?" The corners of Tierney's eyes crinkled, a trace of amusement.

"It's possible you have the wrong guy, isn't it?"

He shrugged off the idea. "I would say the confession and Damon's disappearance have more the ring of coincidence than anything else."

"So, Pierce is your man."

He picked up his pen. "Chad, look. I don't think this kind of talk is going to help us. You're supposing quite a bit, and it's not going to get us any closer to finding your brother."

"But there are too many unanswered questions."

"Like what?"

"Like Perino, for example."

Tierney looked down at his pad and began to doodle. "What about him?"

I watched his pen move, a hypnotizing series of interconnected circles. His casualness was beginning to irritate me. "Is he involved with Pierce?"

Tierney smiled. "Why are you so interested in this case?"

I slammed the table with my fist. "Because my brother is missing!"

Tierney held up his hand. "Hey, I'm here to help."

"Then stop patronizing me!" I could feel my face getting hot.

Tierney placed his pen on the pad and folded his hands. He looked as if he were about to pray. "Chad," he said, his voice calm, "I'm not patronizing you." He sat back in his chair. "I can't really talk about Roger Pierce, but I will say this. There is a connection to Perino."

It was a peace offering and I considered it. "One that makes sense?" I said.

"Yes."

I tried to imagine what connection that might be, but no doubt Tierney was right. There were things he knew about the case that I didn't, and that was the way it should be.

"Now, let's talk about finding your brother, okay?"

"Sure."

Tierney reached into his pocket and pulled out an antique pocket watch. A fob in the shape of a hand-carved horse's head, dangled from a chain. "I think we should mount an organized search of the Turner property," he said. "Your hunch about him going after that buck is a good one. We'll start tomorrow."

"So, you agree with me."

"The part about Damon's hunting, anyway."

I suddenly thought of the cistern and Damon nearly killing himself. "God. I just hope he's not lying out there somewhere."

Tierney stowed his watch in his pocket and got up from the table. "If he is, we'll find him." He adjusted the brim of his hat. "I really want to help here, Chad," he said. "I know what it's like to lose a brother."

I thought about Tierney's comment after he left the farmhouse. That he had lost a brother to drug dealing didn't seem the same as Damon being missing, but I was reminded how embarrassed Tierney must have felt having a brother convicted of growing marijuana. Considering my role in turning Roland in, I was reminded again of how he had always been deferential to me, and I respected him for it. And my respect grew the next day as I watched Tierney put his all into the search; you would think Damon had been his own brother.

All weekend, volunteers from as far south as Manchester combed the Turner property for any trace of Damon. Tierney put me in charge of a group that followed the course Damon and I took the day we went hunting for the big buck, while Tierney himself led another crew beginning in the northeast corner near Tinderhook Mine on Tingly Mountain. Bumps with his people worked their way up from the south, and like a pincer movement, we gradually converged at the center of the property.

Snow hampered our progress on Saturday, and Sunday dawned cloudy and gray. We pushed on, though, and by Monday noon, under a blue sky streaked with cirrus clouds, we finally came together. No one had seen anything.

That afternoon, I was frightened and overwhelmed thinking about Damon, consumed by guilt that I hadn't done more to prevent him from going hunting. I slept for a few hours on the couch and was awakened by a phone call around supper time. It was Bumps.

Damon's truck had been found.

In Boston.

I no sooner hung up the phone when Rachel called. She had heard about Damon's truck on the TV news.

"I had been wondering how the day went," she said.

"Still no sign of him."

"I wish I could have been with you."

"You had to work," I said. "I understand."

"What do you make of his truck being found in Boston?"

My head felt numb with the knowledge of the truck's discovery. Everything I had supposed about what happened to Damon had been turned upside down. "I just got off the phone with Bumps," I said. "I haven't had much time to think about it."

"Would Damon drive to Boston?"

Her question registered, but my thoughts were suddenly on the cell phone conversation Damon had overheard. "Listen, Rachel. Can I come over and talk?"

"Well, I do have a dorm meeting at ten-thirty."

"I'll be gone by then."

"Okay, sure."

I walked through the back door of Rachel's apartment. Cob was on his dog bed, and he barely raised his head at my entrance.

Rachel was in the living room, reading. I liked her glasses better than Traynor's—scholarly horn-rims that suggested intelligence and sexuality. Another of my fantasies has to do with her wearing those glasses and a shirt of mine, loosely buttoned—nothing else. Right now, worried sick over Damon, it was hard to think about that kind of thing.

"What's wrong with Cob?" I asked, assuming a chair opposite hers.

She closed her book, Hemingway's *For Whom the Bell Tolls*, and took off her glasses. "He's been on a toot. Gone two days."

"Probably found an interesting dumpster somewhere."

"I think it's more a bitch in heat."

"Oh. Well, I can sympathize."

"What?"

It took a moment, then I realized what I had just said. "No. I didn't mean you're a bitch. I was talking about Cob. I can sympathize with him."

Rachel harumphed. "Maybe we should get you both fixed." She got up from her chair, came over to mine. "I don't mean that, of course."

"I hope you don't."

She kissed me lightly on the lips. "I thought about you out there today. It must have been cold."

"It was."

"No luck, I guess."

"No luck."

She gave my hand a pat and went back to her chair. She wore loose fitting jeans and a gray sweatshirt that read *Dunston Academy*. She sat down and pulled up her legs until they rested on the seat cushion. "You sounded upset on the phone," she said.

"Yeah. I guess I did."

"What's the matter?" she said.

"I got a little worried talking about this over the phone."

"Why?"

I told her about Damon overhearing the cell-phone conversation.

"You mean you're afraid people are listening in? Your phone is tapped?"

"That's what I mean."

She didn't say anything.

"You think I'm losing it, don't you?" I said.

"No. I just think it's a little far-fetched." She eyed me curiously. "Will you answer my question now?"

"What's that?"

"Would Damon drive to Boston?"

"No. He's scared of the city."

"He have friends there? Anyone you might not know about?"

"You know Damon," I said. "His social skills aren't the best."

I could hear the low murmur of girls' voices in the common room across the hall. "I think it's a ruse," I said. "Someone drove the truck to Boston."

"Why?"

"To get us off the scent."

"But you've searched the Turner property for three days."

"I know. He just had to have gone hunting. There would be no other reason for him to get in his truck in the first place."

Rachel sat forward. "Could he have been hunting someplace else?"

"No. You heard him yourself. He was going after that buck."

She got up and started pacing the room. "Damon may not have driven to Boston," she said, "but somebody could have taken him there."

"Who?"

"Maybe it was a robbery."

I looked up at her. "Damon didn't have anything, and they sure as hell wouldn't want his truck."

There was a knock at the door that led to the common room. Rachel yelled, "Come in."

A young girl, her hair dyed in fuscia streaks, poked her head in. "Oh, I'm sorry, Ms. Spires. I didn't know you had company."

"What is it, Mandy?" Rachel said.

"I just wanted to talk about something," she said.

Rachel glanced at me. "Don't run away," she said. "I still want to talk."

After Rachel and Mandy left I sat back in the chair and closed my eyes. I was tired, but my eyes wouldn't stay shut. I knew I had to rethink this whole thing. Despite what Tierney had said, I couldn't accept that Roger Pierce was really the man. I kept thinking that Damon had stumbled onto something when he was out hunting.

What Rachel had said, though, made just as much sense. Damon could be in Boston if someone had kidnapped him, but I couldn't accept his disappearance as a random act. Somehow it had to be all caught up in this Chambers and Rodriguez thing.

If only Rodriguez would regain consciousness, then he might be able to identify once and for all who shot him—and that knowledge could lead us to Damon.

But Rodriguez couldn't talk. I wondered about the two love birds, Chambers and Rodriguez.

Then it hit me. So Rodriguez couldn't talk, but maybe someone else could. I recalled that both Chambers and Rodriguez lived near Boston. Now there was at least a geographical connection to Damon's truck.

I fumbled through my jacket pocket and found Manuella Silva's crumpled business card.

CHAPTER SIXTEEN

Mandy needed Rachel's attention—something about a phone call from Mandy's father announcing he was divorcing her mother—and I returned to the farmhouse.

I slept well, and morning dawned bright and warm. I lay in bed listening to ice melting off the roof. I'm not one to complain about the weather, but this year the change of seasons affected me more than usual, and it felt like the whole cosmos was out of whack. Fall days had been uncharacteristically warm, and our first killing frost hadn't hit until the first week in November. And here we were back in late summer again—temps predicted to hit sixty, with rain by nightfall.

A snow plow in a rainstorm is a bleak sight.

I drove into town to use the pay phone. I didn't know if the farmhouse phone wires were tapped, but it didn't hurt to be cautious.

It took about a half hour of sitting in the truck before I screwed up the courage to call Manuella Silva. It seemed like a perfectly sound idea last night in Rachel's apartment, but now it rang of futility. But I had to do something. Running through the woods was getting me nowhere. Where the *hell* was Damon?

I dialed Manuella's office, waited for recorded instructions, and punched in her extension.

I got her voice mail and was ready to hang up when she came on the line. "Mr. Duquette. What a surprise."

"Call me Chad."

"To what do I owe this honor?"

"Well, I was sitting here remembering what you said about— you know about ever needing help ..."

"You have some investment ideas?"

"No. Listen, is this a good time? I just had your work number."

"How can I help?"

I asked if she knew about the extensive search for Damon and that his truck had been found in Boston.

"That man is your brother?"

"Stepbrother."

"Well, of course I've heard about what happened, but I didn't realize he was related to you. I'm terribly sorry."

There was silence at the other end. "This is hard to explain," I said, "but I'm running out of possibilities. I think there's a link between your brother and mine."

"Why would you think that?"

"I suspect that Damon stumbled onto something in the woods and whoever shot your brother is involved with his disappearance."

She didn't respond.

"I was hoping we could work together on this."

"I don't understand what you want from me."

"I'd like to see your brother's apartment."

"You want to look at Joseph's place?"

"If that's possible. I mean, do you have a key?"

"I have a key."

There was another pause, too long to be comfortable.

"So can I see it?" I said.

"I don't know if it would be right."

I glanced out the window, trying to figure how to tip her reluctance my way. "Can you tell me this, then: Did Chambers ever live with your brother?"

"I don't think so. Joseph liked his space."

"Do you know if the police have been to the apartment yet?"

"I have no idea. Don't they need a warrant?"

"They do."

"No one's asked me about it."

"They don't have to ask you."

"Oh."

I decided on a new tack. "Manuella, I can appreciate your hesitancy, and if you don't want me to see the place I understand."

"What do you expect to find there?"

"Something that might point to Damon."

"Let me think about it."

"I just hope you won't take long."

"I said I would think about it."

The chippiness in her voice surprised me. I must have been leaning on her too hard. "Thanks, I knew I could count on you." I waited for her to say something else but she didn't. "It's funny how things work out," I said. "I helped save your brother and now you're helping to find mine." It was a cheap ploy.

"All right, Chad," she said, resignation in her voice. "Are you busy this afternoon?"

"Not really."

"Pick me up after work."

***

It's a two-hour drive from Dunston to Boston, depending on traffic, and I made it downtown in just under that.

Manuella worked in a high-rise in Boston's financial district near Post Office Square. In the years right after I mustered out of the service, I gradually learned the Byzantine twists of Boston streets through countless ambulance runs, and I had little trouble finding the place.

But it had been over five years since I had been in the city, and the parking garage I had planned to use had been bulldozed to make room for yet another bank. I chose an underground garage four blocks away. The emergency lights on the cab just barely cleared the height barrier as I eased into the garage.

My instructions were to wait for Manuella outside the building. I made it with twenty minutes to spare. The sun spotlighted the curb, fighting for some presence in this walled part of the city, and I leaned against a mailbox while I waited.

Being in the city made me think of better times. Meg used to love shopping at Downtown Crossing, not too far from here, and we often passed this building where Manuella worked for Brownstein and Hull on our way to the aquarium or a restaurant in the North End.

My thoughts were soon interrupted by a hand on my arm.

"Right on time," Manuella said. She was dolled up in a gray wool coat with the fur of some dead animal for a collar, her hair coiffed, her lips red and glossy.

"Thanks for doing this," I said.

She gave my arm a pat. "I have a dinner engagement, so let's get going."

It turned out that Rodriguez lived in a condo on Dartmouth Street, a converted brownstone. Right away, my expectations were shattered. His place was in the Back Bay area of Boston, land of the Brahmins. You just don't settle there unless you have dough. I had pictured him in a triple decker in Dorchester.

"What exactly did your brother do?" I asked Manuella as she turned the key in the lock.

"Shipping." She immediately disarmed the security system.

"Business must have been good," I said.

We walked in, and a faint smell of disinfectant caught my attention. "You had this place cleaned?" I asked.

"You smell that, too?"

I nodded. We walked through the foyer. A heavy mahogany Victorian piece, a mirrored hat rack/umbrella stand combination, stood sentinal.

We entered the living room. Manuella's spiked heels clicked on the hardwood floor. I followed a few steps behind, noticing her muscular calves drawn up tight. I helped her off with her coat and placed it over the couch.

She tugged at the hem of her suit jacket and straightened her skirt. "Joseph must have had the place cleaned before he left."

I thought about that. It had been over two weeks. The disinfectant smell would have dissipated by then.

"What would you like to see first?" she said.

I glanced around the living room. The couch was a puffy U-shaped sectional that spread across the vast expanse of the room, cornering at an arched window that looked out onto Dartmouth Street. At the opposite end of the room, a big-screen TV sat in front of matching white leather chairs and ottomans. I ran my finger over the coffee table. "This place always this clean?"

"I don't think so." It was Manuella's turn to look around. "Joseph's no neat freak."

"Can I see his bedroom?"

"It's downstairs."

"Just one?"

"That's it. The sofa up here has a queen-sized pull out."

She led me down circular stairs. The place was dark, slate black, and Manuella fumbled for the switch. The lights were on rheostats and she gradually brought them up. Rodriguez must have spent a lot of time down there. It was posh, big enough for another apartment. It ran the same length of the upstairs—open concept—a desk and bookshelves lining one whole wall with areas to read with comfortable chairs. There was another TV on a bracket attached to the wall opposite a king-sized bed Hugh Hefner would kill for.

Manuella slid a closet door open. "Something's wrong," she said.

"What do you mean?"

"His clothes are missing."

I checked out the closet. Nothing but wooden hangers. "You the only one with a key to this place?"

"Chambers had one. That's all I know of." She closed the closet door. "Joseph didn't give out keys." Her brow furrowed.

"What are you thinking?" I said.

"I'm wondering what the hell is going on." She walked into the bathroom. The neon lights that lined a large medicine chest illuminated a jacuzzi-hot tub alongside a sleek commode that doubled as a sitz bath. There were no towels.

Manuella slid open the glass doors of the medicine chest. The shelves had been wiped clean. "I think we should leave," she said. "This place is giving me the creeps."

It didn't take much convincing to persuade me to get out of there. I had seen enough, anyway. This was no police job. They would never have removed the clothes from the closet nor scrubbed the place down.

I wasn't any closer to Damon, and it made me angry that what had once been in this condo might have led me to him.

I gave Manuella a ride to a restaurant called Marlo's off Copley Square for her dinner engagement and decided I might as well have supper in town since the radio told me traffic heading north was moving at the speed of a continental drift.

The sun had long gone and ominous clouds had moved in. I parked in the Boston Common garage and walked in the direction of Arlington Street and the Café de Paris, a favorite sandwich shop Meg and I used to frequent.

I ordered shaved roast beef with swiss, served with chips and a deli pickle. The coffee was still as good as I remembered, strong and black. The café was filled with young professionals—pin-stripes with museum print ties, skirted suits with Reeboks.

I ate and thought about Rodriguez. Manuella had said he was in shipping. I wondered if that meant anything. My thoughts drifted. I studied a young woman with pitch-black hair, eyebrow pierced, and pondered why anyone would elect to wear deep purple lipstick. Her book bag read Emerson College. I checked my watch. I had managed to kill an hour. I went back to the garage.

Before I got in the truck, I refastened snaps that had come undone on the cover on my emergency flashers. New Hampshire law says you're not supposed to have the red lights exposed if you're driving out of state. It sounds silly, probably unenforceable, but it's in place primarily to avoid confusion. Massachusetts' protocols differ from New Hampshire's, and my truck shouldn't be recognized as an emergency vehicle in any place but the Granite State.

I headed out Storrow Drive. The traffic was heavy, but moving. Just as I snailed my way onto the upper deck, the predicted rain started. By the time I reached Andover, it was drubbing my windshield. It didn't improve my mood.

Damon was still missing, and Boston was a bust. I was frustrated, realizing I had little to go on but gut feelings. I had learned absolutely nothing from visiting Rodriguez's apartment, except that someone must have thought it important to sanitize the place.

Who had been in that apartment?

It was just after I passed the exit to 495 that I noticed the car. At first, I thought I might be inventing things, but several lane and speed changes convinced me it wasn't my imagination—someone was tailing me.

I dropped my speed to fifty-five. I got behind a fifth-wheeler camper the size of a three-bedroom apartment and stayed there. The car following assumed the middle lane, keeping pace, at times as close as a car length behind.

I accelerated back into the middle, sliced over to the left lane, and watched as the speedometer crept slowly toward seventy. I tried to gauge if the driver of the other vehicle knew I was aware he was following me. As long as I didn't make a run for it there would still be doubt in his mind. With the pelting rain and glare of lights off my rearview, it was tough to see what kind of car it was, but it was no doubt faster than my truck. Not a good idea to try to outrun it.

It occurred to me that I didn't want to lose him. He might

lead me to Damon. I checked my bearings. I had just crossed over the border. A sign came into view.

Welcome to New Hampshire.
Bienvenue.

I punched the accelerator and maneuvered two car lengths away from my tail. I could see his lights in my sideview mirror as he shifted to the speed lane to catch up. I wrenched the wheel to the right and dove off the exit to the rest area. I flew along the short access road to the information building which housed public bathrooms and jerked the truck into a parking space to its right.

I ducked down in the seat. My plan was to make whoever was following believe that I had stopped to use the bathroom. The information building sat on an oval, the access road scribing the circumference. If he followed me in, I would at least have a chance to take a peek at the car as it passed.

At this time of night there were few cars in the parking lot, and as I lay on the bench seat, I heard the powerful, angry rumbling of an engine coming toward me. The sound moved past the rear of the truck, but I didn't lift my head. I waited, listening as the rumbling varied with distance, and tried to figure out where the car was on the oval. The car passed by again and slowed. When I was sure he was by me, I started the engine, flipped on my lights, backed up, and tore out toward the car.

He was in front of me now, and the game had changed. I was the pursuer. I was close enough to ram his rear end before he realized what had happened.

I gunned it.

I saw the car clearly now as I followed him. It was some sort of muscle-car, a Camaro maybe, a patchwork of gray undercoating and faded yellow paint. He made another pass around the oval and picked up speed. In the light from the lamps overhead, I caught a glimpse of the driver. He wore a hat, but his face was in shadow. I knew one thing: I had never seen the car before.

He picked up speed and pulled away from me. I slammed on the brakes and spun the truck around in the opposite direction. I waited for him to clear the oval in front of me and drove toward him.

He wheeled around the oval, then slowed when he picked up my truck zeroing in on him. Somewhere buried in my brain was the message that a game of chicken was stupid, but I was beyond reason now. I wanted to run over the son of a bitch and ram his hot car into the ground.

As I got closer, he stopped. He gunned the engine a few times, as if to taunt me. I floored the accelerator and bore down on him.

His tires burned rubber as he came at me, then he veered toward the left and flung himself over the curb just as I clipped his rear end with my bumper. He tore over the median, just missed the flagpole, and bounced onto the other side of the oval. He raced away from me. He hit the oval at the far end, and slingshotted himself onto the ramp leading to the highway.

It was nearly 11:00 by the time I got back to the farmhouse. All the way home, I kept checking for signs of the muscle-car guy, but he had disappeared into the night. The episode had left me edgy, and when I finally settled in I paced from room to room, unable to quiet my thoughts about being followed. Had he tailed me all the way from New Hampshire to Boston and back, or did I pick him up in the city?

I don't know when I first noticed it. It could have been the sugar bowl on the counter near the sink, or the chair in the living room moved slightly off its place to reveal indentation marks in the rug, but in my wandering from room to room it slowly became clear that someone had been in the house during my absence. Rachel had a key, but there would have been no reason for her to come in and move things around.

I checked for signs of forced entry, but there were none. I went through my gun storage rack, and everything seemed in order. If it was a thief, it was a lousy one. Nothing seemed to be missing.

But someone had definitely been in the house.

CHAPTER SEVENTEEN

I didn't go to bed that night. I took Grandfather's Marlin from the gun case and loaded it. I sat in the dark in the living room, rifle across my lap, and listened to night sounds. I fell asleep at first light and woke at the sound of the phone ringing. It was Rachel.

"You're home," she said.

"I was in Boston."

"I need to talk to you."

"What is it?"

She hesitated. "I don't think I should tell you on the phone."

Just two days ago she thought the idea of my phone being tapped was far-fetched. "Can you come over?" I asked.

"I don't have a class before lunch. About eleven-thirty?"

"I'll be here."

I spent the rest of the morning thinking with pen in hand. I randomly placed events that had happened in a montage on paper—Chambers floored with a pistol shot, his body suspended from a hook at the mini-mart; Rodriguez in a coma; a scrubbed apartment; pentagram tattoos; Roger Pierce's confession; Damon's disappearance—and the items spread out before me like puzzle pieces that had no hope of fitting together. But I tried to connect them, anyway. I drew lines where I felt there were links.

Damon's truck in Boston made the only nexus with Rodriguez, and as I stared at it, the possibility of its being significant seemed more and more remote. What stood out nakedly, though, was Roger Pierce's confession. It established a motive, but Perino was still a bother to me. I added his name to my chart. I linked him with Chambers and Rodriguez.

I heard Rachel's car in the driveway and went to the door. As I held it open, she brushed right by me and assumed a seat at the kitchen table. "For God's sake, Rachel," I said. "What's the matter?"

"I don't have much time to talk."

"Fine. I'm listening."

"You remember the girl I had trouble with awhile ago?"

"Mandy?"

"No, not her. The one who wrecked our dinner date."

I thought a minute. "Ah, yes. Marijuana in the washing machine."

"I was doing room inspection this morning. I had forgotten she didn't have a first period class." Rachel paused, presumably reliving the experience.

"And?"

"And I accidently walked in on her while she was getting dressed." Rachel took off her knit cap and brushed her hair back. "I can't believe it."

"What?"

Rachel stared at me. "It's the tattoo."

"The pentagram?"

Rachel nodded. "I just stood there gawking at her. Christ, she must have thought I was some sort of pervert."

I lingered by the door. "You're sure you're not mistaken? I mean, it wasn't something that looked like a star?"

"No. It was definitely a pentagram."

"Point down?"

"Yes." She rubbed her arms. "Would you close the door, please?"

I looked down at my hand on the knob. I had been so involved with what she had to tell me I had been oblivious to letting in the great outdoors. I shut the door and joined her at the table.

"What in hell does this kid have to do with Chambers and Rodriguez?" I said.

"Maybe nothing."

"You can't believe it's just coincidence."

"I don't know what to think," she said. "I mean, we don't know about this stuff. Maybe a pentagram is a raging fad now."

"I don't think so." The discovery of the tattoo slowly began to spread in its implications. I stared at the paper on the table where I had scrawled out events and connections. Now there was another link. "What's the girl's name?"

"Angela Warren."

"What do you know about her?"

"Not much. She keeps to herself."

"What about her roommate?"

"She has a single."

I thought about that. A loner?

"She's new this year," Rachel said. "The girls don't like her. They stay away from her. She can be mean."

I rubbed the back of my neck. It was cramped from sleeping in that damn chair. "I don't understand something," I said. "If she was busted for possession, what's she still doing in school?"

"We have a two-strike policy."

"Sounds liberal."

"Maybe. But it's realistic. Kids make mistakes."

"You think she still does drugs?"

"Doubt it. She's on a random piss test. She had to agree to it to stay in school."

I got up from my chair, and, like last night, started pacing the room. Neither of us said anything for a few minutes. One thing was clear: I now had a living, breathing, pentagram carrier. "I want to find out all I can about her," I said. "Maybe there's something in her background that will point to Chambers and Rodriguez—and ultimately to Damon."

"Damon? What does he have to do with this?"

I came back to the table and sat down. I showed Rachel the schematic I had drawn. "These events are all connected in some way. I'm sure of it."

Rachel studied the chart. "You haven't linked Damon to any of them."

"Not yet I haven't, but maybe now I will."

"You mean with Angela."

"You have to help me, Rachel."

"Help you do what?"

"Research."

"You mean you want me to snoop."

"There must be a file on her, right?"

"Of course, but that's confidential stuff."

"But you have access."

Rachel didn't say anything. I picked up the pen on the table and added Angela Warren's name to the chart.

"I'm not sure I could do that," Rachel said, finally.

"Why not?"

"Because it's not ethical."

She was right, of course, and I felt funny asking her to breach professional ethics, but right now Angela Warren was my best shot. "Rachel, let me ask you something. You have a key to the farmhouse, right?"

"You gave it to me."

"Were you here last night?"

"What are you talking about?"

"Well, if you weren't here, did you give the key to someone else?"

She sighed. "Chad. I think all this is getting to you. What are you—"

"Someone was here last night, or sometime when I wasn't. They were very meticulous about it, but they searched the place."

Rachel studied me, most likely trying to find a hint in my expression that would suggest I was kidding. She didn't find one. "You're serious, aren't you?" she said.

I not only acknowledged that I was dead serious, but I also told her about Rodriguez's scoured apartment, about being followed and participating in a mini-version of race day at the Loudon Speedway. "It seems the more I stick my nose in, the more action I get. I know I'm onto something, and I know if I keep poking around, I'll eventually find Damon."

"But this is dangerous, Chad; you could get hurt."

"I'm not going to get hurt."

"Let the police handle it."

"And just what am I going to tell Bumps? What am I supposed to say?"

"Tell him what you told me. Tell him the truth."

"Sometimes the truth can kill."

"What?" She shook her head. "What is that supposed to mean?"

"It means that the less other people know, the better. Besides, Bumps is in no mood to listen to me about anything." In my mind's eye I could see Bumps lifting that dinky pink camera over his head and slamming it to the ground. "And if he finds out I visited Rodriguez's apartment, he'll really get pissed, and I'll be nowhere."

"All right," she said. "What do you want me to do?"

Students at Dunston Academy were required to do a sport or activity in the afternoon. Rachel's hockey squad had an evening practice, and the one player who lived in her dorm was rehabbing in the training room. The fifteen-student dormitory would be empty. I tried to persuade Rachel that a search of Angela Warren's room was in order, but she would have none of it.

"You're on your own," she said. "I don't want to risk being caught in there."

"You have the right to be in her room. You're the dorm mom."

She leaned against the door jamb that separated her apartment from the hallway that led to the common room. "I may have the right, but the political damage would be devastating."

"The what?"

"I'm talking about trust, Chad. I can't chance getting caught going through their things. I get along with the girls because I respect their privacy."

"Sounds like a thin line to walk."

"It is."

"Will you at least tell me the number of her room?"

"Third floor. Room thirty-eight."

"Thanks. I appreciate it." I meant it.

"In the meantime," she said, "I'll go into the office and find her file."

The casualness in her voice gave me pause. "I thought you had a problem with that, too."

"I have a bigger problem thinking about *you* pawing through student files."

"I'd probably bungle it, huh?" I forced a grin, hoping to lighten the weight Rachel obviously felt about the mission, but her expression remained serious.

"Faculty aren't supposed to remove folders from the room," she said. "I'll have to sneak hers out and return it tonight."

The mention of the word "sneak" caused an unexpected pang of concern for her involvement. "Rachel, look." I put my hand on her shoulder. "If you still have misgivings about doing this, I can understand. Maybe it would be better if I took care of it."

She sent me a steely look. "Don't patronize me."

"I'm not."

"I can decide what I want to do. I can even change my mind."

I pulled my hand away from her shoulder. "Yeah, I guess you can."

"I'll tell you something, though."

"What?"

"You get caught in that girl's room, you're on your own. I'll swear up and down I had no idea you were there."

"Then you'd be lying."

"Sometimes the truth can kill."

The stairs were carpeted, and they creaked. The dormitory itself was a recycled Cape, circa 1870. Two years ago the school had gutted the place and finished it off with "bulletproof" wainscoting and textured ceilings, all accomplished and timed with the installation of the computer network that linked the entire campus with E-mail and access to the Internet.

Angela Warren's room was a cramped single tucked in under an eave. I pushed open the unlatched door. There was a stale smell of old laundry. Angela obviously wasn't a stickler about cleanliness, and walking in I was careful not to disturb the detritus on the floor—*Elle* and *Playgirl*, an empty OB tampon carton, and items of clothing—a sweatshirt, blue jeans, and underthings. Angela had a penchant for black lingerie.

I sat on the edge of her bed, making sure the pile of school books and papers didn't slide out of position, and scanned the room. The walls were bare, and even the corkboard above her desk was empty of the usual pictures of family, To Do lists, and heartthrobs. The room felt like a way station, a place to sleep but not to live.

I heard a door slam downstairs. I sat still on the bed, straining to hear. Soon, there were footfalls on the stairs, thumping, heading down, and then the sound of the crash bar on the main door. Somebody had been in and out, quickly.

I got up from the bed, spurred by a sense of urgency. I made a cursory check of Angela's closet. The only article of clothing on a hanger was a surplus army jacket with a letter A on a shoulder patch. Artillery? The rest of her clothes were piled on the floor. The closet was phone-booth sized, so small it was only good for use as a hamper anyway. I half-heartedly pawed through her clothes; there was nothing intriguing.

I closed the door of the closet and brought my attention back to the room. I eyed a Macintosh computer sitting on her desk. It was still on, a screen saver drawing wacky lines in multiple colors. I touched the mouse and the screen jumped to Netscape Navigator. Angela had been surfing the net before she'd left the room.

She had been reading the home page for the rock group Smashing Pumpkins. I grabbed the mouse and clicked on the icon that read "Back." The home page for The Dead Kennedys popped up. I clicked "Back" again, and arrived at the Yahoo search engine where she had typed in "rock groups," global key words that had produced thousands of hits.

I moved the pointer across the menu bar and selected "Book-marks" to see if Angela had any favorite sites. She hadn't tagged anything, a disappointment.

I struck pay dirt, though, when I jerked the pointer to the extreme right and pulled down the menu that indicated what applications were open. Angela had left her E-mail on.

I hesitated only momentarily over the ethics of searching her E-mail. I chose the option, "Hide Netscape Navigator," moused down to "First Class," and her mailbox appeared instantly on the screen. One address immediately jumped out: Julie Hanneford's. As I scanned the screen, it became obvious that Angela had kept in close contact with Julie since she had left the school. There were numerous instances of back and forth communication.

I double-clicked on one letter from Angela to Julie, dated a few days after the incident with the knife. Much of it was a diatribe against the school for having kicked Julie out (not the case, I remembered—her parents had withdrawn her). What caught my eye was the closing line. "But you are not without friends," Angela had written. "Just remember that you have one true family that will not fail you."

I checked out the other letters, short missives that, at times, seemed to be written using special references and codes. It was clear that the weekend Julie got out of the hospital Angela had stayed with her at the Hanneford's. The veiled language also revealed that she and Julie had spent last weekend together, and that Julie's parents were misled about their true location, which was never stated.

My thoughts were so deeply involved with the computer screen that at first I was not aware of the voices in the hall. Then I heard a shrill giggle and the rumble of feet on the stairs. I quickly got out of E-mail, brought up Netscape Navigator and clicked my way back to the Smashing Pumpkins home page. The girls' voices were right outside Angela's room.

I ducked into her closet. The darkness momentarily provided a false sense of safety, for I knew if Angela came into the room and opened the closet, I would quickly be discovered.

The voices seemed to be getting fainter and I concluded they belonged to the room across the hall where the girls had just entered. With any luck, Angela's voice was not among them.

From the closet, I could see the desk with the computer still on. Then, the door flew open and light spilled through the room. I hugged the closet wall. Through the crack in the door, I had a view of the mirror on the wall the same side as the door, reflecting part of the bed and the window on the opposite wall.

At first, I couldn't see Angela's figure, but I could hear her moving about the room. Then the mirror revealed her tossing her coat on the bed. Suddenly, she yelled: "Damn it!" She stormed out into the hallway. "All right! Who's been in my room?"

I could hear her pounding on the door across the hall. "What bitch has been using my computer!"

At first, I couldn't think of what tracks I had left, but it only took a few moments to realize. The screen saver had not come on yet, and the lack of random colorful lines was a tell-tale sign of recent usage.

I stole out of the closet and listened at the door. Angela was still yelling and pounding. The door across the hall must have opened because there were other angry voices raised.

I cracked open Angela's door. There was no one in the hallway. They had let Angela in and the shouting was increasing in volume. I crept down the stairs and made it to the landing of the floor below. Rachel was coming up the stairs.

"What the hell is going on?" she whispered.

"Nothing. It's okay."

"Did you get caught?"

"No. But you need to put out a fire."

Later that afternoon, in the living room of Rachel's apartment, I read Angela's folder. It didn't take long.

"I don't understand," Rachel said. "Usually, there's a lot more information."

"What's missing?"

"There's no evidence of her testing, for one thing. Usually, there's at least a WISC-R. It's required for admission."

"What do you think happened to it?"

"I don't know."

Cob came in from the kitchen and plopped down on the floor beside my chair. I patted his head. "Do students have access to these folders?"

"They can look at them—with supervision."

"So, it would be hard to just walk in and mess with it."

Rachel thought a moment. She sat across from me in her reading chair. "Hard if you don't have a key to the file cabinet."

I studied Angela's transcript from Seekonk, New Jersey High School, one of the few pieces of paper in her folder. "She was a good student. Why did she want to change schools?"

"Well, that's just it. Her father is a friend of one of the trustees, and it was on his recommendation that Angela came here. Apparently, she was falling in with the wrong crowd, had joined a gang, even."

"You know that for a fact?"

"From the girls."

"So, now she becomes your problem."

Rachel sighed. "Usually, she's okay. Except for days like today."

I caught her drift. "Sorry about that," I said.

"You're lucky you weren't caught."

"What were they doing back so early? I thought they were supposed to be gone all afternoon."

"That whole top floor does theater tech for an activity. They had finished building flats and the drama teacher let them out early."

"So, how did you put out the fire?"

"I didn't. There's an uneasy truce on the third floor." Rachel shook her head. "I don't think Angela trusts me now."

"Why? You didn't do anything."

"I know I didn't. But seeing her tattoo ... I don't know. I get the feeling I've violated her privacy."

"Was she good friends with Julie?"

"Yes. Julie was Angela's only friend, really."

I told Rachel about reading the E-mail, how Angela had talked about Julie being a part of a family. "Ever hear them talk like that?"

Rachel thought a moment. "No. They pretty much kept to

themselves." She suddenly sat forward. "You don't suppose Julie has a tattoo?"

I shook my head. "She doesn't."

"How do you know for sure?"

"I've seen her naked, remember? The night she slashed herself."

"Oh, yes."

We didn't say anything for a few moments. Cob broke the silence by breaking wind, stinking up the place.

"That's awful," I said and batted the air.

"He's been like that all day," Rachel said. "Lord knows what he found in the garbage. I've got to tie him up. The neighbors are starting to complain."

"Ah, let him alone. He's not hurting anybody."

Cob let out a groan, as if in agreement.

I looked down at the folder in my lap. Why were things missing? Were there papers that had once revealed something about Angela that she didn't want the school to know? Or had someone else lifted those papers, leaving the folder as clean as Rodriguez's apartment?

CHAPTER EIGHTEEN

My Boston adventure, followed by sitting in a chair all last night with Grandpa's Marlin in my lap, had caught up with me. I slept without dreaming, and I didn't get out of bed until almost 9:00. Temperatures had dropped overnight into the low thirties and light snow was in the air. Back to winter.

Already a few inches had fallen, and the forecast was for six to twelve. The snow was sticking on the ground, but the roads were still clear. I headed out to Holten's Diner.

Cheryl Holten, the petite one, waited on me.

"So, you've been able to save for college?" I asked.

"I was doing okay for awhile. Had to buy a car, though."

"I thought you were driving that little Dodge Omni."

"It died."

"Sorry to hear that."

She flipped a page on her pad and shrugged. "I'm not. Good riddance." She took my order.

"So, what'd you get?"

She smiled, cracked her gum. "A Scirocco."

"Fast, huh?"

"It's hot."

So much for college. Hard to argue with the purchase, though. I remembered the Corvette Stingray I bought when I got out of the service. I'd told myself if I ever made it home in one piece, it would be the first thing I bought. I even carried a picture of one I had cut out of a magazine inside my helmet. I sold the 'Vette and bought a minivan after Meg and I got married.

It was just past 10:00 and the diner had cleared out except for a few tables. The food tasted like chalk, and I pushed it around my plate. The snow falling outside the window, usually a spirit-lifter, depressed me. All I could think of was Damon lying out in it. Where was he?

I was still on my first cup of coffee, even that tasted lousy, when Cheryl came with the check. "That's something else about that guy, huh?" she said.

"What guy?"

"You know. The one you saved. The one in the coma."

"What about him?"

"You haven't heard?" She went to fill my cup but I put my hand over it. "God, everybody was talking about it this morning."

I touched her hand. "Cheryl. Just tell me."

She cracked her gum again. "He came out of it."

"You mean he's conscious?"

"Yeah. It's in the paper."

On my way out the door, she showed me. There it was on the front page.

I headed for Lebanon.

The woman at the reception desk told me that only immediate family could get in to see Rodriguez.

"Can you just tell me his room number?"

"I thought you said you weren't family."

"That's right."

"Then I can't tell you."

She was a woman with fiercely white, freshly permed hair. The fluorescent lights overhead reflected in her glasses, and it bothered me that I couldn't see her eyes. "Do you know if Manuella Silva has been in to see him yet?" I asked.

"Mr. Rodriguez's sister?"

"Yes."

"She's with him now."

"Well, can you tell me where I can find her?"

The woman hesitated, hand on the phone.

"I really need to talk with her," I said.

"I'm not going to tell you the room number." She smiled at me. It was forced. "You can wait in the lobby. I'll page her for you."

"That won't be necessary."

"No problem."

Before I could stop her, she had dialed a code sequence, and the message for Manuella came over the speakers in the lobby.

As I thumbed through magazines I kicked myself for not posing as Rodriguez's long lost brother who just flew in from Borneo, but, in the end, decided the last thing I wanted was to be caught in a lie. Still, it bothered me that a conscious Rodriguez lay just beyond these walls. The odds were good I would finally find out what the pentagram tattoo meant—and that information might lead me to Damon.

It took a full half hour but Manuella finally showed up. "Chad. It's good to see you." She took my hand. I had expected her to be a bit more chipper with the news of her brother, but she looked depressed.

"How is he?"

"Okay, I guess."

"You don't sound sure."

Manuella sat down on a couch in the lobby and I joined her. The cushions were hard. "I really didn't get a chance to talk to him much," she said. "I think the police wore him out with questions this morning."

I thought about Bumps. I was sure he had driven up to the hospital in an eyeblink of hearing the news. I would have to catch up with him right away. "Do you know if your brother remembers much?"

"I didn't ask him about being shot, if that's what you mean." She looked across the room, her eyes listless. "I was more concerned that he was okay, you know, that his brain still worked."

"And did it?"

"His speech is slurred. He's awake ..." Manuella's eyes began to tear. "But he's not the same."

I handed her my handkerchief and she daubed her eyes. This was not good. I had hoped for clarity of recall, Rodriguez's mind refreshed from a long winter's nap. Manuella held out the handkerchief for me to take back. "Keep it," I said.

"Thank you. I'll wash it for you." She stood up from the couch. "I seem to have left my coat and purse in his room."

"That's okay. I'll walk back with you."

She led me down a hallway to a bank of elevators. She slipped her arm through mine as we walked. "Joseph's breathing on his own," she said. We arrived at the elevators and she pushed the UP arrow.

The door slid open and we stepped inside. An orderly with a handful of towels made room for us. I punched the button for the third floor. She leaned her head against my shoulder as the elevator ascended. "I'm glad you're here," she said, and squeezed my arm tighter.

I didn't know what to make of her gesture, but I let it go. The door opened and we headed down the west corridor, the ICU wing. She stopped in front of room 366. "I'll just be a minute," she said.

"Think I could come in with you?"

"He's probably asleep."

"I just want to see him." I tried to make my voice sound doleful. "I haven't seen him since the day I helped bring him in."

Manuella smiled at me. "Of course. I'm sure it's okay."

Rodriguez had a tube running in through his nose. His bad leg was elevated, trussed up in a sling mechanism. An IV drip was connected to a very bruised arm.

Rodriguez seemed to be resting comfortably, and lime green screens revealed a graphic reassurance of the steadiness of heart and lungs.

Manuella ran her hand across Rodriguez's forehead, pushing a wisp of hair back. She leaned over and kissed him on the cheek. Then she gathered her purse and coat from a chair and guided me out of the room into the hallway. "He really needs rest," she said.

"Thanks for letting me see him."

She reached up and touched my neck. Her fingers lingered there a moment, then she pulled my head toward hers. "Thanks for coming," she said. Her breath smelled of spearmint. She kissed me lightly on the lips.

"Are you coming back to see him soon?" I asked.

"Tomorrow," she said. "His doctor thinks he's had enough excitement for one day."

"Mind if I tag along?"

We left it that she would meet me outside Rodriguez's room at 1:00 tomorrow afternoon.

I headed for the parking lot. More than an inch of snow had fallen while I had been in the hospital. It was heavy and wet, and I had to push it off the windshield with my gloved hand. As I let the truck warm, I thought more about Rodriguez and felt intense disappointment over not being able to talk with him. And why the hell was Manuella coming on to me?

I put the truck in gear and started to pull out of the parking lot, but I stopped before I got to the main entrance. Tomorrow wasn't good enough. I had to get answers, and I didn't have time to wait around while Rodriguez had a salubrious recuperation. If nothing else, I knew I had to ask him one thing: Where was this hunting camp that he and Chambers had supposedly come up to New Hampshire to stay in? If it was somewhere on the Turner property, Damon might be there. I had pretty much decided that the truck in Boston was a decoy. Damon had gone hunting on the Turner property. I was sure of it.

I headed back up to ICU, but I took an indirect route through the Emergency waiting room, up the back stairs, and past the birthing unit. The nurses on the floor seemed buried in their work. A large black man in crisp white scrubs eyed me momentarily but was more preoccupied with pushing an insulated lunch cart.

Rodriguez's door was open and I ducked into his room. I walked over to the side of his bed and looked at his face. His eyes were closed, but the eyelids flickered. "Joseph," I whispered.

He stirred.

"I need to talk to you."

He made a guttural noise, then slowly opened his eyes. "Who are you?" His voice had a rasp.

"My name's Chad. I'm an EMT. I worked on you the day you were shot."

Rodriguez grunted but said nothing.

"I just need to ask you a few questions," I said.

He rolled his head slowly away from me. I knew I didn't have much time before someone came in the room. I had to push it. "Do you know who shot you?"

He didn't answer.

"What were you doing in the woods, Joseph? You weren't hunting, were you? You had been staying in some camp on the Turner property."

Then Rodriguez jerked his head, and his eyes, dark and piercing, met mine. "No," he said. "No!"

I watched in horror as he tried to lift himself up.

A nurse stormed into the room. "What are you doing here? Get away from him."

"Don't worry, I'm leaving." I pushed by her.

It took almost until midnight for the snow to stop. I replayed the incident in Rodriguez's room and cursed myself for being so stupid. I should never have gone back to his room. I finished my plow rounds about 3:00 in the morning, but I was too wired to sleep.

I drove around town, thinking I might drop in on Rachel, but I had done enough forcing of issues for a while. Reluctantly, I headed toward home. Ever since I had discovered signs of an intruder, the creaks and groans the house made in the middle of the night felt unnatural, even haunted.

I felt a tug when I passed the turn for Damon's and de-

cided to check on his house. It wasn't so much that I thought I
might find something I had overlooked as it was the need to
see his place again, to get back in contact with stuff that was
once part of him. I flat-out missed the man.

I pulled up to his house and shut off the engine. The wind
had dropped, but the sky was still overcast, the moon a ghostly
crescent of light. Damon's house was dark. I used the key he
kept in his mailbox to get in.

I switched on the kitchen light and felt a pang of loss. It
was so much *his* kitchen—the empty cereal boxes, Coke bottles,
a pan with dried egg in the sink. I hadn't been here since
Damon had first disappeared when I came to check on his
hunting gear; it was gone, of course, all of it—boots, red-checked
pants, fluorescent orange knit cap. He had to be on the Turner
property somewhere, dammit. He had to be.

I didn't stay long. It wasn't a good idea to begin with. I
took the time to clean up the pan in the sink, then drove home.

When I pulled into the driveway I almost rammed Bumps'
cruiser. I backed up the truck, dropped the plow, and jumped
out of the cab. In the time it took to do this, Bumps had exited
the cruiser and was standing by the kitchen door. As I walked
passed the cruiser, I recognized Blaine Haskell inside in the
front seat. It was odd to see both of them on duty at the same
time. I saluted him as I passed.

"Christ, I almost shoved the plow up your ass," I said, as I
approached Bumps.

"Glad you didn't," he said.

"Up awful early, aren't you?"

"You could say that." He held the storm door for me. He
carried himself stiffly, like he did when he had to make a speech.

"What's going on?" I said.

"Need to ask you a few questions."

Inside, I put on coffee. The machine hissed and popped as Bumps took off his coat and hat. He feathered a half dozen long strands of hair over his bald spot. "I'll get right to the point," he said. "It appears somebody doctored Rodriguez's IV."

"You mean he's dead?"

"That's right."

I sat down at the table. "Holy shit."

"They found him about seven last night."

I let the news sink in. "Have any leads?"

"A few."

The coffee had finished brewing and I poured two cups. "Think Blaine would like some coffee?"

Bumps dismissed the idea with a brief wave of his hand. "He's busy."

Busy? Doing what? That's what I wanted to ask, but I checked myself. Bumps had come here for a reason other than delivering the news about Rodriguez. I needed to know what it was.

"You saw Rodriguez yesterday, didn't you?"

"Yeah, sure. I was with Manuella Silva."

"That's true. And then you were seen later in his room. He was upset with you about something. I don't know what you said to him but—"

He didn't have to finish. I finally caught on. "And you think I killed him."

He looked up from his coffee cup. "Did you?"

I searched his eyes for a sign that he might be fooling me, but he didn't blink. "I didn't kill him," I said.

"What time did you leave the hospital?"

"Probably about four in the afternoon."

"Nurse says you were in his room about three-thirty."

"Then that's when I left."

"Where'd you go after that?"

"I drove home."

"Anybody see you? You go to Rachel's when you got back?"

"No. I ate supper and read the paper. I started plowing about nine."

Bumps took a pad from his pocket. He flicked his ballpoint pen. "So between three-thirty and nine you have no corroboration of your whereabouts."

Corroboration of my whereabouts? Bumps' legalese was a sign that this was turning into a formal interrogation.

Bumps shifted in his chair. He smiled at me. "I don't think you killed Rodriguez, Chad." The smile faded, and he kept at it. "Now, you're sure nobody saw you? You didn't stop for gas?"

"I came right home."

Blaine Haskell showed up. Bumps rose from his chair and stood at the door for a few minutes whispering with Blaine. I tried to dismiss the idea that this was serious. I didn't kill Rodriguez. I had no motive. Besides, I had been at the farmhouse. But who could corroborate it? Bumps and Blaine were still talking. An irrational fear gripped me as I tried to ignore their whisperings. I stared down at my coffee cup.

Bumps came back and tossed a plastic bag on the table. "Ever seen this?"

The bag looked like it contained slivers of soap. "No."

"Found it in your truck, behind the seat back."

"It's not mine."

"Have to test it, but it looks like crack cocaine." Another plastic bag landed on the table. It was full of cash. "How about this?" he said. He pulled the money out of the bag and fanned it. "Must be over a thousand dollars here."

"And that was in my truck?"

"Blaine just found it."

Before I could respond, Blaine moved away from the door and walked into the kitchen. "Both those plastic bags were in this," he said.

At first I couldn't see what he had in his hand, but then he swung it up from his side and handed it to Bumps. It was my med kit. The one that had disappeared from the crime scene.

Bumps took his pen from his pocket, opened the med kid, and pulled out a pistol that dangled from his pen pegged through the trigger housing. "And I suppose you've never seen this, either."

It was the same pistol I had found in Rodriguez's hand the day Chambers was killed.

A 9MM.

CHAPTER NINETEEN

"I don't know how all that got in my truck," I said.

"You're sure about that," Bumps said.

"Jesus! Of course I'm sure." I looked at Blaine Haskell who was poised, ready to move in for the kill.

"You're in deep shit," Blaine said.

Bumps held up his hand. "All right. Let me handle this."

Blaine sat across from me at the table and stared.

Bumps put a hand on my arm and drew my attention from Blaine. "Let's talk about this."

"I'm not saying anything." I pulled my arm away. "I don't know how that shit got in my truck. Period."

Bumps turned to Blaine and jerked his head toward the door. "Wait outside."

"What?"

"Just wait in the cruiser."

"You want me to radio in what we found?"

"Not yet."

"Then what do you want me to do?"

"Wait."

Blaine pushed his chair back forcefully. The legs rubbed on the floor with a loud yelp. He left the kitchen.

I stared at Bumps. "I think Blaine's pissed."

"This is off the record," he said.

"How can I be sure?"

"Because I said so."

"I don't trust you."

"You don't trust me?"

"Why now, Bumps? Someone tip you off?"

Bumps' face flashed crimson. "I should just arrest your ass now," he said. "I'm the one taking a chance here."

"You're taking a chance? How does that work?"

"I just sent my deputy to his truck. I don't have a tape recorder." He slapped his chest. "My fucking pen's in my pocket."

I watched him closely for signs he was play-acting. But I knew better. He couldn't dissemble if he tried. I had to be careful, though. He could still use what I said against me in court, and it would be my word against his. "You know I was set up, don't you?"

He took out his handkerchief, wiped his forehead. "I don't know what to believe. But I have to deal with what I've found. I want you to convince me that Christmas in Dunston is over."

"Christmas?"

"I don't like pretty packages. Especially behind seat backs." He used his handkerchief to wipe the sweatband of his hat.

I relaxed my arms. All of this was beginning to sink in. Someone had gone to great difficulty to implicate me, and this was the topper. I had been followed out of Boston, my house searched, watched closely for how long?

"Let's start from the beginning," Bumps said. "Why should I believe you didn't kill Chambers?"

"Because I have no motive."

"You were first to find Rodriguez. You put the nine milli-meter Glöck he had in his hand in your med kit—but no one saw you do it." He used his fingers to tick off the points. "You worked on Rodriguez but Chambers had had enough of helping and walked down the hill away from you. You yelled after him. He turned and you shot him."

"But you're forgetting one thing," I said. "*Why* would I do that? What's the motive?"

Bumps paused. He leaned across the table. "That's what I'm trying to find out."

I kept thinking about the drugs, the money, and the pistol neatly packaged in my missing med kit. It *was* Christmas in Dunston. "I want you to read me my rights," I said.

"You're not under arrest yet."

"Come on! Mirandize me!"

"Why did you kill Chambers?"

Suddenly, the whole idea felt oddly humorous, and I laughed out loud. "Because Roger Pierce and I are lovers."

"What?"

"Oh, yes. We go back a long ways."

"Cut it out, Chad. This is serious."

"You bet your ass this is serious." I slapped my hand on the table. "I thought you had Chambers' killer in custody."

Bumps ruminated.

"I've been followed. I don't know for how long," I said. "At least the past few days. I'm sure someone's searched my house."

"I'm sure they have."

His answer caught me off guard. "You're sure?"

"It was a couple of boys from the Major Crime Unit. They were told to be neat."

Bumps had the house searched? "Under whose authority?"

"Tierney got the search warrant. Relax. It was on the up and up."

"I've been a suspect for a while, then."

"That's right."

"What were you looking for?"

"Whatever we could find."

"Did you have me followed out of Boston?"

"No. What were you doing there?"

"Never mind."

"Better tell me."

"Visiting a friend."

"Manuella Silva?"

"It's none of your business who I saw."

"You two got a thing going?"

"What are you talking about?"

Bumps shrugged. "Nothing. Somebody saw you two kissing in the hallway at the hospital, that's all. Does Rachel know about this?"

I got up from the chair.

"Hey, where you going?"

"Nowhere. I think better when I walk."

"Well, sit down. You make me nervous."

"You think I'm going to take off?"

"Sit down!"

I took my seat, making a show of being deliberate and quiet. I held out my hands to be cuffed. "Let's get this over with."

"In due time."

"Come on, Bumps." I said. "Arrest me if you're going to. Blaine must be getting cold out there."

He picked up one of the plastic bags from the table. "What about this coke?" he said.

"It's not mine, for crissake."

"You don't use the stuff?"

"And you wonder why I've been so happy lately."

He shook his head. "You've been going through tough times. Maybe you wanted to use it to get funny."

I shook my head. "I'm into controlled substances. Stuff the good doctor ordered."

"You don't mind being tested, then."

"Might be a good idea."

I ran my finger over the handle of my mug. "Can I ask you something?"

"Shoot."

"When did I first become a suspect?"

Bumps rooted around inside his ear with his little finger. "Right after we found Chambers at the mini. When we knew he'd been shot with a nine millimeter."

I recalled Bumps' many questions when I had met him in Holten's Diner right after Chambers' body was found. That's why he had pumped me for information, why he made me go through my version of what had happened the day of the shootings.

"But I still don't get how I could have shot Chambers if I was working on saving Rodriguez."

"You didn't put the pistol back in the bag," he said. "You had it with you all along."

"And who took the bag?"

"The same guy who stole Chambers' body. Whoever you're working with."

"You're fishin'."

"You tell me what happened, then."

"Wish I could. I'm still trying to figure out why I would want to shoot Rodriguez."

"Drug deal gone bad? I don't know." He lifted the bag of coke from the table and let it drop. "Finding this stuff did surprise me, I'll tell you that."

"How did you know to search the truck?"

"It was the only place we hadn't looked. When we found out Rodriguez had been iced and you were placed at the scene, we had to move in." He wiped ear wax from his little finger onto his pants. "I guess you could say we got lucky."

"Merry Christmas," I said.

"It's funny, you know. None of us would have thought of you—even Tierney—if it hadn't been for Striker."

"Striker? What did he say?"

Bumps shook his head. "I can't tell you that."

"But he thought I killed Chambers?"

"If you think about it, Striker was the only witness."

"That son of a bitch. And you believed him."

"Let's do this by the numbers, Chad." Bumps reached for his belt. "I had hoped you'd tell me something that would let you off the hook, but now I have no choice but to arrest you for the murder of Glenn Chambers."

"Wait a minute."

"I thought you wanted to be arrested."

"I've changed my mind. I want to talk to Striker."

"I'm sure this will all come out in the wash," he said.

"Where are you taking me?"

"We'll hold you temporarily at the Merrimack House of Corrections in Boscawen."

"Then what?"

"You'll await a hearing at Concord District Court."

"This sucks."

"It could have been worse—publicity-wise, I mean. It was

Tierney's idea to downplay the arrest. Low profile, if you know what I mean."

"Of course. Arresting me makes him look pretty silly, making such a big deal over Roger Pierce."

"Okay. Let's go." He reached for his cuffs.

"No. I've decided you're going to have to shoot me first."

He walked toward me. "Come on, Chad," he said. "Don't make things worse."

"You know I didn't kill Chambers."

He pulled the pistol from his belt and leveled it at me.

"Put it away, Bumps. You're not going to use it."

"Just doing my job."

It was an uneasy feeling looking down the barrel of Bumps' Smith & Wesson, but I waited for him to make the next move. I didn't have to wait long. He fired. The shot zinged by my ear. In the small confines of the kitchen the report sounded as if it came from a cannon. My ears rang. "Christ," I said. "Why the hell did you do that?"

"Just calling my deputy."

I walked toward Bumps, my hands in the air. "Okay. You win."

When he went for the cuffs on his belt, I lunged at him, seizing his gun hand. We struggled. Bumps was strong for an old guy, but I spun him around and ripped the pistol out of his hands just as Blaine Haskell came through the door. He had a shotgun.

"Hold it there, Blaine," I yelled. I aimed the Smith & Wesson at Bumps' head.

"Careful, Blaine." Bumps said.

I grabbed Bumps and used him as a shield. "That scatter shot will do a number on us both," I said. "Put the gun down!"

Blaine let it drop to the floor.

"Hands behind your head." I waved the pistol at Blaine. "Now get over here and handcuff your boss."

Blaine walked slowly toward us. I forced Bumps to the floor, all the while keeping my eye on Blaine. Bumps lay on his stomach, his hands behind, and Blaine put the cuffs on him. I told Blaine to get on the floor, and I did the same to him. I removed the ammo from Bumps' gunbelt. "I can't believe you shot at me," I said.

Bumps didn't say anything. I stuck the Smith & Wesson into my belt and headed for my truck.

The sun was just coming up.

At first, I drove aimlessly and tried to think what my next move would be. Several times, I almost turned around. I was foolish to run. But there was no turning back now. I felt nervous driving, even though the town of Dunston was barely coming awake with only a few cars on the road. I guessed it wouldn't be long before Bumps and Blaine would be discovered. I was sure they had called in their location and dispatch would get suspicious.

The clouds were striated ribbons of fluff, and the rising sun painted them with an orange tinge. It would be a bright, cold day. I pictured myself abandoning the truck and heading into the woods on foot, but I knew I wasn't dressed for staying out. I had boots on, but my jeans would freeze stiff as cardboard by nightfall. Then I hit upon an idea. I headed back through town.

I turned off the main drag after a few miles, down a dirt road until I came to a driveway with a hand-lettered sign that read "Lebeau." I turned into Bumps' driveway.

The original house was a mobile home, and Bumps just added rooms, up and down, and built on whenever he had money.

His wife Grace loved lawn ornaments, gimcracks and gewgaws. In the summer, the front yard was alive with plastic daisies spinning, wind-socked geese, and other assorted whirligigs that flapped, whooshed, and tinkled in wind-inspired frenzy. Now in winter, the only noise came from a bird-feeder with the lonely figure of a propeller-driven lumberjack spasmodically sawing wood on top. Next to the bird feeder stood the statue of a very cold-looking Virgin Mary. She was hunkered down, half-submerged in the snow, in a clam-shell arrangement with a baby blue backdrop, her hands outstretched as if begging for a pair of gloves.

I knocked on the door.

The door curtains parted and Grace's wide face appeared. She opened it. "Why, Chad Duquette. As I live and breathe."

"Hi, Grace. Mind if I come in?"

"Not at all."

The trailer part of the house had a low-ceiling cramped feel that made me immediately uncomfortable, and it was compounded by suffocating heat. The woodstove in the kitchen was cranking, but Grace wore a heavy sweater. She was a squat woman who found most things in life laughable—a suitable balance for her curmudgeonly husband.

"I just put cinnamon rolls in," she said. "Would you like some coffee?"

One thing for sure, she didn't suspect anything. Bumps must not have talked shop at home. "I'd love to, but I'm on an errand."

"Oh?"

"Bumps didn't tell you?"

She opened the oven and peered in. Great. All we needed was more heat in the room. I could feel sweat breaking on my forehead.

"That man never tells me anything," she said. She closed the oven and laughed. "That's the secret of a happy marriage, don't you think?"

"He said he wants me to take a look at his snowmobile."

"The new one?"

"Yeah. Said it wasn't running right."

She paused. "I didn't know you were handy with that sort of thing. I thought Damon was ..." She caught herself, brought her hand to her mouth. "Oh, I'm sorry."

"It's okay."

"No news about Damon?"

"No." I could see tears welling in her eyes. I didn't want to get into a discussion about my stepbrother. "Do you know where Bumps keeps the keys?"

Grace sat in a kitchen chair. "In the jar there, on the chiffonier."

The bureau was antique, with a mirror on top, and looked more suitable for a bedroom than a kitchen. I grabbed the keys out of the jar. If Bumps hadn't been pissed at me before, the discovery of my stealing his new toy would certainly send his blood pressure through the roof. "I need to drive it for a couple hours to make some tests," I said. "Think I could borrow his suit and helmet?"

A smile broke on her face. "You want to wear his snowmobile suit?"

"Well, sure."

"I've got to see this," she said.

She got the suit out, and I tried it on. I had plenty of room in the girth, but when I pulled the one-piece suit up and tried to stick my arms in, the pantlegs rose above my ankles. I wiggled my way in. I stood with my arms extended from my sides like a weight-lifter. "Perfect," I said.

Grace laughed and her body jiggled. "Where's my camera," she said. "I've got to get a shot of this."

"I think Bumps broke it," I said.

Outside, I pulled the black vinyl cover off the snowmobile. It read *Arctic Cat* in white lettering. I straddled the machine and checked the gas: three quarters full. I turned the key, and it roared to life. I didn't wait around. This definitely did not sound like a sick snowmobile.

I headed out his backyard and picked up a trail I knew would lead to a major loop that wove around Dunston proper. Snowmobiling was a sport I had never gotten into. The whine of the machine went against my purist bow-hunting instincts. But I was happy to push them aside now in the name of saving my ass.

Because it was the middle of the week, a work day, I had the trail to myself, and I had to set the track because of the recent wet snowfall. This was fine with me. The fewer people I ran into the better. Just where I was headed wasn't clear yet, but I could at least buy time until I could think of what to do next.

I goosed the engine along a flat stretch and considered losing myself in the vast network of trails that runs through New Hampshire into Maine. It was possible to go all the way to Canada. But the more I drove, the less it sounded like the thing to do. I had to find a way to ferret out who had set me up, and I couldn't do it in Canada.

I stopped around noon, cut the engine, and listened. I could hear a distant engine noise that sounded as if it came from another trail. Overhead, a low-flying single-engine airplane growled in the sky.

I searched through the seat compartment and found two stale candy bars. I ate them quickly and tried to quell the panic that grew the more I sat there idle. I hadn't planned ahead. I had no food. I recalled Grace's cinnamon buns and wondered why I hadn't grabbed a few before I left. I would have to think more clearly.

What bothered me most about the events of the morning was that Bumps had actually taken a shot at me. I could still see the barrel of the Smith & Wesson staring me down. But I remembered what he said after he let fly: "Just calling my deputy."

Of course. Once I had resisted arrest he had no other choice. Sending Blaine to the truck so he could interview me alone was lousy protocol. He'd never meant to shoot me, but he knew it was the quickest way to summon Blaine, and at the same time reassume a professional stance. Taking his gun away had just been too easy. That son of a bitch wanted me to take off. The only possible reason was that he knew I was innocent and needed to be free to find the truth.

But now I was probably fishin'. Wishful thinking.

I drove through the afternoon. I came across one other snowmobile driven by an older man and woman who waved absently as they passed.

The sun was dropping fast, and I had to think of how to spend the night. I thought of building a snow cave, but there wasn't enough snow. No. I needed a base of operations. Some place warm.

The sun had disappeared behind Lucas Hill as I headed

out the Dunston loop that wove close to town. I had been
thinking of Rachel, wondering how she would take the news
of my resisting arrest, when it came to me where I could put
up for the night.

I drove on a trail that led to the back of Dunston Academy,
keeping on a line that edged the playing fields before I dropped
into a gully and onto an abandoned railroad bed. I drove for a
hundred yards, then pulled up and over a knoll. I ditched the
snowmobile in a thicket and started walking.

Soon I arrived at the back door of Georgette Salmon's house.

CHAPTER TWENTY

I approached the back door. The lights were off. My hope was that the house had been forgotten in all the business of Georgette Salmon going into the hospital, but I also suspected that the school's maintenance department would check up on it as a matter of course.

I tried the back door, but it was locked. The windows on the ground level were aluminum combination, the storm glass pulled down tight in each one. I circled the house and twisted the knob on the front door. It was also locked. I went around to the back of the house again, realizing now that if I wanted to get in I would have to break a window. This was especially risky since I didn't know if the house had an alarm system.

I returned once more to the patio at the rear of the building. I took off Bumps' helmet and wiggled out of his snowmobile suit. I placed the pant leg of the suit against the back door window pane, removed the Smith & Wesson from my belt, and punched out the window with the butt end. It made more of a racket than I wanted and inspired a neighborhood dog to bark. I reached through the broken pane and twisted the knob, but the door still wouldn't open. It was deadbolted. I fumbled along the edge of the door, found the bolt, shoved it along the track, and finally let myself in.

As soon as I closed the door behind me, I could see the green light on a console box to my right. There *was* a security system. It just hadn't been engaged. I didn't take it as a sign that my luck was changing—I would need more luck than this.

I had seen this house from the road many times, but I had no idea what the interior looked like. I kept the lights off, feeling my way along a hallway that led upstairs to the kitchen.

From the light that seeped in from a streetlamp outside, I could see the dark forms of a round table and chairs, and the hulking mass of double-sided refrigerator that hummed like a tone-deaf choirboy.

I walked my hands along the wall and made my way into the living room. By now, my eyes had adjusted to the darkness. I found an overstuffed chair and sank into it. The house was warm, but my hands were still numb from riding the snowmobile all day. I let my arms hang over the side of the chair and the pistol fall from my hand onto the rug.

So I was in from the cold, but now what? I considered calling Rachel, but I was sure she would be the first person Bumps would suspect I'd try to contact.

I don't know how long I slept, but I was awakened some time in the night with a loud crashing that came from the patio. I crawled out of the chair and fumbled in the darkness for Bumps' pistol. I crept through the kitchen and down the back stairs.

The wind had picked up since I had come into the house, and the curtain on the door flapped where I had broken the window. I took a few steps and glass crunched under my feet. I held the pistol in both hands, leaned against the wall, and listened.

When the wind dropped, I heard noises I couldn't identify.

At first, it sounded like scratching, then a light metallic tapping. Someone or something was definitely out there.

I dropped to the floor, reached for the knob, and twisted it. A gust of wind pushed the door open and it banged against the wall. I rolled out the doorway with the pistol drawn. At first, I couldn't see what I was aiming at until it woofed back.

Cob was standing next to a toppled garbage can. The crashing must have been his knocking the can over, the tapping, rhythmic sounds, the tags on his collar hitting the edge of the cylinder as he munched away. I approached and he growled at me.

"It's okay," I said. "Good dog."

The wind shifted again, and he must have caught my scent. Cob let out a sharp yelp and rushed toward me, his tail wagging.

I patted him. He barked in sheer joy of seeing me, and I needed to calm him down before he made too much noise. "Come on, Cobbie. Follow me," I whispered.

I walked him into the house, up the stairs, through the kitchen, and back into the living room. I sat on the floor, grabbed both of his ears, and rolled his head, playfully. "So, you out making your rounds, you bad dog?"

His huge tongue washed my face. Because of the dark, I hadn't seen it coming. "Thanks for sharing your garbage," I said. I played with him until we both tired of it. It was good to have him with me. We both eventually fell asleep on the floor.

Cob woke me with his whining, wanting to go out. It was dawn, and a gray light filtered through the living room. The sleep had refreshed me, and I woke with an idea full blown in my head. I found paper and pencil. I wrote: "I'm at Georgette's," folded the paper and fastened it to Cob's collar. When I let him out, he looked back, expecting me to follow.

"Go home," I said.

I stayed in the house all morning. I ate what I found in the cupboards, not wanting to turn on lights or use appliances for fear they might point to activity in the house. I felt like Damon with his cereal as I consumed fistfuls of stale supermarket brand cornflakes. I had no idea how long it would take Rachel to discover my message on Cob's collar, if she found it at all, and by the middle of the afternoon, I was beginning to give up hope. After all, I was a fugitive. For all I knew, she could be tipping off the authorities right now.

Being in the house alone had afforded me time to think, something I desperately needed, and as I ran through my options, I kept coming back to that day when Chambers had been shot. I remembered the chart I had made, tried again to make connections, and couldn't shake the idea that Damon had gone hunting for the buck the day he disappeared. All my instincts drew me back the Turner property.

By late afternoon, I had pretty much decided that my next move had to be out of the house. I would wait for darkness to steal some gas and be moving again by early morning. I would pack whatever food I could into the snowmobile and use the back trails to get to the Turner property.

I felt better with a plan in mind, however broad and tentative, and spent the rest of the afternoon resting up. I dozed, surprisingly relaxed, considering my options were few. It was just after dark, around 5:00 in the afternoon when I heard a light knocking at the back door.

With the Smith & Wesson in hand, I moved quickly through

the kitchen and down the stairs, the route well-worn now in memory. I listened at the door.

"Chad. Are you there?"

It was Rachel. I opened the door.

When she saw me, she threw her arms around my neck, pulled me to her, and kissed me hard on the lips. "Oh, God. Are you all right?"

"I guess my courier came through," I said.

She held onto me tightly.

"Come on. Follow me." I led her by hand into the house, explaining about having to keep the place dark, something she could probably understand on her own, but I needed to talk about something. Her hand felt soft in mine.

We both sat on the couch in the living room in the dark. There was something sexy and dangerous about this whole thing, and we kissed like teenagers stealing a moment, desperate for privacy, hoping our parents wouldn't come home and catch us.

"Chad. You have to turn yourself in."

"It's not going to happen."

"You've been on TV," she said.

"Really?"

"You're sandwiched in between the weather and Pearl Harbor Day celebrations."

I thought a minute. Thursday the seventh, a day that would live in infamy, at least in Chad Duquette's life. "So what are they saying about me?"

"You're a drug dealer."

"I am?"

"What's going on, Chad?" There was a slight tremor in her voice.

"Hey, it's okay." I reached for her, and she came to me again. I held her close. "I'm not a drug dealer."

"I'm just telling you what they're saying."

I pulled her back on the couch and she lay on top of me, her head snuggled in my neck. I felt the wetness of her tears.

"You have to believe me, Rachel."

"Why did you run?"

"I had to."

"You didn't have to. If you're innocent then you have nothing to hide. Nothing to run from."

I stiffened. "You think I did those things?"

"I didn't say that."

"But that's what you meant."

She pushed herself away from me and beat her fists on my chest. "Damn you," she yelled. "Damn you."

I caught her hands. "Hey, cut it out!"

"How could you think that?"

"You said '*If* you're innocent' and I thought ..."

She put her hand over my mouth. "I'm here, aren't I?" She kept her hand there a few moments then released it. "Oh, shit," she said.

I pulled her to me again and stroked her hair. Soon, our breaths matched. I told her of my plan to go back to the Turner property.

"And you're just going to ride around on the snowmobile?"

"Unless you have other ideas. I know the answer to all of this is on that land. It has to be."

"I think it's a stupid plan, Chad," she said. Whatever emotional roller-coaster she had been riding had come to a stop.

"Maybe. But it's all I've got."

She sat on the far end of the couch. "What about Angela Warren?"

"What about her?"

"Confront her about the tattoo."

"What good would that do? She'd just clam up. Besides, I don't want to mess up my only lead." I thought about what I just said. At one point in the recent past—before Rodriguez's murder and Bumps' attempted arrest—I had considered Angela my one big connection with Rodriguez and Chambers. How could I have forgotten her? "Tell me more about Angela," I said.

The dark outline of Rachel's figure stood out in high contrast from the soft backlight of the streetlamp through the window. "I signed a weekend card for her," she said.

"What's a weekend card?"

"Students have to get permission from their teachers and advisor to leave on a weekend. Angela's visiting Julie Hanneford."

"That's interesting."

"Not really. They spend a lot of time together."

I remembered rooting through Angela's E-mail. "So, let me get this straight. Angela's going on a weekend with Julie, and this has happened before?"

"They're good friends."

"How often does Angela take weekends?"

"As often as she can."

"And she's always with Julie?"

"Not always. Sometimes she goes to Boston."

"Boston?"

"Her parents live there."

This information set my mind to work. Maybe tooling willy-nilly around the Turner property wasn't the best option after all. "I need a car," I said.

"What for?"

"I'm going to follow Angela."

CHAPTER TWENTY-ONE

I thought about using Rachel's car but decided Bumps probably had a BOLO (Be On the Look Out) for her vehicle. The school owned two small minivans as well as the larger vans for transportation to athletic events, but I immediately dismissed them as being too visible.

"What about student cars?" I asked.

"Only seniors on honor roll have cars."

"How can I get one?"

"The Dean of Students keeps the plates in her office."

"What about keys?"

Rachel hesitated. "Chad. You're really not going to do this, are you?"

"I'm wanted for murder. Stealing cars is no big deal."

"Students keep their own keys."

I moved across the couch and held Rachel's hand. "Is anyone not going on a weekend that you know of?"

Rachel thought a moment. "A girl on the third floor. She's restricted because of missing classes."

"Could you get her keys?"

"I don't know. It might be tricky."

I knew that what I was asking would clearly make Rachel an accessory. It was bad enough she knew my whereabouts and didn't report me, but adding car thievery to the mix would only make it worse for her. "Never mind," I said. "I'll take care of it."

"No. It will be easier for me."

"Are you sure?"

"I'll do it."

She left about 7:00 and returned about 11:30, keys and plates in hand.

"Have any trouble?" I said.

"I feel sullied."

I pulled her toward me. "How'd you manage the keys?"

"It was easy. Kendra studies in the library. The keys were in the top drawer of her desk."

I ran my hand along her back.

She responded by holding me tighter. "I'm really scared. Is that okay?"

"Of course it is."

"This is stupid, Chad. You're going to get caught."

"I won't." I kissed her, then leaned her back toward the couch.

"Chad. Please."

"What?"

"I guess I don't feel like it."

"Okay."

Then, unexpectedly, she hugged me again. "I'm sorry," she said. "I don't want to lose you."

"You're not going to. That's why I can't give myself up."

"But aren't you the least bit scared?"

"Yes. But there's nothing else I can do, especially if we're going to have a future together."

She pulled away from me. "Is that what's going to happen? We're going to have a future?"

"Sure. Why not?"

"Oh, nothing. You're wanted for murder, that's all. A little thing like that shouldn't—"

"I'm going to get through this. I didn't kill anybody, and I'm going to fight it."

She didn't say anything. She hugged herself. "It's cold in here."

I took the afghan off the couch and wrapped it around her. I held her close. "I want to get married."

"Married!"

"What's wrong with that?" She turned away from me. "You need to know how I feel, Rachel."

She sat on the couch, head in hands. "You think you can talk to me like this when you're about to step out that door and get yourself killed?"

"You believe in me. I know you do."

"You don't know anything about me."

Her words hit hard. "I know enough."

"Name one thing," she said.

"We're good together."

"Name another."

"You like kids. You're good with them."

"Oh, God." She sat back on the couch. "You want kids?" She hesitated. "Let's just forget it. It's stupid to even talk like this."

"No. I want to talk."

"I can't have kids, okay?"

A car drove by and the lights washed through the living room. The car passed into the night.

"Tell me about it."

"What's to tell?" She didn't say anything for a few moments. "Look, Chad. Things have happened pretty fast between us."

"This isn't the beginning of a let-me-down-gently speech, is it?"

"You want too much from me."

"Tell me about Cliff."

"Why?"

"So I don't make the same mistakes he did."

"Okay. Here it comes. Cliff and I desperately wanted a child and tried everything—different positions, peak temperature times. One day we made love five times when I was at the most fertile part of my cycle."

"Wow. I have a new opinion of Cliff."

"Shut up. This isn't funny."

"Sorry."

"Cliff's sperm count was weak, but there was also some concern over the tilt of my uterus." Her voice trailed off.

"Are you sure it's you? I mean, if his sperm count was weak ..."

She hesitated. "I'm not sure about anything."

I waited a few moments. "Is that why you divorced him?" I asked, finally. "Because you couldn't have kids?"

"It had something to do with that." She paused. "That and walking in on Cliff screwing a twenty-three-year-old hair dresser."

"Oh. Well, that might do it."

"And in our own bed."

I expected to hear more, but Rachel grew pensive.

"Do you still want me?" I asked.

"We need to step back a little, I think."

"What kind of answer is that?"

"You have to admit things have changed in the last few days."

"But you still love me?"

"Chad. Be serious. What difference does it make if I say I love you and you take off and get yourself killed?"

"Makes a difference to me."

"I have to get out of here."

"Stay the night."

"No." She made a move toward the kitchen door.

I grabbed her arm. "If you wanted me to give up, why did you get the car keys?"

She pulled her arm away. "That's a damn good question. Maybe because I'm stupid. Maybe because I would hate myself if I thought I forced you into anything."

"You know I'm right about this."

"You haven't a clue."

But I did. At least one. Where did Angela go on the weekends with her little pentagram tattoo? I had to find out.

"You're just like Cliff," she said. "He wouldn't listen to me, either."

"I'm nothing like Cliff. I can't do it five times a day."

"Very funny."

After Rachel left, I sat in the easy chair in the living room. I felt numbed and tired, upset over the way we had parted. I dozed and, curiously, dreamed about the unborn child who had died in Meg's womb. Natalie was dancing again in front of mirrors. She twirled and smiled at me while I sat in a steel folding chair watching her perform. When the music stopped, she came to me and called me "Papa." I showered her with kisses.

Thumping noises on the doorstep woke me with a start.

I fumbled under the cushion of the chair and pulled out Bumps' Smith & Wesson. I was surprised how long I had slept. A cold, gray light washed through the room. I made my way to the kitchen, hunched over in a crouch. Someone was in front, checking out the house.

The license plates and keys were on the kitchen table. I quietly lifted them off the table and made my way to the back door. I realized I had a problem at the last minute: I had no coat; I had left it at Bumps' house when I opted for his snowmobile suit.

I made my way down the steps, mindful to step over the broken glass, when suddenly the door opened and I was face to face with Blaine Haskell. I reacted first. I placed the barrel of the Smith & Wesson against his forehead. "Quiet," I hissed.

He nodded in quick jerks that he understood.

"How many are with you?"

"Just Bumps and me."

"Where is he?"

"In the cruiser."

"Keep your voice down." I pushed the pistol harder against his forehead. "If you're lying to me ..."

"I'm not. We found the snowmobile, that's all. We're just checking the place out."

"Bumps didn't call for backup?"

Haskell shook his head.

"You're lying."

"Okay. He called in."

Shit. Now I really didn't have much time. I caught Blaine staring at the plates in my hand. "Come on," I said, "you're coming with me."

"Why?"

"Never mind."

We made our way down to the abandoned railroad bed and headed in the direction of town. To our right were fields, still hayed in the summer, that bordered Dog River. Blaine walked ahead of me, and I used the pistol to prod him. Snow had fallen overnight. It was a cold and raw day, and the wind blew through my flannel shirt.

"What are you going to do with me?" Blaine said.

"Keep walking."

"You're not going to shoot me, are you?"

"Only if you don't shut up." I glanced behind and no one was following.

We came to an abandoned railroad shed. The door was locked. The wrought-iron handle looked pretty strong.

"Give me your coat," I said.

"No way."

I aimed the pistol at his eyes. "Blaine, you'd better cooperate. I don't think you know how lucky you are."

"Lucky!"

"Yeah. Back at the house I almost shot you." All the color seemed to drain from Blaine's face, and I saw his hands shaking. In that moment, he must have thought I really had killed Rodriguez, and he was next on the list.

"Give me the damn coat!"

There was no hesitation this time. It was a nice black leather insulated one. I put it on; it fit pretty well. I removed the pistol from his gunbelt and tossed it away. "Now your boots."

"My boots? Christ. I'm going to freeze out here."

"Don't be a baby." I gathered his boots. "I'm sure you'll be able to holler loud enough before you die of exposure."

"You're not going to get away with this."

"You sound like a B movie."

"Fuck you!"

"Nice comeback." I waved the pistol. "Now handcuff yourself to the door."

He complied, but not without further observations about how all the cops from the whole state of New Hampshire were going to nail my ass.

I took the key. "You got a watch, Blaine?"

"Yeah."

"Give me ten minutes before you start screaming for help. Understand?"

"Sure."

I held the gun against his head. "I'm not screwing around here, Blaine. I'm a desperate man, so I need you to tell me you understand."

"I understand."

I left Blaine and continued a few hundred yards down the railroad bed until I came to a trestle and hopped across the ties. I threw his boots into the Dog River. When this was all over, I would have to buy him a new pair. Then I heard Blaine's cries. I checked my watch. The bastard had only given me five minutes.

My hands were getting cold from holding the plates, so I stuck them in Blaine's jacket.

I came to a dirt road that led to the main drag through Dunston. I jogged toward the highway and heard the whoop of a siren in the distance. I followed a line through the backyards of homes that paralleled the highway and ended up behind Dunston Academy's hockey rink.

It occurred to me that I had no idea what the car I was

going to steal looked like. The keys told me it was a GM, but that's all I had to go on. I did, though, have a hunch where the seniors parked their cars.

Dunston Academy had one big lot right next to the field house and adjacent to the hockey rink that faculty and staff used. It was too early for the school to be buzzing, and, though I had that working in my favor, I had to be careful.

Finding the car that matched the keys turned out to be easier than I thought. Because of the early hour, there was no one around, and the cars in the lot were only those that had stayed overnight, the plate-less ones belonging to seniors.

The key opened the door of a late model Jimmy, a utility vehicle that looked in pretty good shape. It even had a cellular phone. The only hitch was that Kendra, the owner, had done something with the license plate screws. I searched the glove box and the tray on the console but had no luck. I ended up pirating the screws off another car where they had been twisted back in place after the plates had been removed.

I turned the key in the ignition. It took a few tries to start. There was a quarter tank of gas. I switched on the heater and defroster, got out of the car, and brushed the snow off the windshield.

I got back in and waited for the windshield to defrost. Then I pulled out of the lot. I was tempted to drive by Georgette Salmon's place to see what was going on, but I opted instead for back roads in the opposite direction. I weaved east for a while, not knowing where to drive. The Vermont plates bothered me. There weren't that many in the area. I was only about a half hour northwest of the Vermont border and decided to head in that direction where the plates would blend in with other vehicles and be less conspicuous.

CHAPTER TWENTY-TWO

By mid-morning I had made it to Lebanon. A sign on a bank displayed the time as well as a temperature of twenty-two degrees. Across the Connecticut River was White River Junction, Vermont.

I had traveled without incident, and I was thankful for having a car with a good heater. Driving north, I'd had time to think through this idea of following Angela. I half expected the light of day to put a damper on the idea and force me to reconsider, but the key link was the tattoo. I still felt that this one connection with Angela and Rodriguez and Chambers would lead me not only to Damon, but also to the person who had framed me for Rodriguez's murder.

I pulled into the K-Mart parking lot, figuring the Jimmy would be less conspicuous in a herd of other cars, and I waited with the engine running, watching people going in and out of stores. I didn't know when Angela would be heading out for her weekend, but I guessed that by early afternoon I would have to make my way back to the school to catch up with her.

I drove out of the parking lot. I headed along the back road that led to Lebanon and stopped at a minimart for gas. I bought a newspaper, a cup of coffee, and some day-old doughnuts. The girl who rang me up didn't make eye contact. She went through her routine mechanically, and I was grateful for it.

I parked in the mini-mart lot facing the road. I sipped coffee and read about myself. There was no picture of me in this edition of *The Upper Valley News*, just an article about why a Vietnam vet who served his community as an EMT would suddenly go berserk. The answer was drugs, according to Trooper Manfred Tierney, who was quoted at great length in the article. Then came a sentence that leaped off the page: "We believe Chad Duquette was actually involved in the same drug operation that Roland Tierney, my brother, was indicted for just last year. This has been very hard on all of us, having such a trusted member of the community as Duquette suspected of killing Joseph Rodriguez apparently for what he knew about the drug operation."

What? How could Tierney think that?

But I ran over again the facts in the case as they appeared and could easily see how the hard evidence—the drugs, the pistol—worked against me. I had to trust Bumps to understand that the Christmas package he found in my truck was too convenient, that the doubts he expressed about my guilt that night in the kitchen would eventually help clear me.

As I headed back to Dunston, I became more and more angry over Tierney's theory of motive for my killing Rodriguez. What hurt most was that a man I held in such high regard would so quickly buy into what had to be, to a trained eye like his, such an obvious set up.

It was a little before 3:00 in the afternoon when I hit the outskirts of Dunston. My biggest fear was that the police were waiting for me. But Dunston was sleepy, the only movement coming from kids changing classes.

I parked across the street from the school in a driveway that serviced one of the playing fields. I tucked the car in beside a fence post so that it was difficult to see from the road. From the driveway I had a good view of the parking lot across the street near the field house. When Angela pulled out onto the highway, I should have no trouble catching up to her.

As I waited, the sun tried to break through. In the sky off to the west, shafts of light pushed through dark, broken clouds. I wondered if darkness would work against me and Angela would be able to escape without my seeing her. But there was no other way out of the parking lot, and my chances were good. Why hadn't I asked Rachel what kind of car Angela drove?

I sat there until almost 4:30 with no sign of Angela. Across the street, students had been walking by all afternoon on their way to the hockey rink and the field house, but none of them resembled the Angela I had seen in the picture stapled to her application. She was a darkly attractive girl with coal black hair cropped short. She sported a nose ring in the picture.

I waited another half hour. The sky to the west was now lit with a faint glow. The temperature must have dropped a good ten degrees since I first began waiting, and I zipped Blaine Haskell's jacket to my chin. The street lamps came on, providing foreground lighting, which meant I couldn't clearly see the road that led to the parking lot. This was not good.

I started the car and twisted the heater dial to high. My hands were numb from the cold. I drove across the street and into the parking lot. I backed the car in where I had found it, killed the engine, and waited.

Some of the cars that had been in the lot this morning were gone, and I had the sinking feeling that I had missed Angela. Perhaps she had left before classes were over. It was something I hadn't thought of before, and I silently cursed myself for yet another example of my stupidity. I should have returned to campus earlier.

But before I could chastise myself further, a lone figure walked into the parking lot. I could see it was a girl with dark hair carrying a large backpack. I ducked down in the seat. I waited until I heard an engine turn over. The sound felt like it came from several cars down the row, and when I sensed the driver pulling out, I lifted my head and saw the taillights of a black BMW.

I started the Jimmy and followed, leaving my lights off until I hit the highway, where I proceeded west on the main drag. Even though the girl had dark hair, I still didn't know for certain if it was Angela, but the make of car seemed to confirm it. I remembered Rachel talking about her as being a "poor rich girl." The car looked like a new Beemer, worth over thirty grand.

I followed the BMW out of town. It turned off the highway, down a secondary road, past a new development of low-income housing units, then up Tannery Hill and left onto a dirt road.

If this was Angela, she wasn't leading me to the Turner property. I was again wracked by doubt. It could be another Dunston Academy kid taking a weekend at a friend's house, which meant I really had screwed the pooch. In my mind's eye, I pictured the real Angela getting into the old Chevy I had seen in the parking lot and driving to the Turner property.

The road I was on was familiar. Not too far from here I used to plow a driveway that belonged to a radiologist who worked at Mermorial before he retired to Florida. There were few houses up here, the soil hardscrabble with a preponderance of ledge. The views of Kearsarge Mountain, though, were spectacular.

The BMW nudged along slowly, and I stayed about thirty yards behind, knowing it would be difficult to lose her car since the road dead-ended in another mile. As the houses passed by, I felt a rush of certainty that I was on the right trail, but it left me both shocked and sickened.

There was only one house left that Angela could be heading for, and it belonged to Neil Striker.

I parked the Jimmy below the house at the entrance to an abandoned road that had once serviced a field belonging to Striker's great-grandfather. Secondary succession had long since taken over the field. The snow was knee deep, and I slogged through the woods, following the line of the road until I reached his house, an old clapboard Cape.

Striker had lived there all his life. His family, like mine, had been among the original settlers of Dunston. The furniture-making business Striker owned had been started by his father after the family farm went belly-up.

I skirted along the edge of the driveway until I came to the back of his house. I waited a few minutes, listening. The night was still, the sky overcast, the glow of the stars muted.

Lights were on in the kitchen, and through the window people were moving about. I inched closer, using a large maple for cover. From my vantage point I had a clear view of Striker sitting at a table. There were two others in the room. They were standing, but I could only see half their bodies. Their heads were cut off by the top of the window.

Striker said something and beat the table.

Money appeared and he began counting it, wetting the tips of his fingers now and again as he stacked the bills on the table. He produced two zippered bank bags, separated the money, and handed back one of the bags.

He jabbed his finger at the person who received the money, who then sat down across from him. It was Julie Hanneford. She was obviously angry, gesturing at the other bank bag still on the table. Then I knew. It had to have been Striker in the crowd that night when Julie tripped. He was the one she had pointed her finger at and cried, "You. You."

Striker pushed his chair back with such force it tipped over. He rushed around the table, grabbed Julie, and slapped her face with the back of his hand. The blow sent her out of my sight, but stepping in, fists flying, was another girl with dark, short hair. Angela. I had no doubts now. I recognized her from her application photo.

Striker and Angela struggled, but she was obviously no match for him. This was the same man who had gotten into a squeeze contest with his future father-in-law and broke the man's hand.

Now all I could see was Striker in the window. He was looking down, yelling and gesturing at the two girls who were most likely on the floor. Then he disappeared from the window, leaving only the table and the suspended ersatz hurricane lamp in tableau. The picture was eerily disturbing in its tranquility, given what had just happened.

Striker reappeared. In his hands were coats, which he threw down. He said something and seemed calmer as he put on his jacket. They were leaving the house.

I made it to the edge of the woods and pushed up over a snowbank. I thought of the tracks I was leaving, but I couldn't worry about that now. I cautioned myself to think straight. What mattered was that the Jimmy was too close to the road, easily picked up in the lights of passing cars.

I found my trail coming in and used it to get back to the car. I didn't know how much time I had before Striker and the girls would leave the house.

I made it to the car. There was no wind. The three-quarter moon was barely visible, and the darkness worked in my favor. I didn't hear another car on the road, so I opened the door of the Jimmy and quickly closed it, worried about the courtesy light staying on. The roadhead where I was parked had been plowed, and mounds of snow prevented me from pulling the car deeper into the woods. I had to get the Jimmy out of there.

I twisted the key in the ignition and crept out into the road with my lights off until I was well clear of the roadhead. Then I snapped on my low beams. I'd almost reached the main road when I picked up lights from Striker's vehicle in my rearview mirror.

I dove into the retired radiologist's driveway. It was sheltered by a stand of pine. The house was dark. I cut my lights and waited for Striker to pass. Then I pulled out and followed him.

Striker was driving his truck with the girls in the front seat beside him, and he headed down the hill to the main drag. I followed with my lights off for a while, but when he turned right onto Route 30, I flipped them back on and kept several car lengths behind.

I felt certain that Striker didn't suspect he was being followed. We stayed on Route 30 to the junction of 25A, where he turned right. Striker's route offered few surprises. We were now on the road that went around the old Turner property. Though Angela had not led me to this area initially, I was sure that my hunch had been right. But I was in no mood to celebrate. There was still much I didn't know. I thought about the money on the table and Striker's manhandling the girls. I would have to be careful.

As Striker led me along 25A, I pictured our location in

relation to where Chambers had led us to Rodriguez. The road curved toward the northwest, far away from the woods where Rodriguez had been found, and we were heading toward Tingly Mountain, not far from where Damon and I had hunted the buck.

About ten minutes away from the turnoff to the abandoned Tinderhook Mine, Striker abruptly jerked the wheel to the left and cut across 25A. He pulled the truck onto a dirt road that cut deep into the woods.

It happened so quickly that had I been following closer, I might have rear-ended him. I stayed on the highway, drove past the road where Striker had turned off, and continued in that direction a few hundred yards before I slowly doubled back. I parked the Jimmy on the side of 25A and headed out on foot.

I trudged up the narrow road where Striker had gone. It had been plowed, and beneath my feet it felt compacted from heavy use. The snow was deeper along the sides, and I was forced to walk in the center of the road. In the distance ahead and to my right, lights periodically wagged in the darkness.

Behind me I suddenly heard the roar of an engine. I did a swan dive over a snow bank. The vehicle grumbled past, and the noise stirred my memory. I couldn't see much of what the vehicle looked like as I watched it move by, but it was enough for me to recognize the same muscle-car that had followed me out of Boston.

The road turned to the right, and I heard voices ahead.

I crept closer, and went off-road at the bend. The snow was thigh deep along the edge, with a skin of ice between layers, due no doubt to the recent thaw and refreeze, and I was careful that the crunch of my footfalls not give away my position.

I labored through the snow and took cover in a thicket of spruce. Ahead of me, lit by diffuse moonlight, was the dark outline of a large barn.

I worked my way closer, crawling on my belly until I was able to see shadowy figures standing in front of the barn. Their voices wafted in the darkness, but I couldn't make out what they were saying.

The dull murmur was broken by the whine of a small engine. The light from a snowmobile broke the plane of darkness and spilled over the group, revealing at least a half dozen people. They were dressed in the same type of outfits, robes with hoods covering their heads.

There was little talk. One hooded figure got on the back of the snowmobile, and two more on a sled the snowmobile was pulling. It didn't take long to figure out that I was witnessing some sort of shuttle service.

I was pretty certain that if I followed where the shuttle led me, I would most likely find Damon.

I inched backward out of the spruce thicket, then stood up and brushed the snow off Blaine's jacket.

Tracking the snowmobile wouldn't be too difficult, but I also realized I had to let someone know where I was. It would be stupid to do it alone. I thought of Rachel, but I didn't want her involved any more than she was. I considered Bumps, but he would just sound the cavalry. Whatever this group had planned, I wanted to see it played out.

Then I thought of the only one who could really help me.

I headed back along the road and out onto the highway where I had parked the Jimmy. I used the cell phone to get information, then punched in the numbers for the *Patriot.*

When someone picked up, I said, "I'd like to speak with Natasha Wright, please."

CHAPTER TWENTY-THREE

Natasha Wright was on assignment. I left a message that if she wanted the real story behind what happened to Chambers and Rodriguez she should follow the snowmobile tracks that led from a barn, accessed by a dirt road three miles below the entrance to Tinderhook Mine on 12A.

I could tell that the guy on the other end didn't believe me, but I insisted that if he gave Natasha my name she would understand this was not a crank call. He wanted to know more, but I hung up on him. I had to trust Natasha Wright's terrier instincts to scratch out the truth.

I stuck Bumps' Smith & Wesson in my belt, left the car, and began retracing my steps, still keeping to the center of the dirt road. At the bend, I again entered the woods and crawled on my belly to the stand of spruce. The snowmobile shuttle was still going on. I worked my way along the edge of the road and around the side of the barn.

The barn door was open in back, and the cars that were parked inside appeared as dark, shadowy mounds. I stuck close to the edge of the barn and crept slowly along the side until the voices in front became more distinct. It sounded as if the numbers had dwindled to a few. One of the voices was female.

A snowmobile wound closer, then sputtered to a stop, idling

roughly. Using the sound of the engine for cover, I headed away from the barn in the direction of the trail the snowmobile had marked and hid in a dark culvert. The snowmobile eventually returned in my direction, engine straining, lamp dodging in the darkness. I lay on my belly in the culvert until it passed.

The sky was still overcast, and the moon had a dull ring around it. The cold air was moist, and I could taste snow coming. The trail was visible despite the lack of light, and it was so compacted from the shuttle trips that I would have no trouble making good time on foot.

I set out into the open and began walking swiftly, following the line of the snowmobile trail that ran across a field, extending in a southeasterly direction. I immediately felt the wind on my face. No doubt there would be snow by morning.

After what seemed an interminable number of twists, the trail emptied out onto another field and wound back up a hill sharply to the west. High against the sky stood the dark outline of Tingly Mountain.

I made my slow ascent toward the mountain. The trail led to the abandoned mine. About halfway across the field, I stopped to get my bearings.

Directly behind me, somewhere in the darkness, was the ridge line that marked the boundary of the big buck's territory. The day Damon and I had gone hunting, we had looked directly across this field at the Tinderhook Mine before we made our turn back southeast and down toward the cistern. From that perspective, I remembered the mine appearing as sunken eyeholes in a skull. Now, the openings loomed ahead.

I thought about going off-trail to disguise my approach, but I didn't see anything ahead that suggested someone was on lookout. I was emboldened by the idea of surprise being on my side.

The trail wound toward a high arch cut into the side of the mountain. Part of the mountain in front of the arch had been leveled to accommodate truck traffic, and as I came closer to the entrance, abandoned out-buildings appeared in front that had no doubt served as offices and tool sheds when the mine was in its heyday. I began to pick up a faint muttering of voices coming from inside the mine.

I approached the entrance obliquely, taking a line along the wall of a long shed that faced the mine. I worked my way along the rock, walking my hands across the face, until I reached the opening. The ground was rough with residue rock, like a talus slope, and I was careful not to stumble. I reached the archway and glanced inside.

The cave was lit by torches, flames pluming upward. There must have been an opening on top that created the strong draft. A snowmobile was parked near the entrance. Two figures milled about near the archway. One of them carried a torch. They came together, their hoods meeting and muffling their speech.

Someone shouted something from the rear of the cave. The two figures turned and began walking in that direction. I ducked inside and followed. It wasn't difficult to disguise my movements in the darkness, and I had little trouble catching up.

The figures led me deeper into the cave until they came upon another long shed. A single torch hung from a stanchion near the doorway illuminating other hooded figures making their way inside.

I crept closer.

The only one left outside now was the one with the torch. He began scouring the grounds, making sure the area was secure. As he walked back toward the cave's entrance, I circled behind him and approached the long shed.

Voices broke out in a loud chant. It surprised me, and I made an involuntary noise in my throat. I wheeled around to check on the retreating figure with the torch. The flame was stationary. The chanting became louder and more rhythmic. I was afraid to move. It seemed forever until the figure began walking away from me again, apparently satisfied that his ears had played tricks.

I inched around the side of the building, hoping there was a window I could look through. I found several, but they were all painted black and glowed with strange translucence, backlit from inside. The chanting was still going strong. At the back was another shed, smaller, probably used for storage.

I circled the building and found the figure with the torch returning. I took the Smith & Wesson from my belt and waited by an outcropping of rock for him to pass.

I came up on him from the rear and, like I learned to do in 'Nam, rapped him on the head with the butt end of the pistol. He dropped without a sound, and the torch slipped out of his hand. I grabbed it and let the light rest on his face. It was Striker.

I removed his robe and used the waist cord to tie his hands behind him, leaving enough tail to truss up his feet when I bent them back toward his hands. I took a handkerchief from his pocket and crammed it in his mouth.

I stuck the Smith & Wesson back in my belt, put his robe on, and headed toward the building.

I walked up onto the short porch and listened at the door. The chanting was still going on. I twisted the knob and entered. I bowed my head so the hood hid my face.

The light came from numerous candles spread throughout the room, some large ones on tall wrought-iron holders that stood on the floor. My entrance went unnoticed by those gathered in an arc around what looked like an altar. They sat on the floor, heads bowed, chanting. A mammoth pentagram was drawn on the back wall behind the altar.

I assumed a place at the end of the arc near the door and hoped my joining the group didn't violate some arcane rule about what the guard at the door was supposed to do. But the person sitting next to me didn't seem to notice. I tried to match my voice with his. It was pretty easy to follow the monotone, but to be safe I kept my chanting barely audible.

I counted nine hooded figures in the room. Soon, one of them approached the altar and raised a chalice like a celebrant at communion. The chanting stopped.

"Dark one! Beelzebub! We summon thee!" The voice was deep and resonant.

Others echoed: "We summon thee."

The celebrant continued: "We call upon your powers. There is one tonight who will cross over. A good servant." He lowered the chalice. "Step forward, my child."

A hooded figure came toward the celebrant, fell to the ground, and lay prostrate at his feet, arms spread out. "I am not worthy, Great One." It was a female voice.

"Rise. It is time."

The figure got up from the floor and lowered her hood. It was Julie Hanneford. She removed the robe and stood before the group naked. "I am ready," she said.

Another figure stepped out of the congregation and approached the altar. He spread his arms wide and mumbled something, then nodded to Julie. She approached the altar, climbed up on top of it, and lay on her side.

The figure pulled what appeared to be a thin knife with a bamboo handle from his robe and held it high. On a table near the altar were various bowls and other sharp-edged trinkets.

The celebrant then intoned: "From one blood, the many." He raised his arm and slit a vein with a knife. He held his arm over the chalice and allowed drops of blood to spill into it.

The others stood with arms raised, fists clenched, and repeated: "From one blood, the many."

The celebrant began at the opposite end of the arc, then slowly moved his way down. From each disciple, he collected blood in the same manner. I knew I had little choice but to donate my own when the time came. The EMT in me balked. Hadn't these people ever heard of AIDS?

When the celebrant came to me I bowed my head and raised my arm high. I felt a sharp burning as the knife sliced into my arm. I caught a glimpse of the chalice, as it passed, half full now with intermingled blood. My arm stung, and I fought the urge to clasp my hand over the cut.

The celebrant returned to the altar. He offered it to the robed proselyte wielding the bamboo-handled knife, who proceeded to pour out dollops of blood into a smaller bowl that he mixed with another dark liquid. He then approached Julie Hanneford and raised the knife over his head, holding it in both hands. This was apparently a signal for the others, for they immediately began some sort of incantation in gibberish. It was not done in unison, and it sounded as if the hounds of hell had just been let in the door.

I grumbled some nonsense to be socially correct, while the guy next to me kept saying, "God-Dog, God-Dog, God-Dog"—

apparently blaspheming with the repeated anagram. While all this was going on, I reached under the sleeve of my robe and applied direct pressure to my wound.

The proselyte with the thin bamboo-handled knife stooped over the altar, his back to me. I couldn't see exactly what he was doing, but it was clear from his actions of dipping the slim knife into a mixture of blood and dye and rapidly tapping Julie's thigh with the tip that he was using a crude tattoo technique. I didn't have to guess what that tattoo looked like.

I didn't know much about tattoos. Guys I remembered from the service had it done, and they talked about it being painful until the endorphins kicked in. Then it just became a burning sensation. I couldn't imagine how painful this was for Julie, but I could tell from the grimace on her face that she was fighting hard not to cry out. The process dragged on. The chaotic voices ate away at my nerves.

I felt some vindication for finding the source of the tattoos, and it didn't surprise me that it involved ritual. What bothered me most was that all this tracking of the tattoo hadn't gotten me any closer to Damon. I was caught up in this bizarre sacrament with no idea where it was leading. All I knew now was that Chambers and Rodriguez had once belonged to some church of Satan. But what did that have to do with anything?

While the proselyte continued with the long, painful tattoo process, I shifted my thoughts to finding the best way to escape. Now that the ceremony had begun, I knew I couldn't just leave without drawing attention to myself. I was considering creating some kind of diversion, when the proselyte raised his bamboo-handled knife over his head again and the babble in the room ceased.

"It is done," he said.

Julie rose from the altar. The proselyte and the celebrant helped her stand. She put on her robe and covered her head with the hood. She returned to the arc of fellow disciples, walking with a limp.

The celebrant stepped forward again and began talking. At first, I thought he was continuing in the theme of mumbling inanities, but then I realized he was speaking Latin:

"Orientis princeps Lucifer Beelzebub," he said, raising his hands. *"Inferni ardentis monarcha, et Demogorgon, propitiamus vos, ut appareat et surgat Mephistophilis!"*

The group joined in, repeating at appropriate pauses. It didn't take much to realize he was summoning the devil again, but this time in earnest. I guess the devil understood Latin best.

"Ipse nunc surgat nobis dicatus Mephistophilis!" he declaimed.

The voice was sonorous, an affected baritone, and it sent a chill deep into my bones.

The celebrant lifted the chalice and drank from it.

My stomach churned thinking of the human blood going down his gullet.

"He is here!" the celebrant suddenly shouted.

"He is here!" the loyal followers repeated.

I scanned the room, looking to see if old Lucifer had actually shown up for the party, but there was no sign of him.

"Welcome, Almighty One!"

The crowd began to gush with excitement, but if Satan was there, he was being quiet about it. As I watched the celebrant, I could only conclude the guy was a fake, and he had these poor slobs drinking out of his cup. What made my blood really boil was that he had duped two teenage girls. This must have been the "family" that Angela talked about in her E-mail.

"Master of Darkness," the celebrant continued. "We have

offered you many sacrifices in the past to show our obeisance—the cat, the rabbit. But tonight we prepare for you the ultimate sacrifice."

He waved his hand with a dramatic flourish, like some sorcerer. From the rear of the building a door suddenly opened. Two hooded figures dragged in someone who struggled in their grip. His bound feet trailed behind him. As they brought him closer to the light, I could see it was Damon.

They had taped his mouth. His eyes darted with fear. I reached inside my cloak and let my hand rest on the butt end of the pistol.

The two holding Damon dragged him to the altar. They lifted him up and placed him on his back. He struggled and the proselyte came to the altar to help hold him down.

The celebrant walked to the table beside the altar and fiddled with something. He held up a syringe that glinted when it caught the light. "Beelzebub!" he shouted. "We prepare this sacrifice for you."

I rose and drew the Smith & Wesson from my belt. "Hold it," I said and drew a bead on the celebrant. I could feel heads turn toward me. "Untie him!"

For a moment, nothing happened. I wagged the pistol. "Come on. Move!"

The celebrant nodded to the proselyte who began to remove the rope that bound Damon's feet. I had expected the celebrant to say something, but he just stood there.

While the proselyte worked on freeing Damon's hands, I detected movement toward the rear. I spun around and aimed the pistol at one of the disciples who had crept toward me. "Better tell this guy not to be stupid," I said to the celebrant.

"It's okay," the celebrant said.

It was the first time I had heard him speak in a normal voice. I almost dropped the Smith & Wesson. I wheeled and leveled the pistol. "Tierney," I said.

He pulled his hood back. "That's right."

By this time, Damon was free. He ripped off the tape that covered his mouth. "Chad!" He pointed a finger at Tierney. "He was going to kill me." He ran to my side. "The son of a bitch was going to gut me."

"It's okay," I said. "Right now, he's not doing anything."

I waved my pistol at Tierney. "Get over here," I said.

"What are you going to do, Chad? Shoot me?"

I took the cord from Tierney's robe and told Damon to tie it around his neck. I used the loose end as a leash. "You're going to lead us out of here, Tierney."

"You won't make it."

"Maybe not. But you'll go down first."

I fired a shot in the room just to get the disciples' attention. I told them to lie down on the floor and not move. I led Tierney out onto the short porch. After some persuading with the pistol, he produced a key that fit the lock on the building, and we cloistered the disciples inside.

We headed out of the cave, and I was confident we weren't being followed, that everybody was accounted for. But that was the last thought I remembered.

CHAPTER TWENTY-FOUR

When I came to, I was lying on my stomach, my hands bound behind my back. The side of my head felt on fire. I tried to make out where I was, but it was pitch black. The air smelled musty and close.

I struggled to a sitting position and heard a groan. "Damon?" He muttered something. He didn't sound so hot. I scootched over to him. "Damon. You okay?"

"Son of a bitch," he said. "They're going to gut me."

"Hang on." I leaned close to him. His breathing was heavy. "It's going to be okay."

"Is it really you, Chad?" he said. "You're not a dream?"

"It's really me," I said.

"I thought you'd never come."

"You were kind of hard to track down."

"They kidnapped me."

"I figured that much."

"They're going to gut me."

"No they're not."

"They are. I heard them talking." His voice grew louder. "They're going to put me on that altar and rip my heart out."

"Shh. Don't make so much noise."

"We've got to run away," he said.

He began to whimper, and I had all I could do to control my anger over what Tierney had done to him. If we ever got out of this, it would take a long time before Damon would ever feel safe again. My eyes had slowly begun to adjust to the darkness, and I could see light through the chinks in the wall boards. "Damon, do you know where we are?"

"In a shed. They kept me here."

"Is it the one in the cave?"

"In back of that long building."

He sounded calmer, so I pushed him for more information. "Did they hurt you in any way?"

"No. They told me they'd shoot me if I tried to escape."

"But they never hit you or anything?"

"Not like Striker bashed you on the head."

"That was Striker?"

"Yeah. He was pretty pissed off."

"I guess I didn't tie him so good." I thought about my own bound hands. It felt like they were duct-taped together. "They got you trussed up, too?"

"Yeah. My shoulders hurt."

I wiggled around behind Damon and checked his hands; they were also taped. "Let's see if we can find something sharp," I said.

"Don't bother. There's nothing here."

"You sure?"

"I crawled all over this place." He broke down again. "God. They're going to kill us."

"Stop it, Damon. You can't give in to them."

"But what are we going to do?"

"We'll think of something. Tell me what you know about them. They keep you here all this time?"

"No. They brought me somewheres. A city, I think. I was blindfolded."

"Boston."

"How do you know that?"

"That's where your truck was found."

"Really?"

"Suppose you start from the beginning. You went hunting that day, didn't you?"

"Yeah, I wanted you to go with me, remember?"

"So you followed the same route we took when we went for the buck?"

"I stayed on it for a while. Then I found tracks that headed out and across that field that goes up the back of Tingly."

"And you followed them."

"For a while. I forgot to bring in some water and I was working up a thirst. I remembered you were always getting after me to hydrate. Hydrate, hydrate. Like a broken record."

"You went for water?"

"Damn straight."

"Then what happened?"

"God, will you just shut up? Let me tell the story."

"Sorry."

"You always do that. You always interrupt me."

"Damon. Tell me what happened!"

"So, I walked up the field to the mine to see if I could get a drink. I saw a couple of snowmobiles parked out in front of one of them sheds out near the entrance. I looked in a window and there was a party going on."

"A party?"

"You said you wouldn't interrupt!"

"What kind of party?"

He hesitated before he spoke again. "It was Tierney and Striker and those two girls. They were smoking and drinking and carrying on. That Julie girl was dancing around with nothing on."

I waited for Damon to continue. He was obviously reliving the experience. "And they caught you looking," I said.

"Yeah. It was Tierney, the son of a bitch." He paused. "I saw everything, you know."

"What did you see?"

"I saw what he was doing with that other girl."

"What was he doing?"

Damon lowered his voice. "You know."

I tried to imagine all this, Damon riveted to the window, his face the color of his hunting cap, not able to turn himself away. "So, then what happened?"

"Tierney saw me in the window and ran after me. He dragged me inside. He said I was in a lot of trouble." There was a tremor in his voice. "He put a gun to my head." Damon appeared to be reliving the moment.

"Go on."

"That girl was nice, you know. She screamed at him to stop."

"The girl he was with?"

"Yeah."

"Was her name Angela?"

"I think so."

Angela was old enough to drive, but I doubted she was at the age of consent. No wonder Tierney had to make sure Damon didn't talk. Statutory rape didn't look so good on the record of the head honcho of the Major Crime Unit—to say nothing of satanic rites and murder.

"She wouldn't let him hurt me," Damon said. "She liked me."

"What else do you know about her?"

"She did a lot of drugs."

"And she had to do favors for her supplier."

"What?"

"I'm guessing Tierney made Angela do things she didn't want to."

"They argued a lot. The girls would come to him with money, and they would shout and carry on."

"Julie and Angela?"

"Yeah."

I recalled the scene I had witnessed at Striker's house. It didn't take much imagination to understand that Tierney and Striker had been using these girls as mules for their dirty little drug operation. This explained the sudden influx of drugs at Dunston Academy. But what was the argument about at Striker's? It was certainly over money, and my best guess was that Striker was skimming off the top. I filed that away for future use.

"Chad?"

"What?"

"What are we going to do?"

"We're going to figure a way to get out of here."

"Why did it take so long for you to find me?"

"I looked for you, honest." I remembered tracking him after that heavy snow. "You were always on my mind."

"I thought you didn't care."

"How could you think that?"

"That's what Tierney kept saying."

"Well, Tierney's a son of a bitch. We know that now."

"Yeah, he's a son of a bitch."

Then it occurred to me why the full search party never found any sign of Damon. Tierney had manipulated the whole thing. His sector had been the entire area around the mine. "And we're just discovering what a son of a bitch he is," I said.

Damon yawned.

"Go to sleep," I said. "You're going to need your strength."

"I'm not tired," he said.

In five minutes, he was asleep.

While Damon slept, I assessed our options. There were few. I knew that Tierney would have to kill us; we knew too much. My best bet was to stall him and hope that he would make a mistake. I was encouraged by our still being in one piece. I figured Tierney had kept Damon around all this time to be used as a special sacrifice—the only reason he was still alive—and my stumbling onto the ritual had upset his plans. I guessed he was caught off guard and was scrambling to figure out the best way to get rid of us.

My head began to throb. I lay on the floor, listening to my blood beating, and fell asleep.

We were awakened when the door flew open and light poured into the room. Damon groaned but didn't move. I blinked my eyes against the light and looked up at Tierney.

"I trust you gentlemen had a good night's sleep," he said.

"Floor's a little hard," I said.

"I suppose you could complain to the management."

"Cut the crap, Tierney. Let us go."

"Now why would I do that?"

"Because you're fucked."

"Such language, Chad." He made a clucking noise. "I expected much more from you."

"You set me up, didn't you?"

"You mean with the med kit?"

"Don't play dumb, Tierney."

He smiled. In the gray light of the shed he looked like a tired man. "I don't know what you're talking about," he said.

"You killed Rodriguez. That plain enough for you?"

"I'm not the one running from the law."

"You will be soon."

Tierney's smile faded. "I'd love to talk with you more, but we have things to do." He walked toward me.

Damon drew himself up into a ball.

"Was it because I turned in your brother?" I said. "Is that why you set me up?"

Tierney hesitated. "You're a pest, that's all. One who got a little too nosey."

"You were in on the marijuana growing with your brother."

"It was part of the business." He grinned again. "Just a small part, though."

"And all this planting of evidence happened because you wanted to get even with me?"

"Not really. Not in the beginning, anyway."

"You mean you didn't know I would respond to that call of a man down in the woods. You didn't somehow engineer that?"

"I'm not an engineer. I'm an artist."

"You're an asshole."

He sighed and scratched his head, absently. "Let's just say your being there turned into an opportunity that was unexpected. Getting even with you was an idea that—well—just presented itself. And I couldn't resist."

"Tell me more about it, Tierney."

"Why should I tell you anything?"

"Because you want to. You need to brag to somebody."

Tierney's eyes narrowed. "You really are a pest," he said. "Get up. I have plans for you two."

Keep the questions coming. Keep stalling. "Just tell me one thing first."

"Come on, Chad." He grabbed my arms and lifted me off the floor. The son of a bitch was strong.

"You shot Chambers too, didn't you?" I said.

"Now how could I have done that? I was in charge of the scene, remember?"

I thought back to the event. I didn't know when Tierney had arrived because I was busy in the chopper with Rodriguez. I did know that the Major Crime Unit would have taken some time to get there.

"You shot him," I said. "You were in the woods watching everything. And you had time to get rid of Chambers' body before you came on the scene."

"Don't try to pin that one on me."

"Nobody else could have made that shot using a handgun."

"Except maybe you."

"You know I didn't kill Chambers."

Tierney ignored my comment. He lifted Damon off the floor and pushed him toward the door. "Come on," he said. He walked us out of the shed. I could tell by Damon's silence that he was scared out of his head. His face was set in a grimace like it was carved in stone. We reached the front of the long building and found Striker sitting on the porch. He was loading Bumps' Smith & Wesson.

"Well, if it isn't the traitor," I said.

Striker ignored me. He focused on the pistol.

I looked at Tierney. "He's cheating you."

"Sure he is," Tierney said.

"But you're probably too dumb to understand what's going on."

"You can stop trying to get me riled up," Tierney said. "It's not going to work."

"Better count your money," I said.

Tierney looked over at Striker. "That true, Neil?"

Striker shook his head. "He's lying."

"In your kitchen, Striker. I saw you and the girls through the window," I said. "Two money bags."

Striker lunged for me, but Tierney got in his way. "Take it easy," Tierney said, face to face with Striker. "Can't you see what he's doing?"

Striker's eyes remained fixed on me. He straightened his coat.

"Besides," Tierney added. "It should be pretty easy to check his story."

Striker nodded and smiled, but it looked forced.

I knew Tierney wouldn't hesitate to follow up on my accusation and that Striker realized he was in hot water. "You two are really cute together," I said. "All this devil worship is a bunch of bunk, isn't it?"

Striker leveled the pistol at me. "Let's shoot him now, Tierney."

"Pretty sick," I said. "Just a bunch of mumbo-jumbo to get your rocks off with teenage girls."

"Chad," Tierney said. "I think we've heard enough from you."

"You haven't begun to hear enough from me."

"Oh, I think we have." He motioned with his head toward Striker. "Gag him," he said. "I need to get some things ready for our little jaunt."

Striker didn't hesitate. He reached into his back pocket for his handkerchief and shoved it in my mouth. It was the same one I had used on him, and it was still wet from his saliva. He sealed my mouth with duct tape. "Sick of listening to you," he said.

When Tierney came out of the building again, he wore a snowmobile suit and a helmet. He carried a rifle I recognized right away as Damon's. Striker said it was his turn to get ready and left us. Tierney pushed us in front of him, and we headed toward the entrance of the cave.

Outside, the wind stung our faces. It was snowing hard. We stood next to the snowmobile that had made up the shuttle service last night.

Tierney pulled out a knife. For a minute I thought he was going to gut both of us right there, but instead he twirled me around and cut the duct tape binding my hands. He did the same for Damon.

I ripped the tape from my mouth and removed the handkerchief. "Where are all your little disciples?"

"I sent them home for good behavior."

"No witnesses."

"You could say that."

"What happens now, Tierney?"

"You mean you don't know?"

"You just going to kill us?"

"I could have done that last night." He loaded Damon's rifle. "I'm going to satisfy your curiosity. You're finally going to find out what happened that day with Chambers and Rodriguez."

I eyed him, trying to read what was going on in his head. "So, it *was* you."

"That's what I like about you, Chad. You grasp things quickly." He sighted the rifle and fired a shot at an old tin sign advertising Camel cigarettes that hung from the side of an outbuilding. "Pulls a little to the right," he said.

"You kill us, they're going to know who did it."

"I don't see how. They'll find you with a slug from Damon's rifle. We'll use Bumps' pistol on Damon."

"You actually think people will believe we shot each other?"

Tierney smiled. "I'm surprised at you. People will believe anything when it involves a felon wanted for murder."

The sound of an engine whining came from one of the caves behind us. Striker drove up in another snowmobile. He had changed into a suit and helmet. He idled right next to us.

Damon spoke for the first time since Tierney had awakened us. "What are they going to do to us, Chad?"

Damon's voice got Tierney's attention. He placed a hand on Damon's shoulder. "We're going to finally get rid of you. You haven't been the most cooperative guest."

"Come on," Striker said, putting the plastic shield down on his helmet. "Let's get this over with."

Tierney got on his snowmobile. "Any time, Chad."

"What do you want us to do?"

"Take off."

I hesitated, not sure I heard right. "You mean we can leave?"

"Sure. Start running."

CHAPTER TWENTY-FIVE

Damon and I stuck to the snowmobile track as we raced down the hill away from the mine. The track was solid enough to run on, but the several inches that had fallen overnight made for slow going when we reached the bottom of the hill and headed off-trail into the copse.

Damon was wheezing hard when we stopped in the woods. He fell in a heap in the snow. He wouldn't be able to keep up this pace much longer. He was out of shape to begin with, and his being cooped up these last few weeks had no doubt made his physical condition worse.

Striker and Tierney started after us. I could barely make out the lights from the snowmobiles through the wind-whipped snow as both of them sat, waiting, watching our progress from the top of the hill. The poor visibility was one thing we had going for us.

"We have to split up," I said.

Damon grabbed my arm. "No. Don't leave me."

"Listen. If we stay together they'll just pick us off. Come on." I helped him up.

"Where are we going?"

"We've got to find you a hiding place."

We headed deeper into the woods and started walking uphill again. Damon fell behind several times, and I had to grab his arm and pull him along.

"Chad," he said. "They're after us."

I wheeled and saw the lights from the snowmobiles moving downhill in our direction. Faintly, when the wind shifted, I could hear the whirr of their engines. There was no time left to run. I had to find a place to stash Damon right where we stood.

We were in an area of leafless hardwoods—maple, oak and hophornbeam—mature trees that offered little cover. The dead-fall was sparse, but off to the west there was a scarred stump and the trunk of a large lightning-struck oak lying on the ground.

Damon shivered and flapped his arms against the cold.

"Over there," I said and pointed to the trunk on the ground. "Follow me."

He did so reluctantly. His movements were sluggish, and he muttered under his breath.

The stump was hollow, large enough to fit Damon, and I felt relieved that I had found a hiding place. But something told me it was too good. The stump had jumped into my view when I scanned the area, and it would probably be equally obvious to Tierney and Striker.

I checked out the fallen trunk. The branches had landed cradled in such a way that pockets of space had been created. One pocket along the middle of the trunk was big enough to burrow into. I showed it to Damon. "Crawl in there," I said.

He climbed up on the trunk and slithered inside the cupped burrow and hunkered down. It was a good place. He would be out of the wind.

"Where are you going to hide?" he asked.

"I'm not."

"You can't just leave me here."

I placed my hand on his shoulder. "I'm going to lead them away from you. You'll be safe if you stay put, but you have to be quiet. Understand?"

Damon nodded. He looked tired.

"Hang on," I said. "I'll be back."

I snapped off branches from the deadfall and began walking backwards, swishing at our footprints. On a clearer day, this would have made little difference in hiding our tracks, but I was counting on the eddying snow to help.

It's difficult to judge sound distance in the woods, and I couldn't peg Striker's and Tierney's exact location. But I knew from the increasing volume of the engine whine that they were fast approaching. I got rid of most of the prints near the tree and stopped sweeping where I had first spotted the stump, about ten yards away from it.

Then I stood in Damon's prints and circled back downhill to the west. I moved in this direction for thirty yards or so before I retraced the steps by walking backwards, careful to keep my feet in the impressions made by my boots. When I got back to the place where both our tracks met, I stood in my own and circled in the opposite direction toward the east.

The idea was to get Tierney and Striker believing that Damon and I had fanned out, causing them also to split up to look for us. If I could shake one of them, I'd have a better chance.

I knew I didn't have much time, that whichever of the two followed Damon's prints would soon realize it was a ruse, but judging by how the wind had picked up, our footprints around the fallen oak would be rapidly disappearing and Damon would be safe.

I kept heading east and hesitated when I realized that the sound of the snowmobiles had stopped. I strained to listen. I could hear nothing but the wind whooshing through the trees above my head. My guess was that Tierney and Striker had reached where Damon and I had allegedly split up and were idling, figuring what to do next. Uphill toward the south, the woods emptied into a clearing that I could barely make out through the trees. Slogging through the deep snow had taken its toll, and my legs burned from the effort. Tierney and Striker weren't far from me, and once they figured out what had happened, it would be a matter of minutes before they caught up.

What I had working for me was the terrain. Without thinking much about it, I had followed a course that led me out of the hardwoods and into dense stands of spruce and hemlock, difficult to drive a snow machine through—it would slow them down momentarily.

An engine throttled up in the distance. It sounded like one snowmobile heading my way, gearing down now and again to adjust to the changing terrain. Where was the other machine? I thought about Damon and hoped he'd stay put. If he would only keep quiet, he'd stand a good chance of not being discovered. My worst fear was that he would panic if anyone came close.

I headed uphill toward the clearing. The growth was sparse toward the edge, and if I kept going I would run the risk of losing my cover. I fought panic and, for the second time, backtracked on my own prints. I sought cover a few yards off trail, hunkered down, and waited.

The wind howled now, and the snow was deep where it drifted into the woods.

The lights of a snowmobile suddenly flashed to my left. They darted and bounced, illuminating the whirling snow. The engine slowed as it came close. I couldn't see the driver clearly, just the dark shape of a figure hunched over the handlebars. The snowmobile came to a stop a few yards downwind of my position. The driver stood, holding onto the handlebars to steady himself. I couldn't tell for sure if it was Striker or Tierney. He searched for my footprints, sat down again, revved the engine, and crept slowly in my direction.

I waited until he motored past, sprung from my hiding place, and tackled him from the rear. His hand twisted on the throttle as we struggled. The machine burst forward through the snow, careened up a small embankment, and landed on its side, throwing us both off.

I forced my arm around the driver's neck, but his helmet made it difficult to keep a steady grasp. We wrestled to a standoff until he got an arm underneath and flipped me over. He sat on top of me and pushed his hands against my throat.

I knew from the grip it was Neil Striker.

I grabbed at his hands, but I couldn't budge them. He pressed harder as I kicked frantically, fighting for air, trying to work my fingers under his. I fought to stay conscious, but I could feel my strength ebbing. Striker still hadn't said anything. The slick curvature of his helmet gave him the strange look of a killer bee. When he shifted his hands for a better position, I shoved my knee upward and nailed him in the groin.

It was enough for him to break his hold on my throat. I gasped as I sucked air. I tried to shove him off, but he held me down with one hand against my throat while he fumbled inside his coat with the other. I ripped at the hand pressing against my throat, getting increasingly angry. It didn't seem right that I couldn't free myself, and at this moment every word of the legendary hand-busting episode with his future father-in-law rang true.

Striker pulled the Smith & Wesson from under his coat and shoved the barrel against my forehead. "Relax," he said, his voice muffled from behind the visor of his helmet.

I stopped struggling, feeling the cold metal against my forehead. He released his hand from my throat and pulled the barrel away.

My throat burned when I sucked air. "This isn't going to work," I said.

"Shut up."

"You can't shoot me with my own gun. It'll screw up Tierney's plans."

"Fuck Tierney." He flipped up his visor.

"I don't think he'd like to hear that, Neil."

"I'll kill you any way I want. He's not calling all the shots."

"Trouble in Dodge?"

"Shut up!" He clipped me on the side of the head with the pistol. "Fucking comedian."

I took his advice and didn't say anything.

Striker talked to himself as he walked back to the snowmobile lying on its side. It was still idling, the headlamps pointed upward at a skewed angle. He righted the snowmobile, pulled out a radio from the compartment under the seat, and talked into it.

I couldn't pick up what he was saying, but it didn't take much imagination to figure out he was reporting to Tierney. I touched my head where Striker had hit me. There was a welt but no blood. I was lucky.

Striker put the phone away and pulled out a cigarette. It took several tries to get it lit. He cupped his hands as he flicked a lighter and cursed more with each attempt. Finally, the cigarette tip glowed. He tossed the lighter away. "Fucking child-proof shit," he said.

I had to laugh. "That's what I like about you, Striker. You hate everything."

"Yeah. Especially you."

"Why? What have I done to you?"

"Nothing." He sucked on his cigarette. "I just don't like you."

"Oh, now I understand."

"Good."

I watched him smoke. I had to keep him talking. There was an obvious rift between him and Tierney, and if I could play on it, I might turn it to my advantage. "It must have been hard keeping up appearances that day we found Rodriguez," I said.

"Not really."

"Tierney killed Chambers, didn't he?"

"If you don't know, I'm not going to tell you."

Keeping secrets was not one of Striker's attributes, and I kept pressing. "How long have you been stealing from him?"

The tip of Striker's cigarette glowed. He didn't answer me, so I tried a new tack. "Tierney's going to find out, anyway," I said. "The girls will tell him."

"You don't know jack shit."

"Angela thinks you're an asshole. How long do you think she's going to let you get away with it?"

"As long as I keep her supplied."

"A teenage girl. I'm surprised at you, Neil."

"We have a 'nineties relationship. It's fun for us."

"I bet."

"Almost as much fun as chasing you around that rest area."

At last, the pump was primed. "That was you?"

"I should have killed you then."

"You followed me all the way to Boston and back?"

"No, I was already there. I almost ran into you two coming out of his apartment."

I thought suddenly of Manuella Silva. "Rodriguez's sister's not in on this, is she?"

"What?"

"She didn't tip you off we were coming?"

"No. What are you, crazy?"

A sense of relief settled over me. I wasn't sure why, but it made a difference that Manuella's coming on to me in the hospital had its roots in honest feeling. I saw her now as she most likely was: someone reaching out in a time of emotional need.

"What was in that apartment?"

"Use your imagination."

"Drugs and stuff?"

He laughed. "And kiddie porn."

"Kiddie porn?"

"Chambers and Rodriguez were sick. Even Tierney didn't go for that kind of shit."

I thought about Striker calling his erstwhile partners "sick," and wondered how he could exclude himself. "Is that why they were killed?"

"Part of it. It was a power play. They didn't like the way Tierney was running things and wanted to get rid of him. Tierney got wind of it."

"So, you sanitized Rodriguez's apartment and followed me out of town."

"Well, I let Tierney know about it first."

"Figures."

"What's that supposed to mean?"

"Means you're Tierney's puppy dog."

"It was my plan to follow you."

"Why?"

"You were supposed to have an accident."

I remembered that night, trying to match the dark figure in the muscle-car with Striker. "I've never seen you drive that thing around here."

"Company vehicle."

"A muscle-car?"

He took another pull on his cigarette. "Belonged to Roger Pierce."

"Ah, yes. Roger Pierce. What's his story, anyway?"

He hesitated. "Who knows?"

"You do, Striker. And you're dying to tell me."

He flicked his cigarette away. "It's nothing sexy. Pierce just owed Tierney a lot of dough. Pierce confessed and Tierney wiped the debt off the books."

"A diversionary tactic," I said.

"Yeah, and it would have worked if it hadn't been for your stupid brother."

The reference to Damon made me think again of his hiding place, and I offered a silent prayer that he hadn't moved.

"I'm sick of all these questions," Striker said. "Just shut the fuck up and wait for His Lordship."

My butt was cold from sitting, and my head began to pound. I wondered what His Lordship was up to. I knew one thing. If I didn't do something fast, I wouldn't have much to worry about—ever again.

If Tierney was sticking to his plan he would be coming to

kill me with Damon's rifle. Allowing Damon and me to run away from the mines only to hunt us down made sense. We would be found in the middle of the woods, far away from the mine, the only explanation the telltale slugs in our bodies.

I thought of distracting Striker, but before I could do anything, the lights from Tierney's snowmobile wove along the twists of the terrain, the engine powering uphill. Striker got up from his snowmobile and waved his arm in a wide arc.

Tierney drove up and fixed his lights on me. He left the snowmobile idling, and walked toward Striker, Damon's rifle at his side.

Striker met him halfway. They talked.

I tried to get my head to work, but it felt as numb as my legs. I could always get up and run, but I wouldn't get far. I dug deep inside, but there was no fight left. A strange calm began to settle, and it scared me. Maybe this is what it was like at the end. Acceptance.

"Stand up, Chad."

It was Striker's voice.

I didn't move. They would have to shoot me where I was, like a trapped animal.

"I said, stand up!"

"Go to hell!" I said.

"You bastard." I could hear Striker walking toward me. "Nothing is simple with you."

I felt his hands on my arms. I fought against him, but he was too strong.

I heard the shot, and waited for the pain. Nothing happened.

Then I felt Striker's tough, hard hands relax as he slumped to the ground.

CHAPTER TWENTY-SIX

Striker groaned at my feet, rolled on his back, and was silent.

I waited for the other shot that would send me to the ground beside him, but it didn't come. With the lights from the snowmobile still trained on my face, Tierney appeared as a shadowy, disembodied form. "So I guess this means you believed me about Striker," I said.

"About his cheating?"

"Yes."

He walked over and checked on Striker's body. "Hell, I knew that a long time ago. I was just waiting for the right time to get rid of the bastard."

"Like you did Perino?"

Tierney laughed. He reached inside Striker's coat and removed the Smith & Wesson. "You think I killed Perino?"

"You told me I would find out exactly what happened that day."

"Maybe some other time."

Bits and pieces were coming together. "That morning, you and Perino gave Chambers and Rodriguez a head start and then hunted them down."

"Close."

"If Striker played Perino's role of stalker and we followed the same script, that means you must have killed him."

"If Striker played Perino's role of stalker and we followed the same script, that means you must have killed him."

"That's what I like about you, Chad. You have an inventive mind."

"Then that's what happened?"

"Not quite."

"You're not going to tell me?"

"I'd love to chat, but there's work to be done." He stepped away from me and into the lights of the snowmobile. He raised his rifle and trained it at my head.

"This is beneath you, Tierney. I expected better."

He didn't say anything and appeared to enjoy the moment.

Feeling death so close for the second time in a few short minutes, I expected my whole life to pass before me, but it didn't. I refused to close my eyes.

Tierney swung the rifle away from me and fired.

The shot hit Striker's snowmobile.

"I don't want you following me." He returned to his own machine and cranked it. "I'll come back for you," he said. "Right now I've got to scare a rabbit out of a hole."

I watched Tierney leave, my worst fears confirmed. He had found Damon and had waited to flush him out until after he took care of Striker. Now, he would make a game out of gunning Damon down.

I rushed over to Striker's snowmobile to assess the damage. Tierney had put a bullet clean through the tank, and gasoline was spilling on the snow. I could smell it.

I ran my hand over the tank and found the hole. I tried to stopper it with my thumb, but the gas still leaked. The bullet had entered high on the tank. Once the gas drained below the hole, I might have enough left to at least catch up with Tierney. But then what?

I returned to Striker's body and frisked him for a weapon, but he was clean. I tore off part of his flannel shirt and bunched a corner of it into a makeshift plug.

I returned to the snowmobile and worked the plug into the hole in the gas tank. It wouldn't prevent all the gas from spilling, but it might keep enough in the tank for me to catch up with Tierney.

I turned the key and the engine stuttered. I rocked the snowmobile and gas sloshed in the tank. I tried the ignition again, and this time the engine caught.

I twisted the throttle several times to keep it going, geared down, and set off toward Tierney. I fought the urge to charge after him. I counted on his being more interested in the hunt than the kill—and that would buy me time.

His track was easy to follow. The wind had dropped and the snow was falling in large, meaty flakes—a sign the storm was winding down. The trail back to Damon's hiding place seemed interminable, even though reason told me I had only been rolling a few minutes.

When I arrived at the fallen oak, there was no sign of Tierney. I drove slowly by the trunk and picked up footprints in my lights that led back uphill toward the east.

I found Tierney's snowmobile track, on course with Damon's footprints. I followed them, and it soon became clear that Tierney was keeping some distance from Damon—at least a thirty yard gap between the prints and the track. Tierney was taking his time, toying with him.

The trail brought me farther uphill. Damon must be freaked out of his mind. He would never have chosen an uphill path unless he wasn't thinking. But as I drove closer, I realized he was leading Tierney into our familiar hunting territory, and we were fast approaching the clearing at the top of the knoll where we had stopped that day we hunted the buck.

Perhaps Damon's familiarity with the terrain was driving him forward towards some other place to hide from Tierney. But the nagging sense of doubt crept in again. Damon wasn't planning anything. He was running for his life.

I motored toward the clearing and took my bearings. I had moved in an arc away from Striker's body, and I was now parallel to that position. The clearing was most likely part of the same one I had almost walked into when Striker had been chasing me. I was just approaching from a lower angle.

I throttled down close to the clearing's edge. I listened for Striker's snowmobile but couldn't hear anything above the noise of my own engine.

The snow had almost stopped now. An angry dark cloud leered overhead, but the visibility had improved.

Then I saw Damon. He staggered out into the clearing to my right, at least a football field away.

I shouted, but he didn't react. He stumbled forward. Where the hell was Tierney?

I goosed the engine and shot out into the clearing. Whatever Tierney's game, I had to force the issue. Damon's erratic gait told me he was in trouble.

I skimmed across the snow at full throttle and spotted Tierney's machine to my right. He sped along the far edge of the woods. I had the angle on him, and if I kept going I would reach Damon before he did.

Damon finally saw me coming. He waved his arms frantically, shifted direction, and lurched towards me.

Tierney cut away from the edge of the woods and bore down on Damon.

Damon fell in the snow. He struggled to get up, but his legs gave out.

When I reached him, he was face down. I hopped off the machine and rolled him over. "Damon. Come on. We've got to get out of here!" I clapped my hands once.

His eyes flickered, then opened. "You're alive," he said.

"Can you get up?"

He rolled on his side and struggled to a sitting position. I pulled on his arm and brought him to his feet. Tierney's machine came at us, whining hard.

I helped Damon onto the back of Striker's snowmobile. "Hang on," I said, and straddled the machine. We took off just as Tierney fired. The bullet shattered the front headlamp.

I wrenched the handlebars to the left and punched the gas. Snow rooster-tailed from the rear, and we sped across the clearing, then uphill toward the tree line. Damon clung to my waist.

As we rose up out of the clearing, the engine sputtered, and in my mind's eye I pictured the gas in the tank canted away from the fuel intake because of the incline. I twisted the accelerator, but the engine coughed and died.

"Shit," Damon said. "No."

I ground the ignition but it wouldn't catch.

"Come on, Damon. We've got to run for it."

"I can't. I can't."

"Look. You can make it. We're almost at the top of the rise."

Damon struggled to get off the machine. I could see Tierney now. He was bearing down directly at us. "Move it, Damon!"

Damon tottered off the snowmobile into the snow. As I

reached for his hand, Tierney fired. The report from the Smith & Wesson echoed through the clearing. Damon pitched forward like he'd been smacked by a truck. I ran to him. "Damon. Are you okay?"

The back of his jacket seeped blood. It looked as if the shot had hit him directly through the shoulder. I was about to check him further when another bullet zinged by my head. By the sound of the report Tierney had switched firearms. He was most likely making sure the slugs pulled from my hide came from Damon's rifle.

I zigzagged to the top of the ridge. Tierney fired twice more, but they were half-hearted shots. He was clearly enjoying the hunt and wanted to make it last.

At the height of land I hid behind a boulder and caught my breath. The view across the valley was familiar. The mines appeared as they had the day Damon and I had gone hunting— as eyeholes of a skull.

I thought about Damon lying in the snow and fought to stay focused. There had been only two shots from the rifle and they were in my direction, which meant that Tierney probably hadn't pumped any more into Damon. If Damon didn't bleed to death before I got back to him, he might make it. But it was cold and Damon was exhausted.

Tierney's snowmobile strained uphill. If I was going to help Damon, I had to save my own ass first.

I headed away from Tierney and followed the trail Damon and I had taken when we hunted the buck. I struggled through the snow past the old stone walls and realized the downhill terrain would be tough going for Tierney. There were numerous rills and depressions that he would have to work the machine through to get to me.

I thought of hiding somewhere, but I worried about footprints. No matter where I went, Tierney would only have to connect the dots.

The sky was lighter, with patches of blue exposed behind dark charging clouds.

I took a step, and my foot hit ice on a rock hidden beneath the snow. I pitched forward, tumbled downhill, and caught myself at the edge of a stream. Despite the temperature, water flowed because of the speed of the current, but shallower parts were filigreed with ice.

Tierney suddenly appeared above me. He raised his rifle and fired. The shot flashed snow two inches from my hand. I scrambled to my feet and traversed away from the stream. He fired once more, splitting a sapling to my left.

I circled back downhill and maneuvered out of sight. His engine labored as it fought gravity moving towards me.

The stand of hardwoods was familiar and suddenly I had a plan. I led him deeper into the heavy brush, found the spot I was looking for, and waited.

My heels were on the edge of the cistern.

Tierney took his time. Waiting for him to come to me was a gamble, and if he was familiar with the area, I was screwed. I saw the light from the snowmobile first. Then he appeared, weaving slowly through the brush. He throttled down and came to a stop. He stood on the idling machine and lifted his visor.

"You quitting?" he said.

"Take your best shot."

"Come on. You can't give up now."

"This isn't a fair game."

Tierney checked his surroundings. "How about I give you another head start?"

"How long?"

He checked his watch. "Ten minutes."

"You'll wait right there?"

"Of course."

I headed off a few yards to my right, following the edge of the cistern. Then I retraced my steps and waited. For Tierney to follow me, he would have to negotiate an immediate hard turn, and I was counting on his speed and momentum to make it impossible to react in time.

I didn't check my watch, but I knew ten minutes hadn't passed before Tierney revved his engine and took off. His headlight shot across the yawning hole of the cistern. He kept coming at a low speed, then the light jerked in my direction. It hung in the air a moment, then skewed upward.

The back part of the snowmobile caught on the edge of the cistern, and the belt whirred as it spun for purchase. I sprang out at Tierney, who was fighting to right the machine. He saw me coming and braced himself.

The snowmobile teetered on the edge as we struggled. I pushed hard against him. His front sled rail slipped off the edge.

He battled back. On solid ground, this would have been no match. Even now I couldn't budge him. His arms strained beneath his coat. Then he pulled one hand free and punched me in the face.

I fell backward.

He strove for balance, like a man learning to surf for the first time. His efforts only made the machine more unstable. It was stuck in gear, the engine turning, the back end spinning its way across the edge.

I rushed him again, this time going for a leg. I grabbed his boot. He swung at me, but the effort destabilized him more. I gathered what strength I had left and pitched him off into the cistern.

He fell, bounced off some deadfall, and landed at the bottom. The snow machine wobbled, then careened over the side. It landed on top of him.

I didn't wait around to assess the damage. My only thoughts concerned Damon. I knew Tierney was still alive because I heard his groans and curses as I made my way back uphill. I didn't know if he still had his rifle—or even if he could use it—but the snowmobile sitting on top of him would at least slow him down.

I was working on pure adrenaline because the burning sensation had left my legs. They churned uphill without volition, and I kept a steady pace until I reached the top of the ridge.

The clouds had broken, and the sun darted in and out.

I followed Tierney's track across the ridge and down into the clearing. Damon lay where I had left him, face down in the snow. I rushed to his side and fell to my knees. I leaned my head close to his. "Damon. It's Chad. Can you hear me?"

There was no response. His eyes were closed.

I put my hand close to his neck and pinched his trapezius muscle. He groaned. My heart jumped. He was still breathing.

In assessing LOC—Level of Consciousness—my training called for using the AVPU scale to see if the patient is Alert, Verbal, responds to Pain, or is Unresponsive. Damon's response to pain was a good sign, but he was clearly heading toward the end of the scale.

The back of his jacket was soaked with blood, but the wound wasn't the worst of his problems. He had been lying in the

snow a long time, losing body heat. His brain, like a benevo-
lent dictator, had also been sending signals to shunt the blood
away from the extremities into the core to protect vital organs.
His skin was cold to the touch. If the loss of blood didn't kill
him, hypothermia would.

I kept talking to him as I checked his C-spine. Before I
rolled him on his back, I took my jacket off and spread it out
so there would be some insulation between him and the snow.
I placed his right arm above his head, the left by his side, and
kneeled with my knees close to his back. With my left hand I
cradled his head to steady it and with my right pulled his opposite shoulder toward me, log-rolling him onto my jacket.

He groaned again.

"Damon. It's Chad. Open your eyes. Talk to me."

His lips moved. I put my ear close to his mouth and listened. "Talk to me," I repeated.

"Chad," he said.

"That's it, buddy. You're going to be all right."

I opened his coat and looked at the wound. The bullet
appeared to have gone clean through his shoulder. I ripped off
part of my shirt tail, made a compress, and applied direct pressure. When I pushed on his shoulder, his eyes opened wide.

"Ow. Shit!"

"Lie still, you've been shot."

He relaxed and shut his eyes. "I'm tired," he said.

"Come back to me, Damon. Keep talking."

"Tierney," he said.

"That's right. Tierney shot you."

I placed my hand on his chest and checked his respirations.
I counted for thirty seconds and multiplied by two and got
eighteen. On the high side. Normal range in an adult is twelve

to twenty. Anything above twenty-four is serious. I knew I had to get him out of there fast. He needed oxygen.

I kept applying direct pressure to his wound. He drifted in and out of consciousness. I talked to him, endlessly, trying to persuade him that he didn't want to sleep, when I heard something behind me.

I wheeled, expecting to find Tierney—or his ghost wandering the landscape. "Damon. Look. You've got to see this."

Damon stirred. His eyes flickered, then opened wide. He gasped. "It's him!"

Uphill to our right, rack held high against a cobalt blue sky mottled with dark clouds, stood a magnificent buck.

CHAPTER TWENTY-SEVEN

The buck eyed us curiously, chest out, his coat dappled with snow. Then he sensed something—proud head lifted in the air, nostrils flared—and bolted across the clearing downhill away from us.

"I told you," Damon said. "I told you."

"We'll get him next season," I said. More than any emergency aid I could administer, Damon had received an infusion that might just save his life. He was a changed patient, eyes wide open, no longer wanting to drift off. Now I had something to goad him with. "Keep fighting, Damon. We've got to come back for that buck. Do you hear me?"

"I hear you."

"It's important that you don't sleep."

"I didn't lie about him, did I?"

"You were right on."

In the distance, I heard a high-pitched whirr of a snow machine, probably what startled the buck.

Damon's body tensed. "Tierney's coming back!"

"I don't think so."

The noise of the engine grew closer, and a snowmobile dragging a sled came into view below us. There were two people on it. As they approached, I recognized Natasha Wright on the back. I had forgotten all about my phone call. I knew she couldn't have ignored my message. They pulled up along side of us.

The driver was helmet-less. He wore dark sunglasses and a knitted cap.

"Do you have a cell phone?" I asked.

They exchanged glances, like they were waiting for the other to speak first. "We have one," Natasha said, finally. "But it's in the car."

"Shit," I said.

Natasha took off her sunglasses. "Are you all right?"

"I'm fine. My brother needs assistance."

"Aren't you cold?"

Her question seemed odd at first, then I remembered I had spread Blaine's jacket under Damon. I glanced at the snow machine. "What are you carrying on the back?"

"Camera equipment." Natasha said. She gestured toward her driver. "This is my photo man, Don."

I nodded in his direction. My preferred method for getting Damon to safety was DHART, but without a phone, it was better to sled him out and call 911 for an ambulance from Memorial.

"We found another man dead," Don said.

"Neil Striker."

"Who's he?" Natasha said.

I held up my hand. "First things first."

"Of course. How can we help?"

"You can start by getting all the stuff off the sled."

Don came prepared for a Pulitzer shoot. I didn't know what sort of fast-action pics he had planned with his massive tripod, or how many lenses in the large case he would find useful, but he was definitely prepared. Probably the most valuable piece among the high-tech equipment was a gray army blanket.

"Fantastic," I said.

"You a photographer?"

"I'm not talking about your Hässelblad."

"Oh."

We spread the blanket alongside Damon. I repeated the procedure of placing one arm above his head, the other along his side. Natasha stabilized Damon's head while Don and I log-rolled him onto the blanket. That done, we grabbed the corners and lifted him onto the sled. I wrapped him up like a burrito. We used Don's camera bag straps to tie him in, and a soft accessory case to pillow his head.

I retrieved Blaine's leather jacket and put it on. It was stiff from the cold and I flapped my arms across my chest to get them warm. It didn't help much. "Where's your car?"

"Parking lot at the mines."

"I need your keys. I'm going to take Damon in and have to use your phone."

She threw them to me. The key fob read "Audi."

"Nice car," I said. "News business must be good."

"You going to leave us out here?" Natasha said.

"I won't be long." I glanced uphill toward the ridge. "If you want to follow those tracks, you might get the biggest scoop of the decade."

"What's up there?" Don asked.

"Fellow named Tierney."

Natasha's eyes narrowed. "You don't mean Manfred Tierney, do you? The trooper?"

"The one and only."

"Where?" she said.

"The last time I saw him, he was lying at the bottom of a cistern with a snowmobile on top of him."

"He's dead?" Don said.

"I don't think so. But you should be able to tell by his

hollering. I think he's in rough shape." I stepped onto the snow machine and revved it up. "But if you go up there be careful. He may still have his rifle and probably wouldn't hesitate to shoot both of you."

I gave her a half smile and circled back downhill.

I drove slowly through the bottom land and periodically glanced back at Damon, who was gliding smoothly behind me. I yelled at him now and again about the buck and how he had to stay awake. I pushed the machine uphill toward the mines, past the long sheds, and found the Audi parked at the side of the main road near the entrance to the unplowed parking lot.

I made the emergency call using the cell phone, then returned to the sled to check on Damon. "Help's on the way. How you doing?"

"Okay, I guess."

"Tell you what. When we get that buck, let's get him stuffed and you can keep him in your living room."

"Naw. Naw."

"How 'bout at Christmas we stick him on the lawn and decorate his antlers with blinking lights?"

"That might look nice."

Bumps arrived at the scene first. When he saw me, he drew his pistol and approached the car. "Hands where I can see them."

I complied. "We need to move fast, Bumps."

He looked at the sled and lowered his pistol. "That Damon?"

"He's been shot."

"Who did it?"

"Tierney."

Bumps holstered his pistol. His silence suggested the news was no surprise.

"There's a lot I have to tell you," I said.

D-1, the ladder truck, arrived next, followed by two other members of the FAST squad in separate cars: Town Selectman Wilfred Baines and Josh Morgenstern, road agent.

"Tierney's hurt," I said to Bumps. I described our encounter at the cistern. "Better radio in for snowmobiles. We'll need to drag the Stokes litter."

"How about you, Chad?"

"Never felt better."

Josh and Wilfred were still the only ones who had responded to the call by the time the ambulance from Memorial arrived. They helped load Damon onto a long board from the sled and then to the ambulance stretcher.

It was good to see Lorraine Michaels in the rig. I remembered her professionalism on our last call together when we had Julie Hanneford on board. Lorraine had oxygen running, High Flow at fifteen liters through a non-rebreather mask, and was hooking up a line to Damon's arm before I could get in back and join her.

I recited the details to the driver, a new guy named Ralph, who wrote down the narrative. I gave him the only vitals I had, Damon's respirations, and was encouraged when Lorraine called out his blood pressure, 110/60—low, but better than I had expected. Damon had lost a lot of blood, but his chances looked good.

My hands and feet began to hurt, and for a moment I couldn't figure out why. I was thawing out.

"Let's get out of here," Lorraine said.

Ralph nodded and crawled back into the cab.

"Mind if I tag along?" I said.

"Wish you would." Lorraine glanced at me, as if for the first time. "Looks like you need to be checked out, too."

"I'm okay. Just a little cold."

I crawled to the back of the ambulance and let Bumps know I was leaving. My legs felt stiff and cold as steel pipes.

"What about Tierney?" Bumps said.

"What about him?"

"From the way you tell it, we'll need your help to get him out."

I looked from Bumps to Wilfred to Josh. All three appeared reluctant to go it alone. I suddenly felt the weight of responsibility for Tierney's condition, no matter how much he deserved what he got. I turned back to Lorraine. "How's Damon?" I said.

"Stabilized."

I returned to his side. "Hear that, buddy? You're going to be okay." I squeezed his hand. "I'm staying here to help these guys, okay? Lorraine'll take care of you."

He nodded.

As the ambulance pulled away, I turned to Bumps. "You put DHART on standby yet?"

"No."

"Better do it."

I thought the best course was for Bumps and me to lead the way to the cistern while the others waited for more snowmobiles to come. I figured the clearing had too much pitch so it would be better for DHART to land in the parking lot. Bumps called in for volunteer snow plows. We were about to leave when I said, "Wait a minute. I need to make one more call."

I used the phone in the Audi and dialed Rachel's number. I got her machine. "Hi. I'm on a call at the Turner property. Just wanted you to know I'm all right."

D-1 carried a med kit, a half bottle of O_2, and the Stokes litter, but that was the extent of the medical supplies. I didn't know what we were going to run into when we found Tierney, but my hunch was that he'd suffered a compression injury.

We left instructions for Wilfred and Josh to follow when other snow machines arrived, and Bumps and I crammed the Stokes onto the sled and tied it down. We placed the O_2 and med kit inside the litter and headed for the cistern.

I drove at a steady pace. Bumps held tight to my waist. At the rise, I chose a wide angle and switchbacked slowly down to the cistern. I parked near the concrete edge and cut the engine. Tierney cried out, his voice weaker now than when I had left him.

I peered over the edge and saw Natasha and Don looking up at me. "It's his leg," Natasha said. "He's hurt real bad."

Bumps and I walked down along the side of the cistern. I carried the med kit and O_2, and Bumps maneuvered the litter. When we reached the bottom, Tierney yelped again. We had to get the snow machine off him.

As I got closer, I could see his immediate problem without even moving the machine. He had a compound fracture of the femur, the largest bone in the body. The bone was shattered, the ragged edge sticking up through his thigh. My biggest concern was that the bone might also have severed the femoral artery. If that was the case, then Tierney had little chance of making it.

I turned to Bumps. "Better call DHART," I said.

Bumps got on the radio.

I opened the med kit and gloved up. I told Don and Bumps to do the same.

"Let's see if we can get the machine off him," I said. I didn't look at Tierney as I grabbed the handlebars, but I could hear him whimpering. The injury had to be painful.

On the count of three, Bumps pushed and Don pulled

from the rear while I lifted the handlebars, and we were able to turn the snowmobile on its side. Then we rolled it over.

Tierney screamed as the machine slid across his leg. I had Bumps get the scissors from the kit and the Pampers we used for trauma dressing. I cut away at the pant leg of Tierney's snowmobile suit and revealed the wound. The bleeding was substantial, but the artery wasn't spurting.

"You're a lucky man, Tierney."

"Fuck you," he muttered.

"No, I mean it. It could have been worse."

He groaned.

"I know it hurts like crazy, but I can make it feel better," I said. "Do you want me to do that?"

There was no hesitation. "Yes."

Since the femur is such a large bone, the muscles surrounding it are also massive, which means when there's a complete break, the muscles contract, causing the bone end to dig into the flesh with increasing intensity. The trick is to keep the muscles stretched.

I moved down to the front of his foot and pulled traction away from him. A tremor ran through Tierney's body as the tension stretched the muscles.

"Feels good, doesn't it?"

"Yes."

"You could fall in love me if I kept it up, couldn't you?"

"Up yours."

I suddenly let the foot go.

He screamed.

"Couldn't you?"

"Yes."

I pulled traction again, and he sighed with relief. "Bumps

is going to take over down here at your foot, but only if you're nice. Understand?"

"Yes."

"And while we're working to save your sorry ass, I want you to tell us all a story. And if you're real good, I might even give you some oxygen. I want to know what happened that day we found Chambers and Rodriguez."

As if on cue, Natasha took out her notebook. Don clicked pictures while Bumps pulled traction.

"I didn't kill Perino," he said.

I packed his wound with the dressing and applied direct pressure. "Go ahead, I'm listening."

"Wait a minute," Bumps said. "Let me read him his rights."

"I know my fucking rights."

Bumps ignored Tierney and took out a small card from his wallet. He Mirandized him.

"Okay," I said. "So, who shot him?"

"Rodriguez. Perino's responsibility was to hunt down Chambers and Rodriguez."

"Why?"

"Because they were threatening the organization. Bringing in talent from Boston to tear me down."

"So why didn't you do the job? Why Perino?"

"Let's just say he owed me one."

"Come on, Tierney. Stop being cute."

"I had to see what side Perino was on," he said. "I figured he was in bed with Chambers and Rodriguez. If he could kill both of them, then I would know where he stood."

"But he bungled it."

"He shot Rodriguez in the leg and Chambers took off and hid in the woods. Rodriguez played dead until Perino leaned over to check on him. Rodriguez grabbed him and there was a struggle."

"You saw all this?" Natasha asked.

"From a distance."

"Let me guess," I said. "Rodriguez knew Perino was carrying a side arm. They wrestled over it, and Rodriguez ended up shooting Perino."

"That's right."

Don was leaning over my shoulder now, getting a good close-up of the grimacing Tierney. "Listen," I said to him. "Make yourself useful. Put your hand here, will you?"

Don bristled that I would even suggest his photography wasn't important, but he did what I requested. I had other work to accomplish if we were to get Tierney out of here.

"So, what happened after that?" Natasha asked.

"Nothing."

"Come on, Tierney," I said. "You want me to tell Bumps to stop pulling?"

He started talking again. "Chambers came out of the woods to help Rodriguez," he said. "Chambers helped him to his feet and walked with Rodriguez leaning on him. I followed. They kept going until Rodriguez couldn't take walking anymore. That's when Chambers left him and went for help."

"Why didn't you just shoot Rodriguez?" Natasha said.

"He was hunkered down. He had the pistol and fired it at me."

"The one I found on him," I said. "The one you planted in my truck."

Tierney didn't say anything.

"And this was all because I turned in your brother."

Tierney paused. "You also messed up our business. I didn't like that."

"I bet you didn't."

"Where was Neil Striker while all this was going on?" Natasha said.

"What do you mean? He was with Chad."

"I thought he was your partner," I said.

"Striker was my first lieutenant. Because of my tight schedule he was in charge of the day-to-day operations—too much in charge, it turned out."

"So, why wasn't he with you?" Natasha asked.

"We had a meeting the night before at the mines when a lot of this shit came down. He was there for that. He left in the morning."

"And he had no idea this hunt was happening?" I said.

"No. Perino and I planned it."

"No wonder Striker was acting funny." I stood up and started poking through deadfall. I found a sturdy branch and broke off the end.

"What are you going to do?" Tierney said. "Hit me with it?"

"No. I'm going to make you fall in love with me all over again." I kneeled down and looked at Don. "Got any lens cases in that bag of yours?"

"You know I do."

"I need to borrow two."

"What for?"

"So we can transport Tierney."

He sent a puzzled look.

"For God's sake, Don," I said. "I'm not going to ruin them."

I rooted through his bag and found what I was looking for. If we were going to sled Tierney out, we needed to make sure traction was pulled continuously on his leg. Short of dragging Bumps behind holding onto his foot, this could be accomplished best by fashioning a traction splint. In the regular world, these traction splints are manufactured with fancy gears and ratchets. In the woods, you have to make do.

I measured the stick against Tierney's side from his waist to his boot. It extended beyond the boot, but too much. I wedged the stick between two rocks and broke off another six inches and that did the trick.

I cupped the stick end near his waist with the lens case and tied it securely through his belt loops and around his middle using a triangular piece of cloth, known as a cravat. I fashioned a hitch that went around his ankle and boot with another cravat, and tied a knot beneath his instep.

I placed the other lens case over the other end of the stick, tied one end of yet another cravat to the case, and ran the loose end up underneath the knot at his instep and pulled downward. The pressure forced the stick against both lens caps. I tied off at the end of the stick and told Bumps to release his grip.

The traction held.

I ran my remaining two cravats around Tierney's leg to stabilize the stick against it. He was ready to roll. "Well, it's pretty, ugly, Tierney. But it should keep you happy."

"Clever," Don said.

"Let's get him onto the litter," I said.

Natasha took a step forward. "Wait a minute. I have another question for Tierney."

"Not now," I said. "We have to get him to the chopper."

"I just want to know if he killed Rodriguez."

"What do you think?" Tierney said.

"Of course, he killed him," I said.

"I'm through talking," Tierney said. "Ask my lawyer."

Above us the din of snowmobile engines filled the air. I turned to Bumps. "Looks like the posse's arrived," I said.

He spat. "Save us from hauling the bastard up ourselves."
I looked down at the snow. No tobacco juice.

There was plenty of help to pull the litter up out of the
cistern. Bumps and I made sure Tierney was well-tied in before
the others dragged him up. I put a non-rebreather on him at 15
liters of O_2 and placed the bottle between his legs. I should
have administered the oxygen before I had done anything else,
but I wanted to make sure Bumps heard his story. Wilfred
dropped a rope to aid in our ascent.

We loaded the litter onto the sled. As Bumps and I made
our way back to the mine, a cadre of snowmobiles at both
flanks, I tried to stitch together the events Tierney had related.
I had a much clearer picture of what had happened that day we
responded to the call.

To test Perino's loyalty, Tierney had made him designated
hunter. After giving Chambers and Rodriguez a head start,
Perino, armed with a rifle and his 9MM in a shoulder holster,
took off after them, and Tierney followed on a snowmobile to
watch the game unfold.

Perino shot Rodriguez in the leg with his rifle and Chambers ran into the woods. Perino went to check on Rodriguez to
make sure he was dead. A struggle ensued and Rodriguez got
hold of Perino's pistol and killed him.

Chambers came back out of the woods to help his lover.
Rodriguez leaned on Chambers for support as they set out to
escape from Tierney, who had witnessed the whole thing.
Rodriguez no doubt carried the pistol and Chambers the rifle.

But Rodriguez's wound was too much and he couldn't keep
pace. Chambers left him with the pistol to fend for himself
and went for help. When Chambers reached the road, he ditched
the rifle where I had found it the day we hunted the buck.

Tierney shot Chambers with the 9MM I had put in my med kit. He must have been less than ten feet away from him.

If I were a betting man, I would also lay odds he was the one who took pot shots at hunters to feed Natasha Wright's frenzy and then came to the hospital and killed Rodriguez.

DHART was waiting for us in the parking lot, the prop still turning.

By this time, a crowd had gathered and was being held at bay by the state police. One trooper gawked at us when as we hauled the litter to the chopper.

Right there to greet us was Lefty Birch. He winked at me. "Want to come along for the ride?" he said.

"Not this time," I said.

It occurred to me as I watched them load Tierney in, that we finally did have that chess match. I just hadn't realized the pieces were real people.

I ran in a crouch away from the helicopter and spotted Rachel in the crowd. She broke away from the police, and I raced over and threw my arms around her. She said something I couldn't make out in the whine of the whirring blades, but it didn't matter. All that counted was holding her again.

"Keep your heads down," Bumps yelled.

We turned our backs to the propwash, and I held her around the waist, my head resting on her shoulder. I had the feeling we were going to find out a lot more about Tierney's operations, but I really didn't care about the details. Tierney and Striker were out of business, and they wouldn't be corrupting any more kids like Julie and Angela. That's what was important. The kids.

I held Rachel tighter as the chopper rose and thundered above our heads.